WILLEM DE KOONING'S
PAINTBRUSH

Willem de Kooning's Paintbrush

STORIES

Kerry Lee Powell

Published by Harper Avenue, an imprint of HarperCollins Publishers Ltd

First edition

"In a Kingdom Beneath the Sea" was previously published under another title in the Fall 2013 issue of *The Malahat Review* and in *15: Best Canadian Stories* (Oberon Press, 2016).

"The Prince of Chang" was previously published in the Autumn 2012 issue of *The Malahat Review*.

An earlier version of "Vulnerable Adults" was previously published in *Wild Cards* (Virago Press, 1999).

"There Are Two Pools You May Drink From" was previously published in the July/August 2013 issue of the *Boston Review*.

HarperCollins books may be purchased for educational, business, or sales promotional use through our Special Markets Department.

HarperCollins Publishers Ltd
2 Bloor Street East, 20th Floor
Toronto, Ontario, Canada
M4W 1A8

www.harpercollins.ca

Library and Archives Canada Cataloguing in Publication information is available upon request.

ISBN 978-1-44343-577-2

Printed and bound in the United States
RRD 9 8 7 6 5 4 3 2 1

FOR ANDREW

Contents

WILLEM DE KOONING'S PAINTBRUSH

IN A KINDGDOM BENEATH THE SEA

Today's the day Mitchell Burnhope gets the royal shit kicked out of him. That's the consensus at the bar. Marie-Odile's bear-shaped brothers are already brooding in the rear, chowing down on a late breakfast of corn dogs and Slush Puppies from the Texaco across the road. Every few minutes one of them looks up at the door with his unibrow beetled. I'm still shocked at how many girls allow their own flesh and blood inside this place to watch them grind it out onstage. We had one a few years ago who went everywhere with her little blue-haired grandma until Frank had to kick her to the curb for fencing stolen goods from her jumbo-sized handbag. Crooked grandma aside, Frank is generally a big-hearted guy, likes his regulars to hang out before opening time and after hours, says it makes the club seem more homely. Like one big happy family, where the faces of the daughters who've quit or been fired or disappeared are swapped out with fresh new faces like flower arrangements in a fancy restaurant.

Marie-Odile pushes past me in her butterfly kimono, a trail of bubble-gum vapours and vanilla musk wafting in her wake. Her brothers walked out of a Grimm's fairy tale and laid their woodsman axes at the door a couple of years back. It didn't take them long to get accustomed to life in town. Everyone in the club is terrified of them now, and of Marie-Odile too insofar as she belongs to them. She only flinches a little when one brother reaches out to lightly slap her as she sits back down between them. His rings catch in her hair. He untangles himself while the other reaches for his ringing cellphone. Rumours have been floating around that Marie-Odile is not long for this world, that the brothers have found a spot for her in an upcoming porno flick, are arranging to meet a guy who knows a guy high up in the adult movie scene.

In my day there were girls who dreamed about dancing on Broadway or in the ballet or who just wanted to save up enough money to run away from their crazy boyfriends. Girls who wanted to make the world outside their hotel rooms disappear with a bottle of Southern Comfort and a handful of sleeping pills. But it's all big business now. A whole intricate system that Marie-Odile's brothers have begun to acquaint themselves with. A plum role in a porno will potentially land her gigs in every upscale club on the circuit, and other spinoffs too. Enough to keep a whole host of brothers in Harleys and firearms and cocaine. At the moment, though, she's just a wide-eyed beginner with the odd five-minute spot onstage, panic-stricken and a little unsteady in her six-inch heels. Mostly she sits offside, picking up tricks of the trade from the feature dancers and ignoring the overtures of romantics like Mitchell Burnhope.

Marie-Odile is my replacement. It's unspoken, but everybody knows. Frank's been warning me for ages. I can't remember the last time my name was on the roster. I'm strictly the girl with the cleavage who mothers the old boys at the back blowing their paycheques on overpriced booze. It's no lie that I've been letting myself go of late. And because my mind has started to wander, my body has gone astray, has started to graze on whatever it sets its eyes upon. Wing nights and crinkle-cut fries and every kind of awful snack in the Texaco aisles. Another pound of flab on that ass, Frank tells me, and I'm three deep in the heap, out in the cold. Fine, I tell him. Maybe it stinks less like a gym locker room out there.

Maybe it's no coincidence, as far as any of us is concerned, that today's feature dancer is Destiny. She steps onto the stage, flips her bleached hair, and tilts her head back. She has that heartless hundred-mile stare. The joke around here is that she chose her dancer name after taking a good long look into the future and deciding she didn't give a shit. The daytime regulars are coming out of the woodwork and taking their places at the usual tables. Destiny keeps herself to herself, has no boyfriend or "manager" or bearish brothers to either protect or abuse her or siphon off her earnings. Trying to be friendly, I asked her once where she came from. She mentioned a mining town up north, then clamped her skinny lips shut.

The only other thing we know about her is that she loves her pet cockatiels more than anything on earth, lets them fly around uncaged in her hotel room. It isn't that unusual. A lot of dancers travel from club to club with pets to make life on the road more bearable. The cockatiels shit on the bedspread and on her clothes but Destiny doesn't notice or care. Judging from the amount of bills rolled into coke straws on her hotel room floor and the residues on her dressing table, she's not often in the frame of mind for righteous housekeeping. She's unsteady at the pole today, and Frank is frowning with his fist on his chin while he watches her. A few more false moves and she'll be out on her ass like me except a whole lot faster because she never bothered to get in Frank's or anyone else's good books. Vlada says she's a bad woman. And Vlada should know. She's made a character study of every dancer the Coronet Hotel has ever hired.

"We're all bad," I say. "We're strippers."

Vlada's an odd bird too. With her whiskers and her hooked nose, she looks just like the kind of witch you might expect to mutter curses and have uncanny insights. Over time I've come to realize that most of her pronouncements stem from an obsession with personal hygiene. I guess you pick up some strange ideas about humanity when you spend five years in one of Stalin's gulags. She mutters and leans her mop against the wall to pat my back. But it's not pity that has Vlada clucking over me. A million or so years before I started stripping down in the club I was a chambermaid upstairs, stripping sheets, scrubbing toilets, and helping Vlada heave around a dicky-wheeled housekeeping cart stuffed with towels and miniature soaps. For this, I have earned her undying loyalty. I should get a tin star and a sickle for my hard time.

Back when the town was heading somewhere, before the factories closed and this whole side of the sprawl died, the Coronet was the fanciest place around. I've seen photos of the exterior and the grounds, which had an acre or so of formal rose gardens and a cute little heart-shaped arbour they used for wedding photos. People like the Shriners and the Chamber of Commerce had their conventions here in the sixties, back when all the men looked like Sinatra or Pat Boone. Sometimes I try to picture what the inside was like before they hacked it up into smaller rooms. There are traces of former grandeur: peeling cherubs and the remains of a marquetry dance floor in the storeroom where I sneak cigarettes. But the place is sinking like Atlantis. Any day now they'll paste a CONDEMNED sign on the door. But not before Mitchell Burnhope turns up in his oversized coat and gets himself pounded into Beefaroni in the parking lot.

They didn't have a chambermaid's uniform big enough to fit me when I started. It's not like I was big on purpose, I simply never gave a thought to anything that happened below my collarbone. I wasn't brought up that way. After the receptionist found a cook's apron to wrap around the spot where the zipper wouldn't close, Vlada led me up to a room on the second floor and flung the doors open like she was opening the gates to a lost civilization. Scarves and stockings were coiled around a pool of melted ice cream. A tipped jar of nail polish drooled onto the TV screen. A sequinned belt was curled around some gnawed steak bones and a cigarette-studded slice of pie. Vlada warned me to separate the rotting meat from the clothing, handed me a bucket and a few garbage bags, and pointed to the cleaning supplies on the trolley. Then she handed me a paper sash with the word "Sanitized" printed on it.

"Don't forget to put 'Miss America' on the toilet," she said, grinning.

When Vlada came back we humped the bags of clothes down to a basement storage room crammed full of other garbage bags with the names of other girls written on them, dancer names like Bambi and Barbarella. Every once in a while a girl will turn up in the lobby to reclaim her abandoned things, wild-eyed and rapping her fingernails on the front desk. But it's amazing how many of them just disappear. I asked Vlada once if she thought they'd met some awful fate or just turned over a new leaf.

"Either way they go to a better place," she said, and sucked the side of her cheek.

The pounds melted off and it wasn't long before Frank was smacking my rear and getting me up to audition on amateur night. He still brags about how he saved me from a lifetime of drudgery. I sometimes ask myself what's worse, bumping and grinding in a pair of crotchless panties to a bar full of wing-eating oafs or scooping up Chihuahua shit in an overheated hotel room. Vlada tells me that more and more often these days the girls are neat as soldiers, ordering their brushes and makeup bottles into symmetrical rows, tallying their tips and expenses in little notebooks they hand over to their managers at the end of a tour. For this they earn the unseen respect of a bandy-legged, moustachioed ex-Soviet chambermaid whose chief nervous tic is to stick out her tongue as far it will stretch.

Have you ever had a fish tank? My father had one when I was growing up. He bought it for relaxation but like everything else to do with him, it turned into a horror show. At first it was like a box full of flitting jewels with a little treasure chest nestled in the coloured gravel. Soon there were Japanese fighting fish maiming each other, and hordes of inbred cannibal guppies, and a crab that scuttled around eating the carcasses and lost body parts. He left it like that for a while, a tank full of cloudy yellow water that he stared into looking for signs of life. One night when he was drunk he smashed it with a hammer. I heard the glass crack from my bedroom and then the sad whoosh of water. We never got the sour smell out of the carpet.

When I finally made up my mind to become a stripper, I made a mix-tape of sexy songs and worked out a routine in the basement storage room. The songs sounded all wrong when I finally climbed onstage a few weeks later. I thought at first it was nerves, but the tape was damaged. I got lost in the distortions, and all the walls and faces wavered in the semi-darkness while part of me watched from on high as Helen Blackmore, former member of the First Baptist Church choir, winner of the Calvary Educational Centre inter-school spell-a-thon, transformed herself into a naked trembling creature with jellyfish legs. For months, even years, after that I kept waiting for the big angry eye to fill the window. For the hammer to strike and the cold air to come rushing and the whole place to be smashed into glittery pieces.

Mitchell Burnhope came here for the first time on his birthday with a bunch of other rubes trying to look the ages forged on their IDs. Not for Mitchell Burnhope the ritual jacking off into a wad of Kleenex in the booths at the back. He was going to fall in love. You could see the cupid's arrow hovering a few inches in front of his chest as he gazed around the room looking at all the ladies, which is when Marie-Odile stepped out of the dressing room like a fawn into a woodland bower, then paused to fix a beaded strap on her tiny ankle. The blossom of a smile on those cherry-glossed lips was all it took to plunge the arrow so deep into his chest you could see the tip poking out through the back of his cheap blazer.

The next day he turned up sober and early. He dealt out business cards embossed with his name and the word "Entrepreneur" underneath in shiny letters. It took the brothers the same amount of time it takes to flick a switchblade to measure his worth and turn their backs, bending the cards in half before tossing them into the brimming ashtrays. The next day the flowers arrived, a matronly bouquet of chrysanthemums that sent Marie-Odile into a sulk after she tossed them into the trash.

Later on that day I saw the abandoned flowers arranged in Vlada's old green vase down in the laundry room. Not much happens at the Coronet without Vlada knowing about it. She's always somewhere: a flash of grey, a bent back disappearing around the corner, the sound of a vacuum cleaner in a distant room. I feel her presence wherever I am, the way you might feel mice in a wall or pigeons fluttering in the eaves. The basement laundry room is where she makes herself at home, losing herself in daydreams too painful or lovely to talk about out loud, smiling like a village idiot at the embroidered daisies on a dishtowel while the tumble driers churn. I sat down and asked her what she thought about the unfolding love story upstairs.

"Not good," she said. "For him."

"How long do you think he'll last?"

She let out a little cackle. "Who knows? Ask Destiny."

"I give it two weeks," I said. "Three if he gets her some jewellery."

"Three days," said Frank. And that's when we all started placing our bets.

An idea infects you, occupies your mind like a virus. A St. Vitus's dance that has you jerking and twitching, laughing and weeping for no earthly reason. Makes a holy fool out of you. Has you tossed into vats of boiling oil and thrown to lions. Has you oblivious to the monsters slouching in loosely formed groups in a bar full of muffled grunts and surreptitious glances. It wasn't enough for Mitchell Burnhope to adore Marie-Odile from a distance. He was on a mission to save her.

He came back again and again, alone in his oversized coat, like a man who's found Jesus, smiling and holding out his hand long after the person in front of him has refused to shake it. He sent more flowers. Then the presents started to arrive: a fuzzy heart-shaped pillow with wings, a chocolate astronaut in a box lined with gold foil stars. A googly-eyed teddy bear on a pair of pink plastic skis that Vlada later retrieved from the kitchen garbage canister.

Vlada gave me a tea set from Zellers a few years ago. A blurry willow pattern on cheap grey-flecked china. I was about to hand it back and tell her I didn't even drink tea, when I remembered her endless white coffees sloshing alongside us in the housekeeping cart. I understood then that the tea set was meant to sit on a shelf somewhere looking ceremonial. Because I don't have my own place yet, I keep it in the trunk next to my spare tire. The box is frayed and warped now and stained with salt and antifreeze. Every time I dump it on the curb, I see Vlada's eyes burning holes into my head and I hump it straight back into the trunk.

In the room of an abandoned palace, fires guttering in the streets below, someone has an idea and tells it to an under-secretary, who jots it down and types it into a directive. Some-one has an idea and then the idea has you led at gunpoint to a train station and set trundling across the tundra on a bed of dirty straw. Vlada almost never speaks of those years but when she does there's no overarching story, there's no moral or ending. A battle for a dropped crust. A night search that has her standing like a statue for hours, naked between the winter stars and the piles of frozen excrement at her feet.

I went to her apartment once. There was a bus strike and a snowstorm and because I knew she always walked in to work I offered her a lift. All day and all the night before squalls had blasted waist-high drifts along the streets, and we drove through the white, half-buried town to its furthest reaches. I pulled up at her apartment block just as the streetlights were casting their first sallow haloes onto the unplowed sidewalks. How she had made her way into work that morning was anyone's guess. I stared at her in stunned respect. Childless, husbandless, she was tough enough at seventy to cross the Khyber Pass.

I had a boyfriend once who worked in the merchant navy. I used to take him up to the rooms on the third floor where nobody goes now except Vlada and her rags and feather dusters. He was lying on the bed, a slab of raw pink beef staring up at the ceiling. The harbours in Asia are full of girls, he said. There are so many to begin with, they start them so young and there's so much sickness. Most of them are used up by the time they hit their twenties. What to do, have them crawling the alleys like sick cats? A slit at the throat, a shove off the pier. It's almost a kindness.

I see it when I close my eyes, the sea floor littered with pelvic bones settled into the sediments like spent oyster shells. Once you know something like that, how can you go on fooling yourself about anything?

Every night the club fills up with rednecks and hicks with their hair slicked back as if for church and portly salesmen in polyester suits and half the local chapter of the Hells Angels. The girls undulate under the blue lights and the room is awash in booze and hormones and the smell of genitals and sweat. A slight imbalance and the equilibrium is lost. Algae bloom. Blood spills in the emergency exits and out onto the parking lot to mingle with the asphalt and grit and pieces of other people's teeth. I almost couldn't look when Mitchell Burnhope came into the lobby, a small velvet box in his fist, his skinny neck sinking into his collar as he made his way over to Marie-Odile, who sat at the back of the bar flanked by those burly brothers.

Even the blue lights glowed bluer as he went down on bended knee. The whole room leaned in for a better look. He couldn't have picked a more auspicious moment. There had been angry phone calls, the promising lead to adult movieland had fallen through, and for this Marie-Odile had been dealt a round of blows to her ears and the back side of her head, the only places where the bruising wouldn't interfere with her job. She was in a most evil sulk, which Mitchell Burnhope might have noticed if he wasn't so far in over his head that his vision was blurred.

I don't doubt she would have said no. But if he'd picked a different day she might not have flown out of her seat and kicked him so hard in the balls that he curled into a fetus at her candy-red stilletoed feet. This plus the mirthless chuckles of those two Goliaths would have been enough to snuff out the intentions of the most ardent suitor. But not Mitchell Burnhope. As soon as he could draw a full breath, he picked himself up and brushed himself off and declared that he would never stop. At least he had the good sense to scuttle off before the brothers stopped grinning.

Since then some of us have given up, think that nobody could be that much of an imbecile to risk coming back. Others, like Frank, have doubled down, convinced that Mitchell Burnhope has more of a death wish than a crush.

Destiny spins around the pole and then fumbles. Her knees sag. Frank is now standing in the middle of the room with his arms folded, his legs spread apart as if he's preparing for battle. I know, I know. I've heard him give the speech before. He has the good of the club to think of. She's always been a little unprofessional, even for this dive. She looks over at him and laughs as if to prove the point, sinks a little further down on her haunches. I can't watch anymore. So many awful things happen when you're not even looking, why wait around for the inevitable? The brothers lean back in their chairs, suck the last of the Slush Puppies through their straws, look almost longingly towards the door. I'm sure now that Frank will win his bet that, sloping or straight-backed, Mitchell Burnhope will come through that door and get what's coming to him.

I slip down into the basement to fold towels with Vlada and while away the last of the afternoon. A few minutes later Frank comes downstairs with a troubled look on his face, begs me to give him a back rub. With his red-rimmed eyes and his drooping jowls, he's easy to feel sorry for. Even if he is the boss. Even if he does make a living off our naked bodies. Even if he might fire me any day soon. He sits down at the table and watches me fold towels while Vlada clucks over him and doles out the same flavour cup-of-soup she's just prepared for me. To Vlada, we're all slaves, indentured in a menacing, intricate system she's always aware of even if we're not.

She hobbles out into the corridor with a pile of folded towels. Maybe I'll take her place in a few years when her arthritis is so bad she can no longer hold a mop. Will I be strong enough to survive as long as she has? There's a sharp cry and I run to the door. Vlada is sprinting down the corridor as fast as her bandy little legs will carry her, shaking her fist at the tiny blur of white and yellow that flits and whizzes ahead of her. The escaped cockatiel darts around the corner.

By the time I reach them they're in the boiler room, the cockatiel is flying from pipe to pipe, perching in the warm recesses of the ancient furnace that not even Vlada attempts to dust. She stands there with her hands outstretched, chanting a Russian nursery rhyme under her breath. The bird eyes her suspiciously. Losing patience, Vlada pokes at it with a broom handle. The cobwebs stick to the handle and droop into ragged fringes. The cockatiel flies over to the rectangular window set into the rough concrete wall and flutters there for a moment before flying back to the pipe. Vlada coos, hands cupped and outstretched as if offering the cockatiel a gift. The bird is in a panic, flying back and forth, tapping its little beak on the glass and then returning to cling to the pipe, its tiny chest heaving.

"Fine, you stupid bird," says Vlada. The bird cocks its head. She pushes her footstool beneath the window and climbs up. Even so, she can barely reach the sash. She heaves it open with a grunt and a cascade of paint flakes, dust, and snow settles on her shoulders and the furnace room floor. Vlada bunches her face into a knuckle and steps down. A blast of wind sweeps in another small flurry.

"So go," she says. "Go into the dirty fucking snow and die."

It's a scene from a fairy tale, the cockatiel with its scarlet China doll cheeks perched on a cobwebbed pipe looking down at bandy-legged Vlada with her broomstick and then back again at the window, alive with whirling snow and the sound of the approaching sirens. There is a moment when even the cockatiel seems to understand what has been happening, what is always happening, beyond the borders of its birdy world. And now all eyes are on the grey-white rectangle as it blushes to pink and then cherry red, and the ambulance swings into the parking lot.

Willem de Kooning's Paintbrush

She was still having nightmares about Magic Mountain six months after the attack. Not the amusement park but the roller coaster as it plunged into the lights below. In her dream it was a fall into hell, the pool of neon signs and shapes fluorescing with the intensity of gamma rays. The engulfment left her drenched and upright, reaching for the bedside lamp whose bulb had burned out weeks ago.

They had gone to L.A. for a vacation, their first since moving in together earlier that year. They stayed at a hotel in Hollywood, rented a car and drove out into the burnt-sienna scenery so familiar to them from a childhood spent watching seventies TV shows that it felt like a homecoming. They did the tour of Universal Studios and the Walk of Fame. They went to Magic Mountain on a whim, having run out of ideas about how to spend their last evening before their late flight home.

"Get ready for an eruption of sights and thrills," said Boyd, flipping through the guidebook as if it was a deck of cards.

She had approached the vacation with a sense of irony, wanting to take in the surrounding spectacle in a way that left her feeling if not superior, then at least as a person who had risen somewhat above the callow pleasures of the entertainment industry. But Boyd had loved L.A., had shrieked like a star-struck fan at the Chinese Theatre and gawked at passing limos. He had even insisted they go on a tour of Bel-Air, and for the whole two hours had stared out the bus window like a tycoon on a big-game safari.

He liked it so much she felt she was seeing a different side of Boyd altogether. She started re-evaluating him, appraising his clothes and his hair and his demeanour in a whole new light.

For most of the trip he had also been speaking, awkwardly at first but now with disturbing fluidity, in a series of impersonations that ranged between a basso vampire and the squeak of a cartoon character she didn't recognize. She found herself regarding his mouth as if it was a volatile creature in its own right.

They drove out again into the scenery later on that afternoon, then stood on an acre of asphalt in a crush of loud families before pushing through the turnstiles into the park. She wanted to leave even before the roller coaster loomed above them, but Boyd steered her towards the line of red-faced people. She wasn't good with heights.

"Lighten up," he said, in a tough-guy voice. Then he poked her in the stomach and quacked so loudly that the couple in front of them turned back to look.

What persuaded her to go in the end was the feeling that she couldn't have freed herself from the queue even if she wanted to. With linked arms and adjoining shoulders, the crowd around her was a solid gaudy serpent feeding itself into the flashing vestibule of the Apocalypse mega-coaster, where men in space suits mouthed down at them from angled TV screens.

They reached the front of the queue and were bundled into a car that shunted up the coaster's spine then remained motionless at the apex. Panic-stricken, she stared up at the low-hanging moon, looking down only when she felt the first creaking plunge into the neon maelstrom below. The rest of the ride was a blur of jagging lights and the occasional fraught glimpse of the coaster's wooden stick structure, lit up as if by lightning and looking frail enough to burst into splinters at any moment.

She was so shaken after the roller coaster disgorged them that she stumbled on the ridged metal steps at the exit and fell against the white plastic chain cordoning off another ride. She realized that Boyd was no longer at her side when she reached for his arm. She spent the next half-hour hunting for him among the jangling machines and whirling lights, spotting him at last beside a shooting gallery, where he was watching children with acid-green rifles shoot at cartoon targets. Having now found Boyd, she had an urge to turn and leave him there forever. He looked, to her, like a man about to have a religious vision. Or rather—and she wasn't sure what was worse—a man pretending to have a religious vision. She was surprised that he wasn't drawing more attention from the surrounding crowds, who flowed past him as though he was invisible. Even as a complete stranger she would have noticed, would have singled him out with a snigger or a sarcastic remark about how the enormous stuffed fluorescent animals seemed to cluster around his balding head and beatific face like a kind of deranged nativity scene. She decided in the end that it would be too complicated to break up with him here. She imagined the scenes he might make back at the hotel or airport. She swallowed her rage and went up to him.

"I used to love the shooting galleries when I was a kid," he said. His voice sounded wistful, more like the voice of the old Boyd she knew. Or thought she knew.

On the ride to the hotel, she reasoned that at least the amusement park had the effect of making Hollywood seem more real and less like the delusionary fiefdom ensconced in a sea of tire fires and warring gangs that it actually was. And maybe Boyd was just reacting in his own way to all the false-ness. Maybe once they got home, he would return to normal and everything would be okay.

"Next year we're going to Vegas," she said, watching a man lip-synch to a video camera in an alley across from their hotel. The inhospitable desert, with its lizards and rocks and occasional piles of bleached animal bones, would purge Boyd of his daffy voices and affectations. Or the slot machines would shut him up. He appeared in the bathroom doorway toothbrush in hand and grinned at her with a mouth full of foam. She turned away in disgust and stared at the blank wall until he was packed and ready to go.

At the airport the loud voices seemed to refract off the glass peaks of the vaulted ceilings and break into pieces at her feet. It took several attempts for her to understand from the grey-suited airline representative that their flight had been delayed. With an hour to kill they wandered towards the duty-free shops that glowed on the far side of the airport's aquarium murk. She browsed the aisles and sprayed herself with eau de toilette but the scent was sickening under the hot lights and the roller coaster nausea roiled inside her again.

She motioned to Boyd and crossed the half acre of polished granite to the women's washroom, where she scrubbed her wrists at the sink. The gloomy lighting cast a cowl of darkness around her reflected silhouette. Set against a diagonal slash of maroon wall art and a row of iron-grey cubicles receding into the background, she reminded herself of a dreary, futurist Madonna.

She found Boyd squinting at a magazine by the Sunglass Hut beneath a poster of two smiling models.

She liked to think, looking back on those few moments as she moved towards him, still imbued with the dolorous impression of her image in the mirror, that she approached his figure with something like tenderness. Years afterwards she recalled, or felt that she could recall, the scene with photographic precision: the robin's-egg blue of his button-down shirt, the wolfish smiles of the larger-than-life models above his bent head, vulnerable and boyish despite or because of the shell-pink bald patch on his crown. She liked to think that the irritations and aggressions she had felt during the vacation melted with each step she took towards him, until they were enveloped once again in their familiar cocoon.

The attack began as an awareness of something frayed and blue-grey that flitted, hummingbird-like, a blur of matted hair and faded denim in the corner of her eye. She didn't see the attacker's face until he had flown past her and the two men fell onto the floor, Boyd's head smacking onto the granite with a sickening thud.

When she recounted the incident to the police she told them that she couldn't shake the feeling she'd seen him before. Did Boyd have shadows in his life that the attacker had emerged from? Had he been stalking them for some time? She imagined him trailing through the maze of their doings. She didn't tell them that she felt almost as though he was a figure from a dream she'd once had, come horribly to life. She shook her head at the thought, then wondered out loud if, with his yellow eyes and flaring nostrils and coils of nicotine-tinted hair, he was just such a quintessential crazy guy, an off-kilter Vietnam vet or deinstitutionalized schizophrenic, that he would seem familiar to anyone, would have been picked out of a lineup of casting hopefuls for that role.

While it was happening she stared at him open-mouthed, rooted in shock and a haze of stale piss and tobacco. When the attacker began to bash Boyd's head on the floor, she yanked at the man's shredded jean jacket and screamed at the gathering crowd to call the security guards. The salesgirls leaned out of the Sunglass Hut to watch. Nobody made a move to help. She realized that the onlookers must think that the three of them knew each other. She twisted her head. It was a scene from any one of a million dramas—she could almost see the storylines unreeling in their eyes. It was true that the scene, in the abstract, was mesmerizing. The streaks of blood were vivid against the tan chino and the frayed greyish blue of the man's soiled denim, a portion of which she still held in her own hand. Locked in a hold with their faces purple and straining, the two men looked as if they'd been carved from the same substance. She faced the crowd and tried to arrange her own features so they appeared normal, but felt the panic working underneath, rearranging the musculature to a grimace of horror.

When she saw the flash of a serrated blade, a knife she recognized as the kind her Michigan father had used to gut and clean animals, she let go of the attacker's jacket so abruptly that he fell onto Boyd and pinned him to the ground. She staggered backwards and started to scream, convinced now that the man would slit Boyd from groin to throat.

Then as quickly as the battering had started, it stopped. The attacker stood up, furrowed his brow, and loped away as if he had suddenly remembered something that required his urgent attention. She watched him step onto an escalator and sink from view just as two security guards stepped towards her.

She tried to explain to the guards what had happened, but the suspicion in their eyes told her that they too thought she and Boyd shared a history with their attacker. They stared down at Boyd, whose robin's-egg shirt was wrenched from his chinos and smeared with dirt and blood.

"He's getting away," she said.

The attacker would follow them home, trail his yellow finger down the departures screen to locate their flight number and destination, cling to the plane's undercarriage like that creature from *The Twilight Zone*. They would never be safe again, but always peering between the slats of their venetian blinds before leaving the house.

"I'm fine," said a high-pitched voice. They looked down at Boyd, struggling to his feet. Then he buckled and sank onto the blood-slicked floor, his cheekbone striking the granite. She told the guards about the knife. Reluctantly, one of them unsheathed a radio and held it to his mouth.

She helped Boyd up and they hobbled to the nearest seating arrangement. She settled him into the sling of black vinyl then ran back to the sepulchral washroom, barely registering her hectic silhouette in the mirrors as she unreeled a length of paper towel and moistened it with water and a squirt of pink soap.

Boyd refused any medical attention. "Heads bleed a lot," he said. The bleeding, at any rate, appeared to have slowed or stopped.

The police arrived and she and Boyd were led to an office in the airport's back labyrinth where she dabbed at Boyd's face while they described the attack and their attacker. They were then told that security would scan the surveillance tapes to see if they could spot him on the footage.

They were left in a waiting room until a new flight could be arranged. She nodded off and dreamed about the surveillance cameras, the faces in the crowds moving like fish in a sea of grainy fizzle. She was startled awake when one of the security personnel leaned in through the doorway to tell them that a flight had been found.

"I'm fine," said Boyd, looking over at her. She couldn't remember having asked him how he was.

She held his hand on the turbulent flight home, gazing down through patchy clouds at the canvas of rocky terrain beneath them. Boyd was sweaty and restless, his free arm swaying at the elbow, the hand gesticulating like a sock puppet while he dozed. After they landed he rushed out into the arrivals lounge, sank to his knees, and vomited a pool of brown sludge. Wordless, she looked down at his balding head. The gash on his crown was now a deep burgundy. She watched the slick pool widen on the floor, unable to call out for the attendants. Her face was reflected in the pool, along with a radiant stripe of overhead light.

The next few days were a blur of phone calls and hospital corridors, hours spent in a white cubicle viewing scans of Boyd's skull and brain where a doctor informed her that Boyd's skull wasn't fractured. A disruption to his synapses had caused the flurry of seizures that started in the airport and continued in the ambulance and the emergency ward until he had been medicated and wheeled away. The complications, the doctor said obliquely, were likely to resolve over time.

She had her first dream about the roller coaster back in the empty house, waking into blackness after the whirling lights had sizzled through her body like volts of electricity. Boyd stared at her calmly as she sat on the plastic chair beside the hospital bed the next morning. The left side of his face had deepened to a dull purple and was so swollen that his eye had shifted sideways out of place. There were sutures where the bruises had swollen and split.

"Let's go back to L.A. for a few more days," he said. "We were having such a blast."

When he came home from the hospital, Boyd spent his days in bed watching TV with the blinds down and curtains drawn, claiming that the sunlight gave him a headache. She came back from the grocery store one afternoon to hear him roughly sobbing, the bedroom door locked from the inside. She murmured soothingly through the keyhole but it was only much later, when she'd given up and gone back out onto the front porch, that she heard him moving swiftly through the house, his bare feet slapping on the wooden floors so heavily that the porch steps trembled.

An official called from the airport to say that the attacker had been sighted on several surveillance cameras, had been last seen boarding a shuttle heading back into the city. Wandering the streets of Los Angeles with his frizzled hair like an Old Testament prophet's, the violence crackling through him like lightning down a conductor. She wondered what exactly the attacker had seen in Boyd to turn on him so brutally.

"Do you ever think about him?"

Boyd's face bunched into a fist. He shrugged.

"Don't you wonder why he did it? Why he chose us?"

"Things happen," said Boyd. But his face bunched even tighter and he began to rock back and forth, his tongue bulging in his cheek.

Things happen and can't unhappen. She came into the bedroom one day to find him perched like a gargoyle on the night table. She had read the pamphlet about head injuries and knew that he might behave oddly. She was more troubled by her own state of mind. She had taken leave from work to look after him, but any tenderness she felt dissolved like a mirage by the time she mounted the stairs and turned the doorknob to discern his shape in the gloom, half-buried under a hillock of sour blankets. A knot of fury and revulsion hardened inside her. She had always thought of herself deep down as a good person, that the sarcasm and the deadpan humour were shields designed to protect her sensitive soul. Now, she wasn't sure.

A week later she woke up from her neon nightmare to see Boyd hunched in the rocking chair near the bed.

"Maybe," she said to him in the morning, "you should watch something other than those murder and police shows all day long."

"There's nothing else to watch."

She grabbed the remote and flicked through the channels, landing on a grainy black-and-white image that fizzled on the screen.

"It looks like a documentary about the war," she said.

"Which one?" he asked.

When it became obvious that Boyd wasn't going to get better any time soon, she retreated to the guest room with its mismatched antiques and unwanted housewarming gifts. She positioned a small TV on the dresser across from the bed. On nights when she couldn't sleep she searched out sitcoms starring wisecracking teens, eye-rolling moms and dads with sheepish grins, the kinds of people she liked to think lived in the sea of darkened houses outside her window.

The incandescent lights in her nightmares began to leach into her waking hours, filling them with slashes of violent colour. As if a screen had been pulled to one side, instead of suburban streets she now saw primal violence, in the snarling grilles of oncoming traffic, in the sharp angles of buildings and the sudden movements of strangers. Why would anyone pay to go on a roller coaster when this restless malevolence was everywhere to be had for free? When she told a friend on the phone that she feared she was going crazy, the friend said that the impersonal nature of the attack, the fact that it was such a bolt from the blue, probably made it more disquieting. As if the assault would have been okay if they had known their attacker, or if there had been a reason for it. She pictured the frenetic blue figure and once again had the feeling that he had slipped into the real world from a dream. She didn't mention to her friend that she felt secretly responsible for the attack, that to her mind she had summoned the man up to punish Boyd for being so annoying.

And then there was the smell. What she thought at first was also a product of her imagination grew into a pervasive odour that was most powerful in the master bedroom, where Boyd insisted he couldn't smell a thing. She rummaged through the drawers and closets. When she finally kneeled down and hoisted up the bedskirt, she saw that the floor under the bed was strewn with bones, mostly pork chops and drumsticks and some larger roast and loin bones. She stood up and caught Boyd doubled over, his face contorted in a rictus of ugly mirth. When she walked down to the basement she saw that their chest freezer was almost empty. He was shoving the cuts into the microwave whole to defrost and cook while she was out.

"Has he assaulted or threatened to assault you?"

She was sitting in a restaurant with her friend Claire, grabbing the lunch they'd been postponing for months.

"No. Not yet."

"Are you afraid?"

"I'm horrified," she said. "Is that the same thing?"

"And all the tests come back normal."

"All normal."

They had roomed together in college, had grown so close that people mistook them for twins. Now, although they still shared the same hairstyle, she felt less like a twin and more like a dishevelled imposter.

Claire clapped her hands together. "You can't let yourself go like this. If you don't look after yourself, who will?"

After lunch Claire manoeuvred her into a department store and had a makeup counter artist apply foundation, stripes of blush, and a ring of kohl around each eye.

"There," said Claire, tilting her head back to appraise her friend. "That feels better, doesn't it?"

She was startled by the mask of exaggerated features when she got home and moved warily past her reflection in the burnished hall mirror.

She draped her coat over the bannister and listened intently, trying to pinpoint his location in the house. She was learning not to expect a miracle. What seemed like an improvement always dissolved into tears or that mocking, brutish look. The same ugliness was growing inside her, shifting fitfully at night while she lay awake.

She found him pressed against the farthest wall in the living room. She was shocked not so much by this as by the heft of his marbled haunches beneath the worn blue underpants he had taken to wearing around the house. He looked at her sideways, his face distorted by the living room wall it was squashed against.

She stared at him across the long, low living room with its tasteful furnishings, the walls painted a warm beige to counteract what her decorator mysteriously called the "sterility," past the iron sculpture with its lethal-looking prongs that she had bought expressly for this plunge from their separate city high-rises into leafiness and big lawns, to begin what was called by friends and family the next logical phase in their lives.

But the man had come and infected them with a new way of seeing. She felt her vision blunting now even further, blearing the living room couches and chairs into a mass of cubes and blobs at the centre of which was Boyd, his body filleted by shadows from the venetian blinds, his face bloated with suffering and streaked with mucus and tears.

She could go to him or turn away. Neither of the two options seemed possible at that moment. And so once again she stood transfixed, unable to stop staring.

KINDNESS

I always stop in the park to take in the scenery on my way to work. The green is restful to my eyes, and if you pause long enough a few down-and-outs emerge from the tableau, their dingy clothes blending into the background. A while back some punks, still just kids really, torched one of the frailest guys. He'd been boozing hard and was out cold when they doused him in lighter fluid and lit a match. Hearing stuff like that makes me want to give up on the world altogether. I'm no sentimentalist, you can't afford to be when you work in a bar, but I've got a few old buddies in that park. I'm only ever a couple of paycheques away from ending up under the shrubbery myself.

Lucky for me it's only three short blocks of hustle and bustle from the park to Macy's beckoning gloom. A born skinflint, Macy's only too happy to save a few bucks a year on light bulbs, but if you saw our regulars you'd agree that darkness is more of a public service than a deprivation. Not that anyone at Macy's gives a rat's ass. Except me. No matter how high I propped up Macy's ill-fitting shutter to blot out the bright shapes passing by on the pavement outside, it was still possible to see the tops of people's heads, maybe half the head of a taller person cut off at the nose or lips. Sonny and Wesley and the other regulars made a game out of identifying locals by their hair or the shapes of their skulls. On the day this particular story starts, they'd just spotted the comb-over of the Hillbilly Grill's proprietor frilling like a rooster's crest in the breeze and the beehive of his cashier mistress glittering stiffly beside him when a whole head and neck, wide as a steer's, appeared momentarily in the window.

Framed by a blond wig, the features were pitted with acne scars or what might have been the aftermath of an ice-pick fight. The overall impression was of a face carved from sandstone with a layer of Technicolor makeup applied on top. It was the kind of face, minus the makeup, I might have wanted to draw back in the days when I still did. Charcoal on butcher paper to capture those rough crags and shadows. But striking as the features were, it was the expression—abject and more than a little terrifying—that lingered on like an aura in the space it had only just occupied. We were still staring openmouthed at the window when the face reappeared and stared back in at us so intently that Sonny almost scrambled under his stool.

The door swung open and the figure, dressed in a shocking-pink wool dress, swaggered into the stock-still, spellbound bar.

"Well, it's all fun and games in here, isn't it?" The voice was male and female, light and darkness, a sotto voce interwoven with a bronchial rasp. "Bourbon with rocks. And whatever else these gentlemen over here are having."

It's hard for a poor man to refuse a kindness, especially when his welfare cheque isn't due for four days and he's been eking out a shabby afternoon with a glass of warm, flat beer. Before you could bat an eyelash, the expressions of sly horror had vanished from Sonny's and Wesley's faces and they were shooting the breeze with the Mother of God or Godzilla, depending on which one of them you asked.

"The name is Renée, with two e's."

Which was how we knew she was a woman, or at least preferred to be addressed as one. She held out a raw-knuckled hand the size of a shovel and shook the hell out of ours. She ordered a round, patting her wig while Sonny and Wesley knocked back shots of Wild Turkey.

"That's put the twinkle back," she said.

The flush on Sonny's nose had bloomed across his pinched little face, and Wesley was now recounting a street antic of his involving a troupe of pigeons. Renée was all smiles. The tragic look I'd glimpsed through Macy's greasy, thumb-printed windowpane had vanished. It wasn't long before the three of them were raising their glasses to world peace. An hour or so later she stood up, six foot five in heels, and sashayed down the empty bar towards the washrooms, pausing for full dramatic effect before stepping into the ladies' room. No sooner had that door swung shut than, pantomime style, the hatch behind the bar opened and Macy appeared with a fistful of papers in his hand.

"The great man himself," said Wesley.

Macy grunted, sat down on a bar stool, and spread the papers out in front of him. He groaned and laid his head down. He pounded his hairy fists on the bar top, so engrossed in his display of torment that he didn't notice Renée swaggering back to her place a few stools to the left of him.

"Put me out of my misery," he said.

"You poor man," said Renée. "What on earth can be the matter?"

Macy was an expert at ignoring his customers, who had been pouring the measly contents of their wallets, kids' piggy banks, Styrofoam begging cups, busted meters, and grocery jars into his cash register since he'd opened his doors to the public. He kept his eyes shut and his head, blue-veined and bald as a dinosaur egg, down on the bar top with his papers, which contained columns filled with spiky black numbers and appeared to have been partially gnawed.

"I'm finally going under is what's the matter," he said. "Call an ambulance. Send in the clowns."

His complaints about impending doom were as familiar to us as a leper's bell in a medieval city, so it came as a shock to hear someone take them seriously. Renée peered down at the papers and smiled.

"Call it providential, but I just happen to be a bookkeeper by trade. Perhaps I can be of some help? There would be no charge, of course. We're all friends here."

A camera might have been faster, but only oils could have done justice to the shadings of greed, terror, and disbelief that appeared on Macy's face as his gaze shifted from the ratty papers to her enormous pink shoe, then travelled up the muscular calf to the expanse of pink wool encasing Renée's linebacker silhouette, coming to rest somewhere between her granite-sculpted Adam's apple and pockmarked chin.

"We could just throw a few ideas around," said Renée.

Macy squinted at her and drummed his fingers. I have seen Macy do things to save a few dollars that would mortify the most ambitious martyr. But whatever he'd done in the past, he was married now to a dishwater blonde we'd nicknamed the Duchess who only ventured downtown for the occasional musical and cut-price table d'hôte. Macy now shuttled between his seedy bar and fake-leather-filled behemoth in one of the lower suburban echelons, where the figure of Renée would seem more outlandish than a green-skinned alien. What would the Duchess think? On the other hand, Renée was offering her services free of charge. He squirmed on his bar stool.

"Have you done clubs and bars before?"

"I took care of Athena's books for years," she said. "And Labyrinth and Heaven. Like they were my own children."

The mention of these ancient rivals on the other side of town made Macy bristle. I knew for a fact that they were all doing a brisker trade than his, reinventing themselves on a regular basis. Macy, on the other hand, had been driving his bar into the ground for twenty years. He squirmed some more. To be fair, the downward spiral wasn't entirely his own cheapskate fault. What had kept us going in the past was a regular influx of sports fans from the arena up the road, looking to fortify themselves with cheap beer before migrating to the strip clubs further down. But the arena had closed a year ago and fans were busing out to a shiny new one on the outskirts of town, leaving us at the mercy of strays and lost souls and professional down-and-outs like Sonny and Wesley.

His looked at Renée's pink dress and frowned. "What's with the get-up?"

"It's complicated," she said.

He appraised her again, then made a date to meet in his basement office the next morning. After he'd collected his papers and disappeared back through the hatch, Renée wandered around the bar, taking stock of the yellowed posters of defunct musical acts and the tacky bar paraphernalia obscured by archaeological layers of dust. She ran her hand across one of the graffiti-engraved tables and stroked one of the fake colonial chairs.

"This place has potential."

To say that the whole transaction between her and Macy had an air of unreality was an understatement. I was fine with the idea that she just so happened to be a bookkeeper, but you got the feeling that if Macy had said his ice machine was on the fritz she would have rolled up her sleeves. If he'd said his dog was going blind, she would have rummaged around in that green evening bag and found a cure, maybe even granted the mutt three wishes on the side. She also appeared to be a mind reader.

"I'm always looking for the next big problem to solve," she said, ordering another round. Then she scooped up her green bag, gave me the biggest single tip I'd ever received in my career as a bartender, and left.

"She's no beauty queen," said Wesley.

"Who cares," said Sonny. "She's our hero."

They raised their glasses and clinked.

"To the Pink Lantern," said Sonny.

"To the Pink Lantern!"

Every day for the next week Renée disappeared down into Macy's basement lair and the battle began, quietly at first, then louder and louder, until even the upstairs bar was engulfed by

Renée's hectoring and Macy's answering groans, followed by the occasional loud thwack.

"That's the Pink Lantern," said Sonny. "Throwing around her ideas."

Sonny's nickname proved to be apt, because just like the superheroes in comic books, Renée appeared each day in the same shocking-pink outfit and blond wig and with the same green evening bag.

"What it boils down to is this," she said. "When you find a look that really works, you stick with it."

She stomped down the basement steps for another round of groaning and garment-rending in Macy's office. Later on that day I went down to the storeroom and caught a glimpse of Macy cowering at his desk while Renée waved a grease-encrusted adding machine under his nose.

"I'm painting you two pictures of the future," she said. "One of them is rosy."

A few mornings later Renée appeared upstairs with a clipboard and a pencil. Macy trailed behind her as she took stock. Every now and then she whipped a measuring tape out from her evening bag, stepping back to crook her neck and cogitate.

In my prime, I could have worked the bar at the Astoria, headed an army of slick waiters and potted palms on a half acre of marble. I was a whiz at the drinks but mostly I was that archetypal listener. I could see anyone's side in a story but I also saw the bigger picture. People don't want some grinning dolt telling them everything is going to work out dandy. Nearly every bar or hotel owner in the city tried to poach me from Macy's at one point or another, said I was crazy to keep working for such a pittance. I'm no martyr. The truth is

I had come to savour the long, contemplative afternoons and morose evenings, the ticking Coors clock with the cracked plastic mountain range, and the frail hold that Macy's clientele had on reality. But mainly, I liked working somewhere I wasn't required to be nice. So that on the rare occasions when I did smile or dole out a beer or take a hobo for an all-day breakfast at the Hillbilly Grill, it was out of the goodness of my own heart and not because God or Walt Disney or Mammon in the form of a hotel manager was holding a gun to my head. I could see that Renée was doing her best to help us out of a tight spot, but by the time they'd finished measuring and disappeared down the rabbit hole for another squabble, I was starting to have serious forebodings about my future.

The next day a couple of guys in overalls came in with ladders and cans of paint while Macy stood by the bar and trembled. Renée tapped her clipboard.

"You can't argue with the numbers," she said. "You've got to spend money to make money. You have a month. Maybe two at the most. If you don't want to get turfed out you're going to have to roll up your sleeves and pitch in. Don't you realize how close we are to the abyss here?"

Yes, Renée. And some of us like it that way.

I was one of those kids who could draw early on. I was doing horses and human hands, acing the shading and the perspective and the dimensions while the other kids in my art class were still doing crooked houses with a box of crayons. I got accepted for my foundation year at the Mackenzie School of Art and Design a month after my sixteenth birthday. I had a lot of big ideas back then about what was right and wrong in art. I hated abstracts, thought Dali was a fraud. Picasso made me think of the town bully back home who always took a step back to admire the work he'd done with his fists on my face before roaming off to see what he could make of someone else's. I wanted to do big, dark, moody oils in the style of Rembrandt and da Vinci. Maybe it was because my only skill was to make things look real, but I truly believed the most unsurpassed moment in the history of art was when they beefed up those flat little saints and stick people from the Middle Ages. Even my teachers thought I was a jerk. Fifteen years after I put down my brush for good, I was helping Renée coat walls so adumbrated with nicotine they looked like cave paintings with twenty litres of black latex paint.

"It's the most cost-effective way to make a statement," she said.

The colonial chairs and tables gouged with initialled hearts were herded onto a waiting truck and sleek new tubular sets arrived. The tarps and paint cans were whisked away. Sonny taped a few limp balloons to the mirror at the back of the bar while Renée slung the last of Macy's dented aluminum ashtrays out the back door like Frisbees.

"To the dawn of a new age," she said. She poured shots of Wild Turkey and we raised our glasses and cheered. All of us except Macy. The painters, the lumber, the truckload of tables and chairs, the snakes of new blue neon that blinked his name behind the bar. The pack of dollar-store balloons. It was all too much. He had taken to wandering around compulsively jingling the loose change in his pants pockets, his shell-shocked look now mingled with hysteria.

Renée emerged from the basement later on with an events calendar sketched onto a whiteboard. Charity fundraisers and ladies' nights, every cheap gimmick known to draw in a crowd. Any crowd. Every crowd. I saw my future on the whiteboard and it wasn't pretty. I was just about to throw in the towel once and for all when I looked up at Renée, whose craggy, pockmarked face bore a look of benevolence that rivalled Mary's in Bellini's *Pietà*. I looked at the faces of all my regulars, rosier and more hopeful than I'd ever seen them before, albeit spattered with black paint. They were a team! We were a team! A big, happy family moving towards our mutual destiny with a unified vision. Like the Borgias. Or the Medicis.

She flicked a switch and a brand-new mirror ball spilled its spots onto every surface.

"What the hell," I said, more to myself than anyone. "I'll give it a whirl."

I went to see the Greats in Italy one summer when I was still in school, did a tour of the museums, saw Caravaggio's severed head in the Galleria Borghese and Titian's *Scourging of Christ*. I went to the Sistine Chapel to look at God and all his meaty angels. There was a ruckus just as I was about to leave, then a clearing in the crowds. A kid around my age was writhing on the floor in the grips of what I learned later on was a grand mal seizure. His eyes had rolled to the back of his head and he was foaming at the lips. His friend was calling out, doing his best to beat back the onlookers, but they kept closing in until I lost sight of them both.

I'd seen them before at the youth hostel and I spotted the friend later on that day. Something the kid had seen on the ceiling had triggered his seizure, the friend said. What made it worse, someone had stolen his wallet while he was writhing around the floor. I couldn't get the image out of my mind, this young guy helplessly contorting, and those beefy angels with their big hands looming overhead. And the little hand below, flicking into the kid's pocket fast as a lizard's tongue. I figured it was some kind of pattern or way the light was hitting the ceiling that had triggered his seizure, that he hadn't been stricken down by God. Although lately I'm beginning to wonder if he had. By the time I left Rome, I knew that I was done with drawing and painting. It wasn't just the seizure in the chapel. After an overload of Pietàs and crucifixions, I lost my stomach for the whole thing.

A couple of days after the grand reopening, Renée took Macy down to the local rock station and had him record a set of jingles. On Monday, Macy's had the population of a Neanderthal village. By Friday the crowd had swelled to a heaving, swaying leviathan that threatened to burst the bar stools into sticks with a thrust of its horny tail.

There was even a trickle-down effect. Sonny and Wesley took turns helping out behind the bar, became minor stars, hamming it up on band nights, mooching daiquiris and Long Island iced teas on ladies' nights, dancing Cossack style to "Ra-Ra-Rasputin" on Disco Tuesdays. I turned a blind eye when they ushered their buddies in through the emergency exit after closing time to help themselves to the dregs and the cigarette butts still smoking in the ashtrays. Macy was too busy hauling sacks of cash down the basement steps to notice.

Take someone the size of the statue of *David* and stick them in a crowded bar in a pink woollen dress, and chances are something is going to go awry. But she pulled it off, charming the weekend warriors in from the suburbs, sending the wack jobs in sparkly pants into fits of nervous laughter, plucking the lint from their lapels like a cocktail hostess from a 1940s movie. That's not to say the rumours didn't fly as soon as she stepped out to powder her tombstone of a nose. Nobody knew the slightest thing about her. She clammed up whenever anyone dared ask about her childhood. Some had her pegged for a bank robber, hiding out after a heist gone wrong. Wesley was convinced that somewhere along the line she'd been a criminal mastermind, and this was her way of doing penance for some crime against humanity.

"Whoever she is or isn't, she must be in for a cut of Macy's takings," said Sonny. "Nobody does stuff like this for free."

The funny thing was, instead of enjoying the fruits of her labour, Renée seemed to get more and more depressed. She stopped making jokes and got snappish with the crowds, slumped at the end of the bar picking napkins into shreds. Every now and again she'd bring an equally morose down-and-out from the park in with her and they'd sit together in silence eating beer nuts and downing glasses of draft. The crevices in her face widened and the shadows deepened. I started to see more of that haunted look I'd glimpsed through the window when I first laid eyes on her. After a while she even stopped shaving.

"I guess I'm bored," she said, shrugging her massive shoulders.

When her visits to the bar began to dwindle, Macy was relieved.

"No offence, but she was getting to be a real downer," he said.

"I saw her going into the bar across the road," said Sonny. "But that could have been any old giant in a hot-pink dress."

Macy's ears pricked. While he might not have been enjoying her company of late, the idea that she was transforming a rival bar was worrying. He had bought a new sound system at Crazy Larry's Stereo Warehouse, had given the Duchess the okay to redecorate the family room at home. He had his eye on a second-hand Caddy on the strength of Renée's projections. He had even been toying with the idea of siring a pointy-toothed, stubby-fingered Macy Junior.

"The problem," said Sonny, "is that she doesn't leave enough room for us to be unhappy too."

"I'm trying to run a business here," said Macy. He rapped his hairy knuckles hard on the bar top.

"We can't just turn our backs on her," said Wesley. "Can we?"

He may have had the loyalty of a poisonous frog, but Macy did have a point. In the same manner that a mountain affects the weather of the town it overshadows, Renée's depressions were casting a pall on the more diminutive beings in her midst. Not that she noticed. The Pink Lantern had wanted to save us, and save us the Pink Lantern had. Whereas I would have happily tipped Macy's upside down and let all our new clientele fly to pieces in the wind. Like I said, I'm no martyr.

One of the after-effects of working in a busy bar is that you never really leave. It could be four o'clock on a Sunday morning. The pigeons are ruffling their oily feathers on the windowsill and the bedroom pales to a washed indigo as you launch into the slow drift towards oblivion. But it's no use. The insides of your eyelids burn with visions of Saturday night. It's a scene from the *Inferno*. Red shapes beckon and bang their glasses on the bar. They reel into shadows and surge forward again, a many-headed monster throwing punches in the air. The only thing is to wait for them to disappear. Except they never do.

As it happened, there was no need to make a sudden decision either way, because Renée left off coming to the bar altogether after another couple of weeks. I was beginning to think she'd vanished in a puff of pink smoke when I spotted her standing on the ornamental bridge in the park on my way to the bar one afternoon. The pitted features had been softened once again by that old Pietà-like benevolence.

"I'm looking for Petula," she said, raising her hand to just above her waist. "She's around yay high."

There weren't many female down-and-outs in the neighbourhood, and the few there were didn't tend to last. They faced the same horrors as their male counterparts: exposure to the elements, beatings from roving brutes. Curb crawlers and far worse also loaded them into their cars when they were too drunk to fend them off, dumped them back onto the street when they were done with them. If they were lucky. And so while I told Renée that I didn't know Petula, an image came at once of a squalling bundle of old sweaters and black hair, whose lair of motley blankets was always shifting and reappearing in the denser pockets of the park's woodlands.

"You should hear the stories she tells me," said Renée. "They make me ashamed I was ever born."

We walked along the paths for the half-hour I had to spare, hoping to spot Petula's latest campsite through the leaves. That was the last I saw of Renée for a good long while, until early one evening I arrived outside Macy's to see Wesley standing in the doorway with a stunned look on his face. I pushed past him when I heard something between a wail and a shriek. Renée was at the bar with her hands on her hips and an embarrassed smile on her face. A tiny, dishevelled woman stood in the centre of the room. She wore a clean white dress shirt many sizes too big that was mostly unbuttoned. There was a damp patch of urine in the crotch of her jeans. In her hand she held a single rose wrapped in cellophane, the kind that hawkers peddle from bar to bar on Saturday nights. Like her, the rose had seen better days. The head dangled from its snapped stem beneath the smashed cellophane. She brandished it like a torch, peering into the space ahead of her as if into the mouth of a dark tunnel.

"Fuck you," she said to nobody in particular. She paused to take a deep breath, then turned to me. "And fuck you too. You evil shithead. You stinking bag of pus."

"Petula," said Renée. "You're going to get us into trouble."

Petula spun around and thrust the flower under Sonny's nose, then stamped her foot and screamed again.

"She's crazy," said Sonny.

"Can you blame her?" I asked.

"She's even driven Wesley away," said Sonny.

A couple of customers walked in, took one look at Petula, and walked out. Petula thrust the rose under Sonny's chin again and let loose another tirade of curses. She snatched a beer from the bar top and lurched onto the dance floor, swayed back and forth with her arms outstretched.

"She was screaming blue murder at a vicious bastard twice her size when I met her," said Renée.

"And she hasn't stopped since," I said.

"She'd give the shirt off her back to help a friend," said Renée. "But that mouth of hers is going to get us into trouble."

It seemed that despite her heart of gold, Petula had become a pariah in the nooks and alleyways where her fellow down-and-outs congregated, and had almost worn out her welcome in the park by the time Renée plucked her, kicking and bellowing, out of the undergrowth and took her home for a meal and a hot bath. Renée had sat with her through a few aborted detoxes, but Petula had a bad habit of running out to look for more trouble every time Renée's back was turned.

"She just disappears on me," said Renée. "I can't keep her locked up, but she's getting us kicked out of everywhere we go. Burger King. You name it."

"You sneaky piece of shit," said Petula, peering at Sonny as though through a heavy mist.

"What did I ever do to you?" said Sonny.

"She says that to everyone," said Renée.

"You know what you've done," said Petula.

Another couple of customers came into the bar, caught sight of Petula's enraged face, and turned tail.

"I better take her home," said Renée.

"Come on back soon," I said. "And make sure to bring Petula too."

She was better than a fire bell at clearing the bar.

We got away with it maybe half a dozen more times. Renée smuggled her in like a bundle of high explosives, glad to have somewhere warm to take Petula, who had taken such a dislike to being confined to Renée's apartment that she had even once climbed over the balcony and threatened to jump. I got the sense she tried her best to behave for Renée's sake.

She held off the hard stuff, sat at the back with a glass of beer, belching in a lady-like manner and staring at the black-painted wall. Nobody could tell what the trigger was but she always raised hell in the end, cussing and scuttling from customer to customer, clearing a wider and wider berth for herself until it was just Renée wringing her hands, a few strays staring open-mouthed in the background and Sonny muttering and twisting a dishcloth into a garrotte. And me, revelling in the newfound emptiness.

I knew the jig was up when Macy appeared out of his hatch clutching a fresh set of papers, the veins in his forehead more prominent than the coils of blue neon behind the bar. He grilled me about the crazy lady he'd been hearing about from an unnamed source, who was scaring away his customers. But we both knew the numbers had been steadily declining well before Petula ever set foot in the place. Every bar has an upswing after a grand reopening. The truth was that all the cheap gimmicks in the world weren't going to save Macy's from sinking back into the dump it really was. The sooner we were teetering on the brink of oblivion, the better, was my view on the matter. But Macy had the Duchess and her new decorating scheme to worry about. He had his Crazy Larry's Warehouse payments. He had his stubby unborn progeny. Petula had to go, and if Renée had to be banished alongside her, so be it.

"I'm trying to run a business here," he said.

Sonny slipped off his bar stool and slunk towards the emergency exit. In my mind I painted a long black lizard tail on his rear.

You can't save the world. You can't save even one tiny bag lady without a cascade of unintended consequences. Despite

Macy's threats and lamentations, I didn't turn them away the next time they came. What kind of person does that make me? I took a bottle of Wild Turkey off the back shelf, poured one round of shots and then another. And then another.

She was like a half bag lady, half owl swooping from one customer to the next, retching out curses and farfetched threats in the raggedy blankets she'd switched back to instead of the clean clothes Renée tried to coax her to wear. The customers smiled and made fun at first, which only made her more furious. After Renée excused herself to go to the ladies' room, Petula got hold of a broom and starting waving it around like a light sabre. By the time Renée got back, half our customers had disappeared. And it was almost funny, watching her flit between the few remaining people, her face partially hidden by a blanket so that she looked like a miniature ninja or monk from a kung fu movie. The blanket fell back when she started cussing me out, and because it was afternoon and she was standing in the sole shaft of available light from Macy's shutter, I saw that her eyes weren't focused on me but at the space a few feet above my head. And I saw also that she wasn't just angry. She was terrified. She waved her broomstick, battling against whatever she believed was looming overhead.

"She thinks she's still asleep," I said. "That we're all figures in a nightmare."

And we are. Red shapes beckon and bang their glasses on the bar. They reel into shadows and surge forward, a many-headed monster throwing punches in the air. The only thing is to wait for them to disappear. Except they never do.

Macy arrived, with his usual comedic precision, just in time to see Petula crack his precious mirror ball in two. He charged at her like a bull, nearly butting Renée in the solar plexus as she stepped between them. There was a lot of hollering and accusations and vigorous wavings of the broomstick. There was Macy grabbing the broomstick off Petula and snapping it in two over his knee. There was Macy banishing both of them, threatening to call the police if either of them darkened his door again. There was Renée raising herself to her full height, screaming back at him.

"How could you do this to me," she said, "after everything I've done for you?"

The bar is silent as they stare each other down. A thousand years pass. Villages are razed, wars fought and won. Cities rise up on the plains and by river deltas. Others crumble into ruins. A cathedral is built and then bombed and rebuilt. Then there's Renée with her face like a low-hanging moon overhead, and the expression it wore, haunting and hunted, as she bundled up Petula and led her out of the bar for the last time.

"I'm trying to run a business here," said Macy.

I always stop in the park to take in the scenery on my way to the bar. The green is restful to my eyes. Sometimes I'll spy an encampment through the leaves, disturb some bundle of old blankets that never turns out to be Petula. I've heard rumours that she cleaned up her act, hitched a ride back up north where she came from. I hope it wasn't in the trunk of some sleazebag's car. And for all the trouble she's caused me, I like to think Renée's still out there doing good somewhere else in the world.

FIREBIRDS

Maureen always slowed the car to a crawl on her street in order to better take in the view. The flanked shrubs and expanses of greenery were graceful enough to adorn the covers of the design magazines she kept splayed on low tables for her clients to browse at the showroom. Nearing her own house, however, she began to frown. Her next-door neighbour was out tending the red-bloomed azalea that was the centrepiece of his garden. To her eye, the azalea was a blot on the muted landscape. It was even more of an eyesore in winter, shrouded in burlap so that it looked like an upright corpse jammed into a snowdrift. She waved abruptly at the old man to register her dislike. Then, worried she might have seemed too imperious, she leaned out and smiled. But by that time the neighbour had turned away, his head immersed in the fleshy leaves as she pulled into her driveway. Although they had lived side by side for several years, she didn't know his name to call out.

This wasn't entirely her fault. It was the kind of place where neighbours rarely spoke, a well-groomed suburb with its own vacant blue swimming pool and greens, and a tennis court that was only ever used by the white-haired couple a few houses down. To speak might break the spell of lush good fortune that hung overhead like a summer haze.

In spite of the clamour that assailed her at the front door, Maureen paused to give her white-carpeted living room its habitual once-over. She aimed for perfection, agonizing over each piece. She believed in the power of decor the way some people believed in Jesus or Apollo, was convinced that it brought grace and purity into the world. She set her groceries on a slab of marble in the kitchen and then walked up the half flight of stairs to the source of the racket, frowning again at her daughter's sole contribution to the household: a small round badge of a fanged goblin that she'd crazy-glued to her bedroom door.

She marched past the girl, who lay spread-eagled on the pink bedroom rug, to where the stereo, volume turned so high that the speakers pulsed and crackled, stood and flicked the switch, then turned to face Dawn, who had by then hoisted herself upright to sit yogi style, an open palm on each of her thickset knees.

She was a large, solitary girl who seldom brought friends home. As a child she had contorted her face into bizarre expressions that made her parents laugh. The habit had stuck and was now a tic, her face bunching into random fists, the tongue straining on the end of its stalk in mid-conversation, the brows wagging comically above bulging eyes. They did not resemble each other in the least, but every now and then Maureen caught an unsettling glimpse of herself in Dawn's expressive features.

"I'm going for a stroll by the golf course," said Maureen. "It would do you good to get some exercise."

"Exercise is for assholes," said Dawn.

Maureen resisted the urge to scold, envisioning the tantrum that might ensue. Her daughter's rages had begun to flare with an alarming intensity. She noticed that Dawn's fingernails were caked with dirt, but racked her brain instead for something nice to say.

"How did it go with Mr. Vittadini? Are they giving you a part in the play after all?"

"They hate me," said Dawn. "Everybody does."

"You really ought to scrub those nails," said Maureen.

She changed into her walking clothes, closed the front door just as the stereo began to throb again, and headed for the canopy of trees that lay between the golf club and suburb. She loved the woodland paths encircling the golf course with its fairyland vistas. She had never played herself, but felt sure there was something magical about golf, some act of localized wizardry that suspended the unlucky laws of destiny, allowing the tiny balls to whiz through the air and land with any precision near the place they were aimed at.

Broke, living in a one-room apartment with a howling newborn, Maureen and her husband had dreamed of one day belonging to the fancy clubhouse, a white-pillared mansion mirrored by an artificial pond, its paired swans circulating among the reeds. She was rich enough now to join the white-clad members on the high stone patio, but something held her back. The prospect of losing that wishfulness, the sense of longing for an enchantment she might be worthy of one day.

The call came the next day while she was draping upholstery across her desk for a client at her showroom. Her assistant, Belle, a nervous, freckled girl whose job included keeping nuisances at bay, handed her the phone with a look of feigned helplessness.

It was the school secretary asking to schedule a meeting with Dawn's guidance counsellor. The client fussed with the fabric, holding it up to the window and then back down into the shadows by the desk while Maureen flipped through her diary, recalling Dawn's most recent tantrum, the sound of late-night sobbing, the piles of crumpled Kleenex she'd found at the back of Dawn's vanity the week before. The paranoia. The accusation that she'd been searching through Dawn's things, which was, of course, true.

"How bad can it be?" said Belle. Maureen shook her head and set the phone down.

"It doesn't grab me either," said the client.

She voiced her fears that evening to her husband, Terry, a plump, pink-cheeked man who wore his sweaters draped across his shoulders. He began to pace the white carpet in his sock feet, something he always did when she demanded a heart-to-heart. He had grown up in the same bad neighbourhood as Maureen, with an alcoholic father who brutalized his family so brazenly and often that he became a local legend. Terry was doing his best not to follow in his father's footsteps and apart from some colourful threats made under duress, the only blow-ups he'd had with his wife concerned Dawn. He tended to dismiss what Maureen saw as disturbing flaws.

"She's a sensitive kid," he said.

"They don't call for no reason," said Maureen. "Remember when the Lawrence girl accused her of bullying?"

"That was just a set-up," said Terry. "I'll bet you it's the drama group. We'll have to go down there again."

"You can't make them give her a role," said Maureen.

They had gone to see the drama teacher, muscling their way past a swarm of girls in fairy wings and pastel leotards to the prop room behind the gymnasium stage, with its cut-out silhouettes of trees and hollow pillars and the crude outline of a Greek temple sketched onto pasteboard, which Maureen found particularly unsettling.

"She had her heart set on that play," said Terry, walking back to the living room window. He parted the long white curtains, peered out onto the street, and let out a long whistle. "You don't see too many of those around here."

"See many of what?"

"A Pontiac Firebird." He wrinkled his nose. "With a big, tacky gold bird painted on the hood."

She reached the window just in time to see the tail end of a red car round the street corner onto the main road.

The guidance counsellor gave Maureen an unfriendly smile as he let her into his office, which was cluttered and dusty and painted the same flaking peppermint green as the outer corridor where Maureen had, for the last twenty minutes, been subjected to various alarm bells and shrill announcements from the loudspeaker above his door. He waved at a chair across from his desk without a hello, then fingered through Dawn's file while Maureen looked for somewhere clean to set her bag.

"Her grades have been okay until this year," he said. "Is there something going on at home?"

He read from the file before Maureen could answer. Dawn had been cutting classes. Faking mono. Had rigged up a system of sick notes and forged letters. She'd been spotted by a teacher at a gas station with a couple of tough-looking guys.

"Which gas station?" said Maureen. "How tough?"

"Tough-looking," said the counsellor. He met her gaze for the first time. "How well acquainted are you with the town's Vietnamese community?"

"For the millionth time," said Maureen, "I'm not racist."

"Why else would you just assume he was in a gang?"

Dawn's face was mocking and lobster-bright as she sat, cross-legged again on the pink rug, surrounded by ornaments she'd yanked or flung off shelves, fluff from an antique doll, feathers from a torn cushion. She gnawed on her lip for a moment and widened her eyes in a show of innocence.

"We met at the food court," she said. "He was new so I showed him around. His name is Kuan. We went to Peoples Jewellers. He bought me a milkshake."

Maureen leaned against the door, relieved. The story sounded innocuous enough, the kind of thing two teens might aimlessly do at the mall.

"It's not the Vietnamese side of things that worries me," she said. "It's the lies. Who is this guy, that you're forging notes and skipping class and hanging out in gas stations for?"

"Like you ever cared about the truth," said Dawn. "Your whole life is a lie."

Maureen had an urge to rush over and shake this stocky stranger with the mocking smile and lobster-bright face and command her to release the little daughter who was surely being held hostage somewhere inside that thick casing of flesh.

Like her husband, Maureen had been estranged from her own family for many years. Her parents had taunted her as a child, made fun of her finicky nature and high-handedness, couldn't mask their scorn even when they'd started asking her for handouts.

You let people go. When they keep hurting and disappointing you. You let them go and make their own way in the world. She was happy not to see her knock-kneed relatives lounging on her white leather couch, squinting uneasily at her collection of abstract prints. But they came back in dreams. She saw them bickering as they drifted out to sea on ice floes, or crossing the desert dressed in loud clothes, her father's face with its permanently annoyed expression a pinprick on the horizon. She felt a prickle of panic looking down at her daughter. Maybe Dawn had picked up on their philosophy but wasn't mature enough yet to appreciate the nuances or reasons behind the estrangements. But this wasn't the time to delve into ancient history.

"Look," said Maureen. "If it's about the play—"

"It's not about the play. Although the play *did* make me realize a lot of things. Like just how terrible this place is." She waved her arms at the ruins of her bedroom and the view beyond her low-hanging window, now denuded of its floral drapes. "Anyhow, you can't stop me from seeing him," she said. She poked her tongue out and made a popping noise with her lips. "We're in love."

Maureen told Belle about it the next morning while they were matching upholstery swatches to wallpaper samples.

"She accuses everyone, even the wacko guidance counsellor, of being a racist. And then just tells me she's in love. Like that gives her some kind of immunity. Like she even knows what love is at her age."

"Like anyone does," said Belle.

"It's not the Vietnamese I have a problem with," said Maureen again, thinking of Dawn's scarlet face and goggling eyes.

"Of course it isn't," said Belle.

"Do you know what she said when I asked her to bring him up to the house? That he wasn't interested in meeting us."

"Maybe he's shy," said Belle. "Just because he doesn't want to meet a girl's family doesn't mean he's a drug lord."

They had both grown up in the town, had seen the Vietnamese groceries and noodle restaurants and the stores full of baskets and braided palm-leaf murals that had begun to appear among the dollar stores and muffler service centres in the seedier areas after the first wave of migrants. They had heard about the rumoured gangs, the rackets and the ruthlessness, but they also knew there was a way in which a boy named Kuan might weave himself into their lives, might aspire to live in a suburb like Maureen's one day, where differences were subsumed in a sea of muted greys and tacit beiges.

"She's not *acting* like a girl in love," said Maureen. "She's barely even bathing. She lies around on the floor staring up at the ceiling. The rest of the time she's having fits, heaving things around. Expensive things. Carriage clocks. China."

"She's going through a rebellious phase," said Belle.

"Rebellious doesn't describe it," said Maureen.

There were movies that captured the sense of dread she felt when she heard Dawn's footsteps in the house. Movies with monsters lurking in the basement. Maureen had the phone number of a child psychologist in her bag but was starting to wonder if she needed a psychologist of her own.

She had gone to Dawn's room with some books about self-esteem and self-improvement and a brochure about a spiritual retreat nearby, if that was a path Dawn wanted to tread. But she'd swerved into the master bedroom after catching a glimpse of Dawn's furious reflection in the hall mirror and dumped the books into her own underwear drawer.

"Terry's losing his marbles," she said. "He keeps a baseball bat by the front door now in case 'they' come around. This is our life now."

When she turned onto her street that evening after work, she saw the tail end of a red car disappearing around the bend and knew before opening the front door that Dawn wouldn't be in her room.

"Many of them, as you might imagine, have suffered unimaginable atrocities," said the guidance counsellor. He pushed back his swivel chair, put his feet up on the desk in front of him, and smiled. "Beheadings. Rapes. Whole villages with their throats slit."

"Yes, but is he in one of those awful gangs or not? How else could an ordinary boy afford to buy himself a fancy red Firebird?"

She had come to see him without an appointment, not knowing where else to turn.

"It's a delicate situation," said the guidance counsellor. "I don't think we should rush to judgment."

He went to the window and stared out at the field below his office, where a few delinquent students were picking up litter under the supervision of a bored-looking teacher, their rain ponchos slick with the drizzle that had only just stopped. It was a large and prosperous town, settled by Mennonites and German farmers who had drained the marshes and driven out millions of wild pigeons whose ancestral roosts were spread across the surrounding lowlands. Over the previous century the townspeople had built row upon row of tall Gothic houses and white civic buildings and churches whose steeples needled the heavy clouds. She had worked hard and grown rich here, painting over the oaken gloom of historic homes, faking rustic charm on the blank canvases of new suburbs. She hoped that instead of mocking her, Dawn would come to understand the efforts and sacrifices behind her success. She was trying in her own way to make the world a better place. A streak of sunlight unfurled behind the domed town hall.

"You have to consider what they endured to escape," said the guidance counsellor. "The camps. The diseases. Imagine drifting in a leaky boat, the gulls circling overhead like vultures. People don't just get over experiences like that."

Maureen locked up the showroom after work and drove out to a group of weather-beaten buildings on the town's outer limits, parking in front of a convenience store with a dusty window. She had been here before, lost and looking for the show home a contractor had hired her to decorate in one of the subdivisions overtaking the farmlands.

The front aisles of the convenience store were full of chewing gum and chips but at the back it was an Asian grocery, with sacks of jasmine rice, bottles of sauce with cockerels emblazoned on the labels, and a dirty paper dragon hoisted above a glass-topped freezer full of odd packets and chicken claws bunched into bouquets. The smell—like a meat wrapper left too long in the sun—was more rank and primeval, and the old woman behind the counter more bent and gnomish, than Maureen remembered. Clearly the new suburbanites were giving the store a wide berth. She tossed a packet of mints onto the countertop's battered lottery display.

"Do you remember me? I was here a while ago."

When she'd asked for directions to the lost show home the woman had simply blinked and squatted back down on her upturned milk crate to stare at the tiny TV blaring behind the counter. Normally, Maureen would have bristled at the woman's rudeness but something about the raw construction outside, the new road winding through half-uprooted corn fields familiar to her from childhood trips out to the countryside, had lent the moment an air of unreality. Instead of storming off she had entered into a tortured conversation, stressing each syllable so heavily that her own words felt alien and indecipherable in her mouth. The Vietnamese woman had been— for Maureen was convinced now that the woman was one of the very earliest of Vietnamese immigrants to the town—obviously keen to get back to the tiny TV. Nonetheless, Maureen had left the store feeling as though she'd triumphed over their differences. After all, they were both women with wares to sell.

And hadn't Maureen's ancestors also fled from some blazing village across a different sea to build a new life, a new town, a new world?

The woman gave no sign that she recognized Maureen from that earlier encounter, snatched the bill from Maureen's hand with a grunt, pushed the change and mints across the battered counter with a scornful flick of her wrist, then sat down on her crate, leaving Maureen with her palm open and trembling.

She knew the link she was seeking to re-establish was tenuous. But back in her car with the smell of old blood and dust still clogging her nostrils, she felt robbed of even her own humanity. She had an urge to go back in and smash the tiny TV screen, drag the old harpy back up to eye level by the roots of her hair. The ride home, directly in the path of the setting sun, seemed to take an eternity.

The next day they found the dents and scratches on Dawn's window along with the blade she'd been using to let herself out.

"Or letting them in," said Maureen, remembering voices she'd heard a few times over the last couple of months. Back then she'd assumed, after Dawn had complained of not sleeping well, that it was the TV.

"We would have known if they were in here," said Terry. "Instinctively." He stroked the blade with his finger. "It must be kind of weird for them to come here after all the godawful stuff they had to do to survive. Making man-traps out of bamboo. Eating rats and whatnot. But what are we supposed to do with them potentially lurking around every corner? We don't even know who they are."

For the last couple of weeks he had been prowling around the house off and on, sniffing the night air like a forest animal in his piped navy pyjamas. That morning he had spiked his hair hastily with too much gel and slit his upper cheek while shaving, slapped on a flesh-coloured bandage that already looked grubby from his, to her mind, unnecessary excavations under the shrubberies near Dawn's window ledge. Now his sweater came unknotted from his shoulders and slithered onto the grass.

"I don't even know who we are anymore," said Maureen.

In her dream that night, Maureen saw the Firebird and knew that it had come and would keep coming to spirit her daughter away like a fairy-tale princess under a cruel spell. The Firebird had no wheels, hovered a foot or so above the asphalt as she drifted out through the open window and down the front path, her nightgown trailing behind her. When she reached for the door handle the car zoomed above her head, the gold-blazoned bird on the hood glowing so brightly she had to shield her eyes. When the car swooped down and settled beside her, she peered through the window and saw her own face staring back at her from behind the steering wheel.

She woke up late in an empty, sun-flooded house, blinking at the refracted dazzle of her crystal glasses on the cabinets as she walked into the kitchen. Dawn had evaded them by leaving early for school, a message in shaky red felt-tip pinned triumphantly to the fridge. Maureen poured herself an orange juice as Terry came in from the side door after his morning patrol around the house. He led her out to where a circular section of their lawn had been burned away in the night.

"It's a warning," he said. "I know how these guys operate."

He arranged to have the turf replaced, while Maureen called a home security company.

"You've got to hand it to them, those guys are stealthy as hell. Nobody saw a single thing," said Terry. "And I was up five, maybe six times checking on the window. On her."

"This isn't *Apocalypse Now*," said Maureen.

But she found herself hunting them on adrenaline-fuelled drives through town, holding her breath each time she caught a flash of red or gold rounding a corner, cruising down streets choked with weeds and abandoned furniture, a tire iron at her feet.

She found what she was searching for, on a rainy morning at a doughnut shop facing the out-of-town bus terminal. There were six in all, boyish and slim-hipped under the eaves beside a pair of red-and-black Firebirds. They had long hair and wore tight jeans and fringed leather jackets, each with a brightly coloured feather roach clip attached to the front zipper. She had seen these feathers before in fairs and at mall kiosks. There had been one lassoed around Dawn's bedpost that Maureen had made her get rid of because it was tacky.

In the fantasies that replayed themselves while she drove around, Maureen recognized Kuan instinctively, either shook hands with him in a show of cordiality or shook him violently by the shoulders and warned him to keep away. A hundred feet from six possible Kuans in the rain-soaked parking court, her hands trembled on the steering wheel. She had expected jeering, at least. The young men, however, barely registered her as she swerved past them and stumbled into the doughnut shop, joining the crush of shift workers from the town's remaining factories, damp and mottled as raw pork from the cold drizzle.

The walls were tiled with rural scenes, red barns with hexed doors set among stylized blades of wheat and farmers with sloping foreheads and slashes for mouths who looked both moronic and sinister, the kind of blockheads who might mob together with pitchforks and start a burning. The mugginess and smell of the fryers made her nauseated, and the wall of doughnuts behind the counter began to whirl like a carousel as her turn came at the counter. She steadied herself and asked the cashier about the huddled men outside.

"Oh, the worm pickers," said the cashier, waving in their direction as though attempting a magic trick. Through the fogged window they were only just visible. "They pick worms for the tackle shops," she said. "There must be money in it. Look at those flashy cars."

"I can't believe people do that in this day and age. In this town. It's medieval," said Maureen as she slipped between the bedsheets that evening.

"It's probably a cover for something else," said Terry.

"What could be worse than that?"

"Some kind of racket. Drugs. Trafficking."

She turned away from Terry and saw them as soon as she closed her eyes, black-jacketed and long-haired, bent over fields that stretched endlessly into sleep. Then she sat upright, remembering the crescents of dirt wedged beneath Dawn's fingernails.

"It's fun," said Dawn. She sat with her white blanket heaped over her head and shoulders, blinking at the overhead light her parents had just switched on.

He drove her to the gas station where a truck waited to take her and the other pickers out to the fields.

"What kind of a person would encourage a young girl to do this kind of work?"

"I like it," said Dawn. Her voice was matter-of-fact. "I feel safer out there than almost anywhere. It's more real than anything here, that's for sure. And besides, Kuan doesn't *make* me do anything. Half the time he isn't even there himself."

"So where is he when he's got you crawling around in the dark?"

"Like I said, he's a busy guy," said Dawn.

"I'll kill him," said Terry. "If I ever lay hands on him."

"The idea that she would get in that car night after night and be driven out into the darkness, into those fields," said Maureen.

"It *is* like one of those fairy tales," said Belle. "But you still don't know what's really going on. He could have eaten nothing but Cheetos for a year to buy that Firebird. She could be lying or exaggerating to get attention. A couple of kids living in a dream world."

"Do you know what she told me? That she was getting really good at it."

The two women sat on a pair of wingback chairs that had been delivered to the showroom that evening. Belle poured wine into glasses, locked up, and turned off the overhead lights so that no latecomers might rap on the window to disturb them. A cluster of dimmed lamps glowed like a small village at the far end of the showroom; all else was in semi-darkness. This was Maureen's domain, each object chosen and placed at

KERRY LEE POWELL

its ideal vantage point. In darkness the things took on a life of their own, their forms rippling and distorting like sea creatures. Maureen kept her eyes trained on the swarming dark. She had been terrified, ever since she could remember, of mice, and the phobia sometimes, when she was anxious, became unmanageable. She often saw fleeting shapes from the corner of her eye, bristles of fur that made her shudder but turned out nearly always to be products of her own imagination.

She took a deep drink.

"Everything is fake. Nothing is real. She hates the school and the neighbourhood and the whole town, and everyone hates her. It's like she has a persecution complex or something. She hates the house."

"She can't possibly hate the house," said Belle.

"According to her, it's another example of how I always dominate over everything. But she knows damn well there are rules. There are principles of design," said Maureen.

"Maybe she's just feeling lost and lonely," said Belle.

"Who isn't?" said Maureen.

She blinked back the tears that had begun to blur her vision, and stared hard into the showroom's murk. Neither she nor Terry was sleeping much. Maureen kept slipping into Dawn's room to make sure the girl was still beneath her mound of blankets. Terry patrolled the windows with his bat in hand, waiting for the Firebird to reappear. His paranoia was infectious. Maureen felt eyes peering at her through the shrubberies and the fleshy leaves of the neighbour's gaudy azalea. She felt them hunched in the rough grasses, flattened behind the artful trees surrounding the golf course on her evening walks.

"At least if he's picking worms then he's not likely to be

some gang lord," said Belle. "I mean, at least the kid is industrious."

"The problem is that nobody knows who Kuan is. Or nobody's telling. Nobody at the school. Not the Vietnamese. Not the police. Not the fishing tackle stores. He's nowhere and everywhere," said Maureen. "He could be doing this worm thing and a dozen other things on the side. Terry is convinced of it. Dawn said he was a *busy* guy."

They had collared Dawn's classmates in the flaking green corridors. They had gone into the new Vietnamese community centre and the noodle houses and the stores full of tatty baskets. Terry had braved the pool halls and the parking courts and all the other haunts where the gangs were said to go. They had gone to the police station, where an officer had glanced and shrugged at Dawn's photograph.

The two women sipped in silence. To calm herself down Maureen had been mentally spinning through the colour wheels she kept on her desk, spotting flecks of peacock blue and carmine red in the pooling shadows. After a few more sips from her goblet a tentative geometry began to emerge from the showroom's expanse, like the figured patterns in an enormous rug. She was tempted to describe it out loud and make Belle see it too, but the illusion dispersed into an unruly mass before the words left her mouth.

"What are you going to do?" asked Belle.

"Terry's taking her to Wonderland," said Maureen, resisting an urge to giggle. "On a father-daughter date. He wants to establish trust."

They left early and came home late. Maureen was in the bedroom when she heard Dawn's heavy footsteps in the hall. She waited a few minutes, then pulled on her robe and went down to find Terry slumped in front of the TV watching the highlights of a boxing match with the sound turned down. The date had been a disaster. Dawn had spent the day with her mouth clamped shut as she was shunted back and forth on the various rides.

At a rifle range booth he had won her a rainbow-striped tiger the size of an Alsatian dog, which she abandoned at a gas station on the way home. He noticed its absence and turned back, enlisted the gas station staff to join in the search while Dawn sulked in his BMW. He spied the rainbow tail deep in the garbage can by the gas pumps and pulled the tiger out, sodden with wiper fluid and cola dregs, then shoved it back in. He had gotten no information from her about Kuan.

"I couldn't even get her to smile," he said.

He meditated on the screen in front of him as the boxer re-entered the ring against a backdrop of gesticulating arms.

"Who in their right mind would throw a brand-new tiger in the garbage?"

"It's a symbol of renewal," said the guidance counsellor. "The phoenix rising from the ashes. Think about how they've come here with nothing to start again."

"And the gangs," said Maureen.

"A lot of rumours flying around," said the guidance counsellor.

"Newspaper articles. Reports and statistics. And the idea

that they would take a young girl out into the fields at night when she should be asleep in her bed."

Terry and Maureen had spoken to Dawn the night before about their dreams for her future. They had sketched grim scenarios about what was sure to happen once Kuan and his crew had cast her to one side or worse. Dawn had plugged her ears with her fingers and sung the "Eensy Weensy Spider" song under her breath.

"You don't know what this specific Vietnamese person has done wrong other than date your daughter, take her along with him to a job you disapprove of, and drive her around in a car you don't like."

She knew it had been questionable to bring up the Firebird with the counsellor. But there was a world beyond morals she felt he always skirted around.

"I'm not saying he's evil," said Maureen. "Life makes people dangerous sometimes. I want that danger kept at a distance. Why wouldn't I?"

Backing out of her driveway the next morning, she saw that a wobbly red "Fuck You" had been spray-painted on the garage door. She phoned Belle to explain why she'd be late.

"They're redecorating the house again," she said.

"At least now you know he speaks English," said Belle.

"It might have been one of his minions," said Maureen. She went over to the fridge. Glancing at the kindergartenish note that Dawn had pinned there days earlier, she knew who had sprayed the letters on the door and who had burned the lawn and wheeled the lawn mower into the gulch.

"I'll wring her neck," she said.

While Maureen and Terry restored their garage door to its muted beige, Belle took the second call from the school, leaving a note with the counsellor's telephone number on Maureen's desk.

Maureen arrived at the counsellor's office a breathless hour later to see Dawn hunched on the radiator, rubbing a bandaged cheek with her raw knuckle. Two male students had, she claimed, pushed her into an empty classroom. One held her in a headlock while the other punched.

"They warned me there was worse in store," said Dawn.

"You should know that the students are denying that they attacked her," said the counsellor.

"There must be a place she can be sent," said Maureen, turning to the counsellor. "If only for her own protection."

"A child's entry into the adult world can be disturbing," said the counsellor.

"To who?" said Maureen. "The child or the adults?"

He stepped away from his desk and stared out at the needling steeples and civic buildings, his hands clasped behind his back.

"She accuses us of having no charity. No kindness or humanity. Then I have to tell her there's a world where that simply doesn't matter."

"I'm sure she's already aware of that," said the guidance counsellor.

In the struggle, Dawn had bitten the flesh of one student through to the bone.

"Nothing matters anymore," said Dawn, smiling and suddenly self-assured. "Because Kuan is going to make mincemeat out of you all."

"You seem to be doing a pretty good job of that without his help," said Maureen.

Walking back down the green corridor with Dawn trailing stubbornly behind, Maureen thought of her own brief years in high school before the pregnancy had forced her to drop out. Pausing at Dawn's locker, she noticed the look of wariness on the surrounding students' faces and wondered how often Dawn had threatened them with Kuan's vengeance before. Her locker stank as though rotten food was wedged among the bunches of crumpled paper and gym socks and textbooks with twisted spines. A few loose sheets drifted down onto the floor. They were images of the Firebird on the hood of Kuan's car, crudely sketched and messily coloured in. There were dozens more in the locker. Maureen felt a surge of irritation as she gathered up the papers. Surely Dawn was able to draw better than that. When she stood up she saw that Dawn was picking her nose, staring fixedly past the looks of disgust on the faces of the students closest to her. By the time they reached the exit Maureen felt like pulling the fire alarm by the door, losing herself and Dawn in some larger chaos.

"We should buy a boat," said Terry. He stared into the open fridge and took out a carton of milk. He took a long slug straight out of the carton, smacked his lips, and smiled. "I'm serious," he said. "Nothing fancy. A thirty-six-footer. We could take off for the whole summer." He fumbled in his robe pocket for the brochure. He had penned an asterisk on the one he wanted, a white-and-navy cabin cruiser with a family lounging on the deck, their faces tinted such a deep bronze that it was difficult to make out their features. "There are places we've never seen. We could go out into the wilds. Get back to basics."

Instead of Kuan and his Firebird, there would be snakes and bears and unknown dangers, other boaters seeking respite from whatever unhappiness had driven them out of town. And Terry would be at the helm with his chest puffed and his chin squared like the captain in the photograph, thinking he'd saved them from an awful threat. She folded the brochure into a tiny square and slipped it back into his robe pocket.

You let people go. You can't make them stay. You let them walk out into the wind, onto the ice floes, into the deep woods, across the Gobi Desert. Let them find their way in the world.

The last call came when she was alone in the showroom. More or less unharmed, the nurse had said, although the strangeness underlying her tone sent Maureen flying out to her car and across town. She spotted the Firebird in the hospital parking lot, its golden bird casting prisms up and out into the warm air. She peered briefly through the windows and saw, beyond her own squinting grimace, the bloody fake-fur covers like two slaughtered animals slung over the bucket seats. She bolted for the doors, found Dawn in the emergency room hallway. Her face was expressionless under the fluorescent light, her gaze fixed on an open door.

"He was trying to protect me," she said.

"Come home with me now. He'll find someone else." Maureen put her arm around the girl.

Dawn flinched and ducked away, brushing her shoulder as though it was contaminated. "You don't understand," she said.

Maureen remembered the blood-soaked pelts in the Firebird and stepped into the room to find out what had happened. He was lying on the bed with his eyes closed, an exposed side heavily bandaged. He had, since the time Maureen had seen him outside the doughnut shop, grown a whisper of a moustache. He seemed diminished without the worn leather jacket, which was draped over a chair next to the bed, its gaudy feathers tipped in blood. Standing over him, Maureen felt ungainly, her hands and feet the size of shovels, her neck long and scrawny as a rubber chicken's. A Vietnamese nurse came in and he raised himself up onto his elbows and spoke with her in Vietnamese for a few moments. Then they both looked up at Maureen, their expressions a blend of curiosity and pity.

They had given Dawn a tranquilizer, the nurse said, and would admit her for observation over the weekend. She turned again to Kuan and they spoke. The nurse explained to Maureen that Kuan had understood something was wrong with Dawn. That she was suffering, said the nurse. Kuan stared at Maureen intently, as though she held the answer to some confusion he had been trying to understand.

He spoke again to the nurse. He wanted to make clear, to the hospital, to the police if necessary, that Dawn had not hurt him on purpose, the nurse said. "She had been trying," said the nurse, "to defend him against a spirit. A creature that wasn't there." She fumbled for words. "A creature only Dawn could see. The accident happened while he was taking the knife away. He was able to drive them both here. It's a superficial wound."

"What does he mean, a creature that wasn't there?" said Maureen.

He reached for his jacket, pulled out the knife, and handed it to the nurse. Maureen, heart plunging, recognized it as the one she'd confiscated from Dawn a few weeks earlier and carelessly tossed into her own sock drawer. Kuan lay back on the bed and began to speak again, the nurse translating while he spoke.

"Dawn was a good girl. She liked to laugh and she worked hard. Then she stopped laughing. The troubles came. And she was not like her old self anymore."

They were interrupted by a doctor who asked Maureen to talk with her in the hall. Dawn, she told Maureen, had been given a brief assessment. It was crucial, however, to determine if there was a point at which her behaviour had started to seem bizarre. The shorter the gap between frank psychosis and treatment, the better the chance for recovery. Had there been signs, and if so, when had the first ones occurred?

Maureen's mind froze at the word "psychosis" and then reeled backwards. Had there ever been a point that had *not* been leading up to this moment? There had been signs. Signs that mockingly told a different story, whose ending Terry kept a baseball bat by the front door in panting anticipation of.

She sagged against the wall. Her life was a kind of lie. Dawn had at least not been deluded about that. She and Terry had sacrificed years to cast off their own crude beginnings, transform themselves into something else. Would she have seen any more clearly if she hadn't painted over all those oaken panels, hadn't patrolled the boundaries of her own tastes so ferociously, hadn't kept within view some shining ideal of perfection? Would she have had a better grasp of the unravelling drama if she'd been more down-to-earth?

The woman squatting on her crate at the convenience store, she thought bitterly, wouldn't have fared much better. She would have banished Dawn to the streets for bringing shame on the family or attempted some primitive witchcraft. The conjecture made Maureen blush. Drug lord or worm picker, this boy, this actual Vietnamese boy with his blood-tipped feathers, had brought Dawn to the hospital, had looked upon Maureen with pity. Had explained the situation lucidly enough, first to the nurses and doctors and now again to Maureen, so that Dawn was now dozing peacefully in the corridor, her gauzed hand cradled like a doll in her lap.

Maureen told the doctor about the time at the high school when she'd turned to see Dawn picking her nose as the badly drawn Firebirds fluttered down around her feet. But that look of wary disgust on the other students' faces must have grown over time, like Dawn's illness, under cover of the guidance counsellor's Romeo and Juliet gloss. She aimed deeper and deeper, remembering the silly faces that had made her and Terry hoot with laughter, the gauche solemnities of early adolescence that Maureen had ascribed to her daughter's bulkiness. The falling apart of the stereo after over a year of blaring, the speakers blown because, as Dawn had confessed to the doctor moments earlier, only the highest volume stopped the voices from whispering at her.

When she left the hospital a few hours later, Maureen drove recklessly towards home, got stuck behind a dump truck hauling loads on the way back to her suburb. She looked out at the new development going up and it seemed, for a moment, that the brightly clad construction workers were yanking the vinyl siding down, undoing the wooden frames plank by plank. Soon they would strip the pavement, roll up the golf course's green lawn as though it were a magician's tablecloth, cart each item of the manicured landscape off until nothing was left but rock. She thought it might not be a bad idea.

PROPERTY OF FATTY

My biggest mistake was going on vacation with a buddy I met at the Boogaloo. A guy who all the strippers make fun of behind his back by oinking and puffing their cheeks into balloons. Who sings the lyrics to "Almost Paradise" while jacking off in the dark. Ask me how I know.

What comes to mind when you hear the words "tropical vacation condo"? Palm trees, balconies? Women oiling up poolside or bringing you drinks with dinky parasols?

Now picture a place that looks like it's been bombed, invaded by tanks, ravaged by goats to the point of desertification. Picture my buddy Calvin from the Boogaloo, ankle-deep in gravel and Marlboro butts, beer gut bobbing into view beneath his Mötley Crüe T-shirt, a warm beer overflowing in each fist.

"It would have been nice," I say to him, "if you'd mentioned that your condo hadn't been built yet. I might have brought a sleeping bag. A flashlight. A couple of sticks to rub together."

Calvin looks hurt. Can't a man dream? Use your imagination, he tells me. This is just the pre-developmental phase, he says. A while back he divvied his property up into plots with wooden stakes that have been chewed down to the nub by the local wildlife. Human or otherwise. Almost Paradise.

Don't get me wrong. I'm grateful. I'm so grateful I'd offer myself on a platter to old King Coconut himself, if he ever dips his beard into the square of empty sky above my head. I'm grateful Calvin picked me up at the airport in a cardboard sombrero with a WELCOME sign drawn in crayon by one of his best girls, a different colour for each fat letter. I'm grateful Calvin didn't kill me on the drive back from the airport, what with him jabbering non-stop while his jeep swerved between ruts and bomb craters and kids selling woodcuts of pot-bellied women, and a bazillion other islanders in flip-flops and straw hats, empty-handed or bent over wheelbarrows full of fruit the size and shape of medieval weapons, or bikes buried beneath clouds of blow-up beach toys.

After twenty minutes or so he slowed the jeep to a crawl.

"The thing you have to remember about this place," he said "is that you could pretty much fuck any one of these people if you offered them enough cash."

Grandpas, panhandlers, former statespersons, mothers of five, all just waiting to bend over for a few bucks, according to Calvin.

"I'm telling you," he said. "They don't have hang-ups about sex out here. Unlike back home, where even the strippers are uptight know-it-all little bitches. Even when you ask politely."

He frowned and tugged his gizzards through his khakis. I asked him to prove it, pointed to a girl and told him to pull up beside her. Calvin squinted and told me he didn't like the look of her from where he sat. Then he stepped hard on the brakes and gave me a serious look. Possibly the most serious look anyone has ever given me.

"You can tell a lot about people by the shape of their ass," he said. "It's like a second face."

It's pretty much Calvin's whole philosophy.

Lucky for him there's a lot of ass around here that he does approve of. There hasn't been an unbroken night of humping and oinking since I got here. I don't know who, or how, or what anymore and I don't want to. I never thought I'd be the one to say this, but you can have too much of a good thing. It's got so when I hear the jeep crawling up I take a nosedive under my blanket and dig myself down into the gravel. But no matter how deep I go, I'm waking up to the sound of skin spanking on skin. It's in my dreams. It's in my bloodstream. It's what I hear in the bush when I drag myself the boiling mile down the dirt path to the so-called beach.

It's what I hear right now, watching Calvin waddle out and plunge his deck chair into the shifting dunes of what he sometimes designates as the living room.

"Cities are crumbling," he says. "Chunks of overpass are falling out of the sky and flattening folks into Silly Putty. And you're bitching about a little old unfinished condo."

There are walls, I'll grant him that. Four cinder-block walls and a strip of corrugated tin over what Calvin calls his master bedroom every time I so much as squat there to sneak some shade. Which I'm not even going to do anymore.

"Civilizations are sliding into the sea," he says.

His eyes are bugging out even more than usual. And I think to myself, let the freaking civilizations slide into the sea.

What did civilization ever do for me, except land me right back here with hairy old knuckle-dragging Calvin? When it really comes down to it, though, I blame Lotta, and people like Lotta, for the whole stinking mess. Or at least the mess I'm currently in.

The guys I've rented rooms out to in the past have always ended up stealing straight from my wallet, or passed out drunk in the hallway with their pants around their ankles. Have jammed up my plumbing or just been pigs in general. So when pink, doughy, four-eyed Lotta shows up looking for a room I think: Bingo! Home-cooked meals. A little light housework. As a landlord you expect a few perks.

She moved into my place three months ago and never stopped. First, it's your usual beat-up coffee table and junk wrapped in garbage bags and duct tape. But the vanloads kept coming. Look at this box of doorknobs I picked up on the corner, she'd say. How could anybody throw out a dented but otherwise perfectly okay hamster cage? Why, there's hardly a speck of rust on this rebar. The sheer waste, she'd say, bowing her head and folding her doughy hands together. It's not just a crime against humanity. It's a crime against the Lord and his host of heavenly angels. Because every inch of Lotta's firmament is chock-a-block with angels. I'm still waiting for her to stuff the house with feathers. She has a big old book somewhere in her pile upstairs that she kept trying to shove under my nose. It's called angel-o-lo-gy, she'd say, mouthing the word at me really slow, like I was stupid. Which I am. Sweet Jesus, I am.

Soon my yard is filled with busted flamingos and three-wheeled baby buggies and a heap of planks that only need the rusty nails pulled out to make them good as new. Everything is sal-vage-a-ble, because anything can be turned into something else, or put to an as yet unknowable use. Think of the potential, she'd say, holding up a piece of buckled sheet metal with a gleam in her beady eye. Next thing I know my porch is sagging with the weight of all the broken dishwashers and microwaves that Lotta has somehow managed, in spite of being about as round as she is high, to drag up the steps because she's worried some other salvagers are going to poach them if they're left street-level.

"You have no idea what those bastards get up to," she tells me.

"I'm starting to get a pretty good idea," I say.

By the end of the month she's filled my chest freezer with packets wrapped in butcher paper and dirty string that I don't have the stomach to defrost and find out if they're chops or baby heads or severed limbs or what. I'm not saying she's a killer, just that if anybody is going to drag home human remains from the bottom of a dumpster or the back of an abandoned warehouse, it's Lotta.

It got so everywhere I looked I'd see her big rump bent over a garbage can. I'd see her poking around in her dirty pink sweatsuit in every alley I passed. I'd see her rounding the street corners with her van door open and something bulky strapped to the roof. When I told her it had to end she sat around for a week in her house robe, picking at the wad of gum stuck to her elbow. Then she's sneaking stuff in through the basement hatch, filling up the furnace room with clock radios and dud lamps. A few more days and she's backing her van into the driveway with another pile of crap.

The neighbours start coming around in concerned groups. She's a one-woman wrecking ball, they tell me. Knocks a grand off the value of every house on the street any time she swings by to dump another load. I tell them how she pulls the waterworks on me every time I try to kick her out, starts squealing how she has nowhere else to park her ass. They ask me if I'd consider hiring someone to break her legs with a crowbar, a tire iron, or maybe one of the many busted, duct-taped baseball bats she's collected up and got leaning against my back shed. I tell them hiring someone is not an option in this household. I'm on a strict budget, in the first place. And the thing is, unlike all my previous tenants, she was paying her rent. Right up until the moment she wasn't. Then she's six weeks overdue and there's not so much as an IOU in my envelope.

I put the boot in. Next thing you know, she's shifted her piles out of the bedroom and into the hallway and along the stairs. She's rigged up a dirty canvas tent at the bottom of the yard. She puts a sign up out front offering psychic readings for ten bucks. I poke my head under the flap and she's sitting there at a fold-up table with a scarf wrapped around her head, thumbing a grimy pack of cards.

"This isn't some shantytown," I tell her. "This is a private house in a private neighbourhood."

Then she's calling me a scuzz and a pighead just because I've come into a bit of my own land, squawking that she's never so much as seen me step onto this section of the yard before so what's the big fat deal? Which might be true, but you don't have to trample on every inch of a thing for it to belong to you. My other big mistake was letting it slide when she promised me a cut of her earnings. Because it turns out not many people want to stroll through head-high piles of scrap metal and rusty baby buggies down a path lined with artificial yucca plants to have their fortune told by a chain-smoking butterball in a dirty pink sweatsuit. If I had thought about it long and hard enough I could've predicted that myself.

"It takes time to build a solid business foundation," she says, divvying the cards into two piles and shuffling them like a pro.

A couple of days after that I'm squeezing past a box spring and a crate of vacuum cleaner parts on the front path when I see a blonde carving a heart onto my porch step with a penknife. When she looks up and asks me if I'm the one meant to read her fortune, I almost fall onto my knees and praise all the angels in Lotta's heaven. Because every square inch of that body, from the look in her blank little eyeballs to the pigeon toes in her pink sneakers tells me she possesses the kind of pure, God-given dumbness that falls from the clouds into a man's lap once, maybe twice in a lifetime if he's lucky.

"I don't need a pack of cards to see love with a stranger in your future," I tell her.

She jabs at the space in front of my crotch with a smile, tells me her mama always told her to beware of strangers. I grab the knife, fold the blade, and put it in my pants pocket.

"Hey," she says. "That was a birthday present."

"Let's celebrate indoors," I say. "Where it's more private."

You know how one thing leads to another. Soon we're peeling our clothes off and banging so hard Lotta's boxes take a tumble down the hall stairs. All the gewgaws and muffin pans she never uses are rattling off the counters and the big old buffet. Her collection of plastic ducks is flying off the top of the bathroom cabinet. Her stack of *National Geographics* is toppling onto the shaggy old carpet she dragged in off the curb. And I'm saying to myself, I'm screaming to anyone within a five-mile radius: let it all end now in a blaze of fire and glory. Or at least let me. Because sweet Mother of Jesus, it was that good. It's only when she's down on all fours that I see the words "Property of Fatty" tattooed in thick black letters on the hollow space above her crack.

"Don't worry," she says, twisting her head around and giving me that sweet empty look. "He isn't getting out for a whole other month."

She must have mixed her dates up because a few days later a guy who looks not so much fat as forced to surrender his steroids for a while at the penitentiary check-in is circling my block in a Chevy Blazer with one tinted window rolled down. I ask Property what Fatty did to get himself incarcerated.

"A little bit of this," she says. "And a whole lot of that."

Grievous bodilies, assaults with dangerous weapons. And he got way more time in the clink than his two brothers or his cousin Bubba did for the exact same crimes. Which isn't exactly fair, she tells me.

A few days later Property of Fatty stops taking my calls.

My problem is, I never got a good look at his face. So everywhere I go, Fatty might be. Fatty or Fatty's crew. At the back of the bowling alley, behind me at the drive-thru. Waiting to bust out of the gas station bathroom with their flabby Popeye arms. Which is why I had to change my whole routine. I'm sneaking out back to climb the fence behind Lotta's tent every time I need a six-pack at the store I normally don't go to. Which is how I get my pants stuck on a nail in the fence and gave myself a wedgie so hard I bawled like a baby.

"You've been sticking your business where you shouldn't," says Lotta, not even bothering to wipe the smile off her face while she unhooks my belt from the fence. I follow her into the tent, picking the splinters out of my palms.

"I see suffering in your future," she says. "And a Chevy Blazer with tinted windows."

Then she has the balls to try and charge me her friends-and-family rate for a reading. No way, I told her. I already knew all that and more. Because every black car coming at me out of the corner of my eye, every black car nosing around every curb, every black speck speeding at me on the horizon is a Chevy Blazer. I've got Blazers in my bad dreams, rising up out of lakes with water gushing from the windows. I've got Blazers revving their engines outside my window at 3 a.m. I don't even go anywhere near my usual spots because I can hear the Blazers lining up outside waiting to drag me off to a secluded place where my arms and legs can be broken at leisure. Which is how I ended up at the Boogaloo on a Tuesday afternoon, in my humble opinion the lowest-ranking club on the strip, watching a broad in pigtails with a beer gut spin herself around a pole until she's a blur of fake tan. Which is when the bouncer comes over and tells me he thinks a guy came in looking for me the other day. The news almost made me happy, because it was the first real proof I was right to be shitting my pants all along.

I contemplate my beer. I contemplate disappearing into thin air. Which is more or less the exact moment when Calvin comes up to me.

"My friend," he says. "You look like you've got the weight of the world on your shoulders."

Pretty soon I'm offloading the whole story to this stranger. About Lotta and her hoarding. About Property of Fatty and how and where I stuck my business and just how temporary that was. About Fatty and his probable crew, reaching out to clobber me with their beefy biceps. How I couldn't even walk around my own neighbourhood anymore without expecting to pay a visit to emergency.

"That's no life at all," says Calvin, while we watch the dancer scuttle off stage.

"Your problem," says Calvin, "is that you're too big-hearted."

"You don't know the half of it," I say to him.

I tell him how I got married, got a nine-to-five and a house in a not-so-great suburb. Then my wife maxes out all the cards on wall hangings and puffy couches and a big shaggy bedspread she hates after a week and stuffs to the back of the closet, and which makes me jump out of my skin every time I reach in for a fresh towel. Then she's bored with the house and the suburb and stupid me and my office job. She joins a softball team to pass the time. It's great, she says. Team spirit and rah-rah-rah. We all have hot dogs and beer and crawl into the hot tub after a tough game, she says. Give each other rubdowns with this special oil.

Boy, I say. Wish I could be a fly on the wall for that.

No way, she says, punching me hard on the arm. Burt and Chuck have a strict no-hangers-on policy.

Burt and Chuck. Hot tubs and rubdowns. When I close my eyes I'm seeing big, bristly moustaches, I'm seeing hairy arms and muscly torsos packing the steam-filled air instead of naked women.

They don't usually allow girls on the team, she tells me. But they made an exception for me on account of my skills. Wasn't that nice?

After the big corporate takeover the management started going on training camps every other weekend. They built human pyramids and went on group scavenger hunts to build team morale. Then they're coming back and laying people off left and right. I don't even see my wife anymore because I'm chained to my desk trying to get the zigs to zag on the diagrams my boss draws on the whiteboard every Monday morning. All so she can climb into a vat of steam and testosterone.

I'm staring at my wife and the big fat pieces of my life click into place like a jumbo puzzle. How she was dressing like a hooker and humming "We Are the Champions" all the time. The jokes my boss kept making about gangbangs and swingers. The whole office looking at me sideways on smoke breaks. I'm the dumb bub, the rube with the loosest skank in town. On no account, I tell her, is she getting up to that kind of behaviour again. Next thing I know she's moved out and I'm getting letters from Bonehead and Bonehead, specialists in family law. I'm getting big-assed hoarders and smart-aleck psychics to move in with me so my house doesn't get repossessed. Which I couldn't care less about anymore. I tell Calvin that, straight up in the strip club.

"Give those types an inch," he says, "and they take a mile."

"I'm the little guy here," I say. "I'm getting shafted."

"You know what you need? A vacation," he says. "You've got to go where you're appreciated."

A tropical vacation condo, he tells me. In a tropical vacation paradise. I can picture the whole place while he's describing it to me, right down to the WELCOME sign sewed out of coconut husks. I can feel the ocean breeze. No Fatty. No Lotta. Calvin's flying out the next day, and the sooner I get there the better, as far as he's concerned.

An hour later and we're still clinking glasses to my Fatty-less future. The next day I'm in Payday Loans. I'm trading in the last of my gold at the pawnshop. I'm tacking the ROOM FOR RENT sign back up at the 7-Eleven, telling Lotta I want her and every last mother-loving scrap of hers off my property ASAP. I'm phoning sick into work, thinking I'll forge a doctor's note when I get back. If I ever come back. Because Calvin has plans out there on that island. All that's required is a huge enough vision. And a willingness to get behind it in a big way.

Even on the ride in from the airport, he's outlining scenarios for the future between potholes, one hand on the wheel and the other hanging on to his paper sombrero or rearranging the crotch of his khakis. Which is why I'm just a tiny bit surprised when he asks me to spot him a twenty for gas. It's almost dark when we pull up outside of what looks like a cross between a fallout shelter and an ancient ruin. The condo. There's this little old problem, Calvin explains, called a cash flow situation.

And the WELCOME sign sewed out of coconut husks, the dinky parasols, and the soothing ocean breezes? All that's down in the gated resorts with the centrefolds and the sports celebrities on the other side of the island, where I hear there's a reef that keeps out the barracudas and great white sharks. On this side it's half-naked Calvin pleasuring himself on a mound of gravel, lording it over his acre of scrub.

What he doesn't see, or doesn't want to see, are the expressions on the islanders' faces. For the whole week I've been here, the louder he gibbers, the harder he honks his horn or grabs his balls, the more faces scowl out from the shacks or overtop of the ditches. So even though he tells me it's all in my head, I'm scanning the scenery every time I leave Calvin's so-called condo. Which is what I was doing coming back up from the scrubby little strip of beach today when I saw my own 100 per cent silk boxer shorts running through the bushes ahead of me.

And I'm everywhere. A woman in my pyjama bottoms with Calvin's Flintstones beach towel wrapped around her head pushes past me on the path, smiling ear to ear. Through the trees, I see my favourite red T-shirt with Calvin's khakis goose-stepping underneath. Two kids dressed in the top and bottom halves of my Nike sweatsuit are playing kickball with my shaving kit. Deeper in the shadows, I see my dress shirt toss my key chain to the guy with a big grin wearing my home-team jersey, who slips them into the pocket of his camo Bermuda shorts. Which are my camo Bermuda shorts, the seams straining from his bulky thighs. I start running back to Calvin's, guessing at the bright blurs of colour along the way. The burgundy blur by the banana tree is Calvin's bathrobe, the baby blue squatting in the flower-bush is my stonewashed jeans. The green and orange and black is my Hawaiian shirt with the macaw pattern, which is the last thing my wife ever gave me.

Back at the condo, bottomless Calvin is sinking deeper into the gravel and staring at me with his yellowy eyes. He chased the girl they sent as a lure halfway across the island, he says. Then they nabbed his pants while he was getting down to business. The only thing they didn't take from the unmanned condo were a few loose bottles of beer half-hidden in the mounds. I'm looking over at where my pile used to be. The wallet, the suitcase, the toothbrush. The return ticket. I'm thinking about the way my watch face and the embossed gold on my passport used to shine when they caught the light.

You've got to use your imagination. That's what he said when the jeep pulled into his no man's land for the first time, right before he palmed another twenty off me for supplies. And to be perfectly honest I have seen, in little flashes here and there, how glorious it all could be.

Calvin plants an empty into the gravel and upends the bottle in his other hand for a last guzzle. I'm not going to tunnel down to the fiery lakes of hell that I now know exist. I'm not praying for a military reconnaissance helicopter, for a team of venture capitalists in shining armour or the Horsemen of the Apocalypse. I'm just a slab of grilled meat with nothing but a Speedo to my name, and nothing on my mind but a chunk of empty blue sky.

So come get me, Fatty. I'm all yours.

Moon Cakes

The first time I saw Findlay was from the second-floor window of a classroom packed with the other immigrants who'd just enrolled, mostly Asians, Italians, and Greeks. The back rows were filled with Colombian girls who whispered among themselves in Spanish and knit christening blankets and baby bonnets from mounds of white wool they kept half-hidden in bags under their chairs. The needles paused whenever the teacher looked up from the magazine on his desk, then started up again when he looked down. All the rich kids went to the segregated girls' and boys' colleges in a leafy neighbourhood on the other side of the junction. The rest of us—a mix of immigrants who didn't speak English, aboriginals, bronzed surf nuts who'd flunked out of their final year, and pasty-faced teens from low-income families—were crammed into the bunker-like high school, whose urine-stained stucco perimeter surrounded a central courtyard without an inch of shade. The teacher—whether out of prejudice, incompetence, laziness, or an unwholesome combination of all three—made it clear from the start that he had no intention of teaching us a single thing. Every hour I'd spent in the classroom so far had been like this, with the clock and the needles clacking, and the motionless teacher with his stiff moustache and even stiffer expression.

It started as an inkling, a taint in the air that quickened to a surge in the gravel parking lot below. There was a rattle of chain links and we flew from our desks to the window. A gang of boys was pushing him so hard against the fence that his cheek, red as a raw flank steak, bulged through the wires beneath his round eyeglasses. They stayed there frozen and straining, like statues depicting a scene in an epic battle, until the bell rang and everyone except the oblivious Colombian girls elbowed past each other down the rough stucco stairway to the parking lot. By the time I got there Findlay had vanished and the brutes who'd penned him in were scratching their heads. Even though I was new, I'd already heard about how he finagled his way out of situations. How he appeared and disappeared at the drop of a hat, and never seemed to incur any punishments beyond the pink detention slips for truancy that he—or so it was rumoured—turned into paper cranes and launched oceanward on the nearest beach. Having already had a few encounters with the bronzed gods who ruled the courtyard, I was more keen to meet him than ever.

By the school's exit I met up with a little Scottish girl as new as I was, a sunburned redhead with a disoriented expression. We followed some Asian girls into the junction and bought pieces of battered fish wrapped in Chinese newspapers, biting off pearly grease-slicked chunks as we walked.

For years her redhead family had dreamed of immigrating to Australia, lining up at the visa bureaus and government offices. Now all they thought about was going home. And rain. Rain on the cobblestones and the mossy rooftops. Rain in slow rivulets on the window. Cool rain collecting in the ditches. I held her fish while she dabbed at her tears with a wad of greasy napkin. I also dream about rain. When I lie in bed at night, when I dart from shade to shade in the blazing daylight, when my throat is choked with dust.

Unlike the Scottish girl, I was there because of a mix-up.

My mother suffered with her nerves, and was never one to order either her household affairs or her inner life with any great success. Her breakdowns meant that my brother and I were sent to live among our extended family, who were scattered across the globe. Sometimes we ended up together, but more often than not we set off in separate directions, reunited when my mother felt well enough to resume a family life.

Even as a small child my brother had a passion for Australia. His most treasured possession was the tooth of a great white shark, which he kept in a tin box lined with felt. I once saw him fiercely haggle over a mangy-looking kangaroo paw at a flea market with the last of his allowance. It was decided among the various family members that my brother would go to my grandparents in Sydney while I was to be sent off to a great-aunt who lived in a real chateau in France with actual turrets. Sad though we were to leave our mother, we were delighted with our individual prospects. Her breakdowns frequently required a lot of interference and involvement from well-meaning outsiders, and on this occasion the visas and papers were mixed up. My brother was sent to the francophile aunt, while I embarked on the two-day plane ride to the land of spiders and snakes and the great whites my brother adored. We never quite forgave each other for that turn of bad luck.

Every now and then I received a photograph of him venge-fully tending our great-aunt's prizewinning rose gardens with the fairy-tale chateau half-cloaked in the misty background. I reciprocated by sending him postcards from a series entitled "Poisonous Spiders of New South Wales."

You'd think with over a dozen schools and as many changes of abode under my belt I'd have picked up a few tricks to cope with always being the new kid. I was underdeveloped for my age, and could have passed for either a girl or a boy, which garnered me bullies of both sexes. At the last school the word "hermaphrodite" had been bandied around in tones of sotto voce dismay, but so far the kids here were too dull witted to use the term or too poorly educated to have heard of it.

My Scottish friend was too wrapped up in her own nostal-gia to worry how I might affect her popularity, and was happy to reminisce with me during lunch hour about the grey misty village her people came from. We walked together, lost in sepa-rate worlds, when there was a disturbance at a market stall across the street. She grabbed my arm but I looked up a second too late, catching what looked like the shadow of a horse rounding the corner into an alley. A lemon rolled onto the pavement and then the whole stall collapsed, its array of fruits and vegetables cascading onto the pavement. The angry stall owner looked left then right for the culprit, shook his fist in the air, and began to chase after the tomatoes rolling downhill towards an open sewer grate. Fish spilled from the red-haired girl's open mouth.

"It was the boy at the fence," she said.

Findlay.

Even walking me home in our school uniforms, Findlay attracted attention. It's hard to say why. He was tall and thin with a freckled baby face and round wire glasses shaped like moons. There was something about the way he moved, as if he was always on his way to somewhere wonderful. Like he really believed it.

My grandparents' bungalow was brown and crammed with junk and antiques. The only new things were my grandmother's medical implements: a walker and a stiff plastic bib to stop the food falling onto her blouses. The bungalow went on forever, each room leading into another, all of them dusty and almost always deserted. We stepped into the shuttered parlour where my grandfather kept his gramophone collection, each horn like a blast of music frozen in mid-air.

"Play something for me," said Findlay. The horns on the high shelves loomed overhead. He threw himself into a wicker chair, his brown bangs flopping over his eyes. "It's like a tomb in here."

We both knew it was better than his mother's place, a tiny glass condo in a smooth-sided complex on the other side of the junction. And we had plans to discuss.

"Do you think we'll get caught?"

"They'll banish us to the middle of nowhere," said Findlay. "With nothing to eat except dried snakes and dirt pie."

Because Findlay was always looking for new ways to get into trouble, his mother was always threatening to send him to an uncle's remote sheep station to teach him a lesson.

"They're not going to let us in," I said. "They'll arrest us for having fake IDs."

For all my world travels, I'd never tried to get into a club underage. And with my puppy fat and baby-smooth skin, I had more to worry about than him.

"It's a masquerade ball," said Findlay, rolling his eyes. "*Everyone* is going to be false impersonating."

I cleared away some books and old magazines from a trunk and took out the bags Findlay and I had hidden there. The black material inside of them slithered onto the floor.

"Head to toe in black," said Findlay. "With black masks. We'll simply disappear."

It was Findlay's idea to make outfits instead of buying or renting them. His mother worked in a fabric shop. I went with him and fingered the gingham and upholstery material while he stole us a bolt of sheeny black cloth. He worried that it was too stiff to drape well. He didn't know how to fix this. His mother made herself matching skirts and short-sleeved blazers in lavender and sea green, but she never taught him how to sew.

Just to be sure we wouldn't get caught, Findlay decided to use the park across the street as a changing room and as a place to hide our bikes. He stuffed the material back into the bags and headed to the side of the bungalow to get our bikes. The park is full of stumpy palms with frilled leaves that sweep to the ground like skirts, but so many drunks and children hide under them it was hard to find one empty. We pushed our faces between the leaves and found a bearded man curled up like a dog. In another we found a girl with hair to her waist and a boy already reaching down to pull his jeans up from around his ankles to chase after us.

We pedalled away and leaned our bikes against a gum tree. Findlay threw himself onto the ground and closed his eyes. In spite of the spiders and sharks, it was the most beautiful place I've ever seen, maybe even more beautiful than the misty chateau. I couldn't stop looking at the flocks of pink cockatoos in the loaded fruit trees and the coloured lizards darting between the rocks. I was on the underside of the whole world. If I closed my eyes I'd fall off and wake up grabbing at the clouds. I clutched a handful of grass and stared at Findlay's dreaming face, the sky reflected in his round glasses.

We hid our bikes in the wooded shrubs along with the black material, the masks, and the fake IDs. "We'll meet here at midnight," he said. "Remember this bench. Remember the gum tree. Remember this fountain."

That night I lay in bed fully dressed with the sheets pulled up to my chin until our Filipina housekeeper, Flordelisa, shuffled down the corridor in her straw slippers and out into the choked garden where she lived in the converted pool cabana. I waited until I heard the sound of her television before I inched the window open and squeezed out into the darkness dividing our house from next door's, the black wet nose of their German shepherd snuffling at me through a loose board in the fence.

Thanks to the postcards I sent my brother, I was painfully aware of all the deadly creatures that could kill me. But it was my grandparents' neglected pool I had nightmares about, sinking beneath the layer of green fuzz into the cloudy water below. I edged past it with my shoes in my hands, tiptoed past the cabana, and climbed over the back wall.

I zoomed through the park's unlit spaces. There were slivers of light from under the drooping palms, and the sounds of coughing and transistor radios. It felt for a moment as though

I was running into outer space, with no earth or sky but only a silky, damp-scented darkness. Then I saw the bronze fountain's silhouette and remembered.

Findlay's legs dangled off the wooden fence that separated the shrubs from the path. The light from the lamppost made moons of his eyeglasses. His face was already made up and his lips looked black in the semi-darkness. We stripped down to our underpants. He took out the flashlights and the swathes of black material cut out in the shapes he'd dreamed up earlier. He wound the fabric around me, tying knots and pricking me with safety pins. He took out a makeup bag and powdered me, applied deep red lips and false eyelashes. Then I draped him in his fabric while he yanked and twisted. Finally, we put on our wigs, tucking and straightening.

"Findlay," said Findlay, "you've outdone yourself."

We fished our bikes from the shrubs and threw our shoes—candy-red heels—into the baskets and pedalled barefoot towards the river of red tail lights at the furthest end of the park.

Findlay's mother threw a surprise birthday party for him once and sent out invitations to all the kids in his class. She made cupcakes and had balloons and had pin-the-tail-on-the-donkey, but the kids had a secret game in mind, which was to draw as many swastikas as they could in books, on walls, behind the bedroom doors. Findlay and his mother found them for weeks afterwards, his mother screaming each time because she thought they were spiders.

The heels were almost our undoing. We'd never walked in them before. What seemed like a jaunt from the bushes in the park where we'd once again stowed our bikes became an unbearable journey, our feet blistering after a single block. We stumbled and bled. The black material unravelled, and Findlay tripped and sprawled into a flower bunker, his blue underpants and long knobbly legs splayed out for all to see. It took us forever to put him back together. I brushed the pebbles from a raw patch on his knee. He pushed his glasses back into place and we tottered past a fancy hotel with a striped awning and a bolt of red carpet.

By the time we got to Chinatown we were carrying our shoes in one hand, stooping down to rub our blisters in between gawking at ducks hanging in the windows and tiny plucked chickens with their legs tucked primly behind them, big-whiskered fish, and vegetables with prickled dragon skin.

"I want moon cakes," said Findlay, holding two blank white cookies in front of his eyes. "I want everything and nothing at all."

He handed me one and ate the other before the shop owner caught sight of us. The market stalls gave way to café windows and bouncers in black leather slouching against the lintels of nightclubs. Findlay raced towards a cluster of people at the far end of the street, stopped short half a block up to put his heels back on.

There were men in Dolly Parton wigs and women in Batman costumes. There were clowns and Victorian gentlemen and World War Two pilots. There was an Elvis and a Buddy Holly and a man dressed as Madonna. Findlay was in his element. Because the thing about Findlay was that he didn't want to decide who he was. Why rule anything out? The bouncers barely glanced at our fake IDs and nodded us in. Findlay threw himself onto a sofa and struck a glamorous pose.

And then he was everywhere. Whirling with the ball-gown-and leather-clad figures on the dance floor, hoisting himself onstage to walk like an Egyptian. He was heading up a conga line and then was draping half his black skirt over his head like a mantilla and screaming out the lyrics to "Like a Virgin." He was fixing his lipstick in a gilt-framed mirror so big I thought it was an archway into a whole other bar.

Then he was out of breath and barefoot beside me, our red heels lost in the crowds hours ago. When we left, everybody was patting him on the back and kissing two times on each cheek French style and saying they couldn't live without him. Then we were whizzing down the bike path in the park with the black material flapping behind us, the city lights blurring behind us. And I wanted every day and every night to be like that, with Findlay's eyes like moons and his long brown bangs frilling like a horse's mane in the wind.

It was still dark by the time I crept past the cabana and into my grandparents' garden. I had just reached the green pool when the neighbour's German shepherd squeezed through the loose board in the fence and stood in front of me with teeth bared, ears and tail rigid. The dog growled each time I tried to take a step. I was still standing when the sky turned from indigo to washed ink, and the frangipani unloosed the last of its sweet night fragrances overhead.

The dog sat back on its haunches but kept its eyes fixed on me, not even flinching when the electric light to the cabana switched on and Flordelisa stepped out with a wide, flat broom. She used the broom to shoo the dog back to the loose board and back under the fence. Then she turned and her eyes travelled down the length of my costume, which had come unknotted in places and was hanging in wrinkled loops around my legs. She put her hand over her mouth to stifle her laughter and led me into her cabana, where I stared at a wall of framed family photographs—she had children and cousins and a whole raft of people she sent money home to—while she fried us both some rice and salted red eggs. I was so tired by the time I finished that I don't remember her sneaking me in through the back of the house to my room, minus my black costume.

There was no Findlay in the courtyard at school the next day or the day after that. There was no Findlay in the park or in the market at the junction or out by the smooth-sided complex where I rang and rang the buzzer. After another week had passed I made my way to the fabric store and waited for Findlay's mother to look up from her measuring board and tell me that there was nothing wrong with Findlay at all.

The Scottish girl and her family got so homesick they moved back. She sent me a letter saying how there were wet bundles of laundry mouldering behind doors and socks drying on every radiator. It never stopped raining, she said, and every day there were more wet clothes, and all she dreamed about now were sunny courtyards and flocks of cockatoos.

My days settled back into their old routines, with the girls in the back rows knitting christening blankets from mounds of white wool and the needles pausing when the teacher looked up from his magazine. And every day was more or less like this, except that sometimes when I was lonely I sidled past the old green pool to see Flordelisa in her cabana and ate salted red eggs and rice while she told me stories about her kids in Manila.

It started as an inkling on a hot afternoon, which quickened to a surge in the gravel parking lot below. I looked up a second too soon, caught what seemed like the shadow of a horse rounding the corner. I ran down the stucco steps into the school courtyard.

He tossed his brown bangs and squinted at me behind the round glasses. He told me how he must have lost his key in the park. Rather than wake his mother he went back and scrambled in the shrubs and all along the paths where we'd cycled but instead of finding the key he found a gang of thugs heading home after a night out. They knocked him down and took the bike, along with all the daytime clothes he'd planned to change back into. Being Findlay, he managed to wriggle free before they beat him to a pulp.

"I swear to you I actually flew," he said.

He lost the gang on a side street near the condo, then he tried to scale the smooth-sided wall, grabbing onto a trellis of bougainvillea. He was around halfway up when he fell onto the lawn below, snagging the black material of his dress on a spike. The noise woke up someone who triggered the burglar alarm and then the security lights. His mother heard the alarm, leaned over her balcony, and saw him sprawled on the lawn, his black dress half unwound, lipstick smeared to his chin.

She kept him locked in the condo for the rest of the week. Fed him saltines and bowls of cup-a-soup brought to him on a tray in bed.

"Like I was sick," he said, rolling his eyes.

She sent him on the four-day Greyhound trip to his uncle with a suitcase full of rugged clothes. I asked him if it was as bad as we had imagined and he told me that his uncle taught him how to mend fences. He showed him how to chase kangaroos on a motorcycle. He showed him how to castrate baby goats with a rubber band.

He saved every penny he could get his hands on for the bus fare back.

"Did your mother forgive you?" I asked.

Findlay snorted. He didn't care if she forgave him. It was his mother's face, stiff with disgust, staring down at him from the balcony that he couldn't forget all those long blazing days at the sheep station. Even though she'd taken him in and washed the makeup off his face, unwound the torn fabric from his body and bandaged his grazed knee. He couldn't forget. He wouldn't forgive.

When I asked him where he was going, he shrugged and squinted at me through the moon glasses, as though he was already far away. Then he's slipping past the bullies in the courtyard, slipping past the chain-link fence. In my dreams he's tossing his brown bangs back like a horse's mane, running down the street and up into the air. He's drifting up over the horizon. He's winding himself in an acre of black cloth and disappearing into the night sky.

Findlay, you outdid yourself. It feels like I've spent my whole life since then going wherever I've been sent. But where are you? Who are you now that so many long, dusty years have passed?

Scenes of Acapulco

Walt and Troy sat on the Maple Leaf's yellow bar stools, their legs splayed, the remains of two heart-clogging Trucker's Breakfasts in front of them. Walt stared at his sagging orange peel and parsley garnish, an innovation since the Denny's had opened up off the highway. Then he leaned forward to catch a glimpse of Donna's ass as she rooted for coffee filters under the counter.

"They say the only place he didn't shoot her was in the face," he said, elbowing Troy hard in the gut.

Troy grunted and filled his mouth with the last of his sausage. That bony elbow of Walt's was good at finding soft spots.

In reality, Donna had been shot four times by her husband after he caught her in bed with Rudyard Delaney, who had then run naked into the woodlot outside their pre-fab while Donna's husband took potshots at him from the back door. Rudyard moved in with Donna after her husband went to jail but, being just as bad tempered as Donna's husband, had run her over with his pickup truck a few years later.

"Happens once, it's an accident," said Walt. "Happens twice, you got to think she's a ball-breaker."

"Or worse," said Troy.

"What could be worse than that?"

Remarks like these had been traded among the Maple Leaf clientele for the last fifteen years. To their minds, and maybe also to hers, there were two Donnas. One was the horror story of patchwork and scar tissue they whispered about behind her back; the other was a homely waitress doling out wads of rocky road from the cake dome on the counter. Once in a blue moon, always after too many rum and Cokes, Donna hoisted up her shirt to give onlookers a show. She claimed the only thing that had saved her life was the tooled leather handbag decorated with scenes of Acapulco she'd held to her chest while he was shooting. She'd never, on the other hand, showed anyone the damage done to her legs after the pickup backed over her. The story was that Rudyard had, in addition to various bones, broken Donna's heart. She had a jerky way of walking that made Walt wonder, not without pity, what the hell was going on under those polyester slacks. He squinted at Troy.

"You ever see under that shirt of hers?"

"Nah."

Walt swallowed his last mouthful of coffee. "I bet her husband wishes he'd cut himself a bigger lawn into that woodlot of theirs when he saw Delaney's guilty white ass disappearing into the trees."

He speared the orange garnish with his knife, plopped it onto his napkin, then smeared the egg yolk on his platter with his last piece of toast while Troy went up to the cash register and paid. Troy was the son of a fishing buddy, a moon-faced kid who'd grown into a mass of silent, six-and-a-half-foot muscle-bound manhood. He was getting married on the coming weekend to one of the other Maple Leaf waitresses, a skinny girl named Bonnie who was recently back from being away in the city. Walt gave him a playful shove as they left the diner.

"Nervous, wedding-boy?"

Troy shrugged and zipped up his jacket. They lit cigarettes.

The Maple Leaf overlooked the smoky brown river and an old warehouse that some city goons had tried to convert into an antiques barn. Each of the partners had tried to rip the other off, and now the antiques were gathering dust while the court case dragged on. The barn was broken into by teenagers and vagrants who looted the smaller items and carved their names into the furniture. Walt knew this because he had been appointed an auxiliary caretaker and he used his key every once in a while to let himself in with a flashlight and take a slow, triumphant inventory of the burgeoning rodent colony.

They tossed their butts onto the sidewalk, climbed into Walt's pickup, and headed out towards the construction site. The morning was cold and fine and all the leaf-choked gutters sparkled with bullet casings. It was hunting season.

"Are you sure it's safe?"

Shelley held her gown up and stepped over a log. The gravestones were visible through the trees.

Bonnie pushed ahead through the undergrowth towards a small clearing with a blackened firepit. She turned to frown at Shelley, who stood stock-still with the hem of her gown clenched between white-knuckled hands.

Because no licence was required, hunters sometimes came to shoot the feral cats infesting the woods behind the graveyard. Bonnie and Shelley had seen a few of the cats already, their heart-shaped faces and wild eyes peering out at them from the leaves. Bonnie had chittered and crouched until her thighs went numb but hadn't managed to lure a single creature into her outstretched arms.

Shelley glanced through the trees at the graveyard and let her gown drop to her ankles. Her grandparents were buried out there under a pricey granite headstone that her parents still argued about. Her mother came once a year, like everyone else, to replace the plastic flowers on the grave. The bouquets were visible through the trees from where Shelley stood.

"Do we have to do it out here in the open?" she said.

Bonnie laid her bag down by the firepit and began to gather kindling, using her long skirt as a wood apron. Shelley watched. They'd known each other as little girls but then Bonnie had gone away to the city and come back a witch. Shelley remembered the day Bonnie got off the bus with her duffel bag, skinnier and more hollow-eyed than ever. When she asked her what life was like in the big city, Bonnie had stared off into the distance and shaken her head.

She'd explained all about Wicca one night to wide-eyed Shelley who nodded and nodded while the shivers coursed up and down her spine. The plan was to build up their coven in town and then spread out with sub-covens across the whole county. To be sure, that wasn't how Bonnie explained things exactly. But to Shelley's mind the coven seemed like a kind of mystical Tupperware party. A local hockey star had started a burger chain and now had a row of vintage Corvettes. Who knew where the coven thing might end? So far, though, it was just the two of them and a big hazy blank between now and the future.

"I would definitely feel more comfortable indoors," said Shelley. She loved Bonnie's tiny apartment with its figurines and sticky amber bottles of myrrh and patchouli. Anything was possible in Bonnie's darkened living room, incense in the air and *Oprah* flickering in the background with the volume down low. Out here, though, Shelley was starting to feel more like an ordinary weirdo than an apprentice witch. She stared at her gown, a muddy brown vintage Laura Ashley with stained armpits and a frilly skirt that had been impossible to iron. She hoped nobody had seen them slipping into the woods.

"You can't think about it like that," said Bonnie. "Remember the pagans. Remember the Druids." She dumped the kindling in the firepit and began to realign the rocks, her mouth pinched into a grim circlet.

"It's nothing personal," said Shelley, glancing over once again at the bright specks of plastic dotting the graveyard. She hugged her elbows. "I'm cold. And my shift at the Leaf starts in an hour and a half."

Bonnie stood up and looked at Shelley, her eyes wide with hurt and something else. Maybe it was the jitters about the upcoming wedding. Nobody in the town expected her to follow through with it. The rock in Bonnie's hand thudded onto the ground. Bonnie was so frail, her shoulder blades knife-sharp above the black lace neckline. All the magic, Shelley realized, could disappear in an instant and they'd be back to where they started, with just the Maple Leaf and the town with its one main road and rickety bridge. Without another word, she gathered the hem of her gown in one hand and stepped across the firepit to help.

Six hours of stick-straight pine and the mind starts to crave the logged enclaves full of bald stumps, the glimpses of copper mines and their trickles of blood-red leachate.

In and out of sleep, awakened by the engine's thrust or a hard twist in the road, Bonnie felt as though she was travelling not through time or space but deep into the mystical inner realm she had spent so many months reading about. By the time she stepped off the bus with unsteady legs a few hours later, it wasn't even into her own past. The loggers and weathered buildings of her childhood, the pickups and chainsaws and the umber statue of Queen Victoria, even the smallest objects at the corner drugstore were laden with new meaning, like the trinkets of explorers that become the centrepieces of lost forest religions.

For the first week she slept in the wood-panelled basement rec room of a childhood friend. Then she found the tiny apartment with the miniature Dutch windmill by the front path that made her feel like a giantess each time she swished past in her long skirts. It was a full month before she got the courage to visit the grimy vinyl-clad bungalow where her mother still lived.

"I heard you were back," said her mother, retreating into the cave-like front room. "And now here you are," she called out, disappearing into the back kitchen.

From the vestibule she could see the old wall unit stuffed

with TV magazines and stray ornaments, the carved coconut head from a long-ago trip to Florida.

"I've changed," said Bonnie. She stepped into the living room, took a cigarette out of her mother's pack on the coffee table, and lit up. She cupped her free hand around her mouth and called out, "Things have changed."

"Like hell they have," said her mother.

It was an Indian summer, so blazing hot by mid-afternoon that the men had stripped down to the waist. Walt's bronzed beer gut swayed across the construction yard while a guitar solo wailed out of the ghetto blaster. Gordie and Jolly leaned against a rough concrete wall and shared a joint while Troy polished off the last of a king-sized Mars bar.

"I've seen her saggy old titties more times than my ex-wife's," said Walt, returning to the raw pine frame with his nail gun.

"Which ex-wife?" said Jolly. Walt grabbed him and held the nail gun to his head, then mussed his hair and pushed him away, laughing. They were discussing what to do for Troy's bachelor party. Gordie and Jolly wanted to wait until the following week when a new stripper was being put into rotation. Troy said he didn't give a rat's ass either way.

"Call me a stickler," said Walt, "but the bachelor party comes before the wedding."

So the strip club was out. In the end they decided on a bush party with a keg and a chunk of stale Moroccan hash that Gordie had been hoarding for a special occasion.

"And a big-assed bonfire," said Walt.

Jolly and Gordie exchanged glances. It was something of a mystery how Walt commanded so much power in the small town. He strutted around on his matchstick legs like a gangland boss, lived alone in a sagging house surrounded by the upturned scarabs of old snowmobiles. He had a way with women. And you could always rely on Walt to get down to the cold, hard, nuggety balls of every issue. You had to admire a man for that. Troy looked down at Walt's distended belly and back up at his squinty eyes, then shrugged once again in agreement. The men stood up and strapped their leather work belts around their bare waists. As soon as the sun sank behind the trees they'd be back in the checked wool jackets they'd worn to work that morning.

"How could you go with an inbred?"

A pickup with a deer carcass drove past, the deer head nodding on the back bumper at each pothole. Bonnie watched the truck turn into the alley where she knew the butcher cleaned wild carcasses for hunters in a back room, bundling the meat into chops and roasts. She turned from the window and stood back on the stool where Candice had been making last-minute adjustments to her wedding dress, a sixties thrift-store find with a green velvet bodice and a floor-length flowered skirt. She frowned and turned sideways in the mirror.

"I've got no tits at all," she said, cupping the loose pouches of green velvet on her chest.

Candice tilted her head back for a moment and then crouched down at Bonnie's feet to adjust her hem. "I mean it,

Bonnie. He's an inbred. The whole family is. And he's dumb. You're smart and should know better."

"It doesn't pay to be smart," said Bonnie.

She stepped out of her dress and Candice disappeared into the cubbyhole where she kept her sewing machine. Shivering in her underwear, Bonnie went back to the window and peered out again. The street was empty this time, filled with slanting afternoon sun, gold leaves, and spent bullet casings.

"He's just quiet," said Bonnie, aware that Candice couldn't hear her. "That's all."

The Cataraqui Hotel was home to a legendary five-foot mounted muskie that presided over the sepulchral lounge, a place where the town's more illustrious tourists had been served watery beer across the decades by a succession of plump, pimpled teenage girls, as tremulous as sacrificial virgins in their starched aprons. This was where the staff of the local newspaper and radio station queued at Christmas for bleeding slices of prime rib and sundry buffet accoutrements. It was where Bonnie and Troy's wedding reception would be held the following week.

It was where Walt and Troy now faced each other under the single tattered pool table's aquarium light, rock anthems thudding through the wall's fake-log facade from the packed saloon next door they'd escaped from at Walt's suggestion a few hours earlier. They were stoned, half-cut on Jack Daniel's and beer chasers, but steady enough to sink an eight ball off the bank, as Troy had just done. Walt was on one of his planned losing streaks. He grabbed the triangle and racked up, then peered through the gloom at the muskie, which the taxidermist had thoughtfully supplied with outsized fluorescent-yellow fangs.

"You don't know what she gets up to," said Walt. "While you're out working your ass off in the back of beyond."

Troy spanked the white hard and sent the balls flying across the table, sinking two stripes.

"I'm just telling you to watch out. Even her own mother doesn't trust her. She took money out of my pants pockets. I woke up and saw her. And she saw me looking at her and took it anyways. Stared me straight in the face. What kind of a kid does that?"

"Hush money," said Troy, grinning while Walt leaned over the table to take his shot.

Everybody knew Walt had boned Bonnie's mother while they were both still married to other people. Everybody knew everything around here. Or so it seemed.

"That's my point exactly," said Walt. "The fruit doesn't fall far from the tree. Speaking of which, one of my boys saw her messing around in the woods. Doing some crazy shit in a cape."

Troy shrugged and sank his last stripe, took aim at the eight and missed. "It's just dumb woman stuff," he said.

"Maybe," said Walt. "Maybe not. I know you like her and you're all puffed up because she likes you back. But don't forget she's a natural-born sneak. You gotta keep both eyes peeled with that one."

He shunted the white across two bands and sank the eight. Troy put on his leather jacket, handed Walt a twenty, and left by the fire exit. Walt watched him disappear down the gravel drive into darkness, the sky faintly green over the mass of trees. He wasn't interested in destroying Troy's marriage before it had even taken place. He could wait.

Bonnie had been accepted at the city art college primarily for an outsized watercolour of her own eye. Anatomically correct, standing out among the skewed portraits and muddy landscapes that made up the bulk of her portfolio, the hazel iris appeared to teem with intricate shapes, mythical creatures, and ghostly outlines that she hadn't been conscious of painting at the time.

She had the eye framed and hung above the unusable fireplace in her room, where it stared down at her as she lay on her damp futon. Each time she looked up at the eye she saw something new: a woman in a trailing gown, a green horned figure peering from behind a shrub. The eye was the first thing she saw when she woke up in the morning and again when she returned from the classes she began to drop, one after the other, convinced she would never create a piece as fine. And she hadn't, nestling deep in her grimy bedsheets with cigarettes and books about angel visits and monster sightings, shamans and satanic abuse networks. She read books about witches and magic, werewolves and wizards until the city's concrete cubes and corporate rectangles and rush-hour tail lights faded into a blur.

One night in a semi-trance she had a vision of the black pine hills around her hometown. Still sleepless at dawn, she headed out to the bus terminal with a duffel bag full of her stuff, the eye scrolled with a rubber band, the shattered glass frame abandoned in the fireplace grate.

"You can't not ask her," said Shelley. "Half the time she doesn't know what she's doing."

The problem was that you never knew which Donna you were going to get. She was fine for weeks and then she snapped. And it wasn't just tears. She got into fights with broken bottles and a pipe end she kept in her purse, had to be escorted home by whoever was sober enough to see their way out to that long, lonely woodlot off the highway. Rumour was that she'd whipped her twelve-year-old boy in the middle of the road with a piece of electrical cord after she caught him masturbating.

"She knows what she's doing," said Bonnie. She poured sugar into the bubbling saucepan. They were making homemade Kahlúa for the wedding party: six flagons of instant coffee, sugar, and grain alcohol topped off with a hand-waving incantation. The two women stared at each other over the saucepan. Shelley didn't know, but Bonnie had already invited Donna because she wanted to ensure enough waitressing shifts to cover her rent after Troy's construction season ended mid-winter. Bonnie wouldn't mind, for example, stealing a couple of Shelley's shifts. She removed the saucepan from the stove and lit a cigarette on the glowing red coil.

"All I know is she'd better behave. It's a wedding."

Bonnie opened a side window and leaned out to smoke. The wind was laced with snowflakes and the sound of Led Zeppelin being played at a distance. She took a deep drag and exhaled, felt a dizzy rush from the nicotine. She was overcome, suddenly, with a sense of the world reeling uncontrollably through space. She shuddered and ducked back inside, took another drag and gazed around the fluorescent-lit kitchen, which was lurid, almost tropical, after the whirling, smoky dark.

"Or else what?" said Shelley.

They met at the Cataraqui a few weeks after she moved back. He was half a head taller than anyone else in the room, his face white and deadpan. Like a golem, Bonnie thought. She had turned to Shelley and pointed at him with her cocktail stick.

Shelley leaned forward and whispered what she knew about him and his family while Bonnie frowned and nodded. She scoured her memory but couldn't distinguish him from the brood of poor boys bused into school from the old farmhouses on the outskirts of town. His face seemed out of place on his massive frame, his arms and hands engraved with raised scars from years of rough work. She smiled and waved at him when Shelley told her that he worked for Walt, her mind working a hundred miles a minute.

Troy had already noticed her, remembered the lanky hair she never shampooed as a child until forced under the tap by her mother. He remembered the rumour she'd spread herself in high school about being born with a vestigial tail. Back at her place his body was solid and hard, like it was carved out of oak. The only thing she remembered of the drunken blur was his impassive face as he thrust inside her, his fists wrapped in her long hair.

He rarely spoke, during sex or after, not even when he started coming over regularly to sit in her tiny living room with the beaded door frame and the dirty brass disc she used as an incense holder. And she really did come to like him. He was her man from a Grimm's fairy tale, with his red woodsman jacket and hunting rifle, and the worn yellow hides of his Kodiaks on the front step. This, she thought, was what life was meant to be. Powerful and mysterious and without a sarcastic running commentary.

She had moved back with a vision of herself making pagan shrines. Collecting herbs in a cloak for potions and reconnecting with Nature and the Divine. In fact she was terrified to go out into the woods. She forced herself on one occasion beyond the town's outskirts and built an altar and a pentacle out of twigs. She was shuddering by the time she placed a silken cord and a little Tupperware bowl filled with salt in the centre of the pentacle. She'd tried to draw him from memory but always screwed up his nose or his eyes, made him look even meaner and squintier than he was in person. She had no trouble summoning up Walt's image in the air above the pentacle. She muttered the rites under her breath, her ears pricked for the sound of approaching predators, human or otherwise.

A cracking branch sent her scurrying but she lost her way to the path and wandered among the densely ranked conifers for hours. She eventually climbed one to see the forest blur into a mass of incomprehensible green in the distance. The men were right, she thought bitterly, to head in and kill things as quickly as possible and haul them in their pickup trucks to Jolly's back-room abattoir. A stroke of good luck had her back on the path but by then it was too late. She had gone out there for communion but felt as though her whole being had been assaulted.

Thirsty and covered in burrs, she emerged from the woods by the back of her mother's bungalow and saw her mother on the back deck with a Fresca in one hand and a cigarette in the other. Her mother was wearing a pair of mirrored sunglasses, so it was hard to tell if she'd seen Bonnie before she smashed out her cigarette, stepped through the sliding patio doors, and locked the door behind her.

Walking back through town she spotted the women gathered outside the Maple Leaf in their mustard-yellow uniforms. They were smoking and fixing up each other's hair, laughing together over a trashy magazine. She had never felt lonelier than the moments she spent staring at them from the other side of the road. Then she spotted the WAITRESS WANTED sign and got the idea for having the coven.

"Did you invite your dad?"

Bonnie and Shelley were unpacking the three boxes of plastic Hawaiian leis for the wedding. The plan was to cut the leis and string them together to make garlands for the tables and the walls. She handed Shelley a pair of scissors.

"What do *you* think?"

When she was fourteen and sick of the silent treatment her mother was still giving her, Bonnie had rooted around in her mother's drawers and closets until she found her birth father's address, then hitchhiked out to him. She decided to pretend she was in town on a school trip and just stopping by for a casual hello. She was surprised at how big the brick house was, and in a nice neighbourhood too. There was a gabled room above the garage that she claimed as her new bedroom as she walked up the winding path and rang the bell.

He was edgy, talked almost non-stop about how broke he was, about how her mother was wringing him dry with alimony payments and child support already. She guessed he was worried she was going to ask for money. She almost had, out of spite.

"Did you really break into his house?" said Shelley.

"I went back when his car wasn't there. I just wanted to get back at him for being so unwelcoming. I'm his flesh-and-blood daughter."

Hurt, she'd accepted the glass of orange juice he'd offered her and then watched her drink with his arms folded, not inviting her past the kitchen into the house beyond. She had hitchhiked back there a month later, rung the bell, and waited. Then she walked out into the backyard through the waist-high grass, climbed up the porch steps, and fiddled at the handle of the screen door until it gave. The house was empty. She had wandered the empty rooms she'd been so curious to see, stepped up into the gabled room she'd imagined she would live in, stopped back in the front parlour with its dusty chandelier to smoke a cigarette that she then stubbed out on the floor. There was no forwarding address.

"I went down into the basement and there was a mask, one of those old Mexican masks everyone used to hang in their living rooms. I put it in the middle of the floor and surrounded it with some old candle stubs. I sprinkled ashes from the fireplace all around it and left. There were still a few boxes of stuff, books and things. I thought he'd come back and it'd spook the shit out of him."

She had also made a deep cut in her arm and spattered the blood over the ashes and the mask.

"What happened after that?"

Shelley knew what had happened. The rumour had spread through the town via Walt, who claimed the story was direct proof of what a weird kid Bonnie was. The father hadn't come back, but the new owners refused to move in and there was a fuss with the police because the couple just happened to be a little superstitious. Petrified, was how the police described them.

"It was a joke," said Bonnie.

She had finally come forward as the perpetrator. Not out of guilt but because she wanted her father to understand that the message was intended for him. She tied the plastic stems together with a twist-tie and held the bedraggled garland out in front of her.

"They'll look better in dim lighting," said Shelley.

Walt tucked his wad of rocky road into his pocket and handed the cash over to Donna. He had just come from the antiques barn where he'd done another slow tour with his pencil flashlight. Donna refilled his coffee.

"I heard a rumour Rudy's out," said Walt.

"He got out last week but I don't give a shit," said Donna.

"You going to take him back?"

"I told him I was waiting for my husband. I might be."

"Take old Rudy back. That way your husband can have another pop at him when he gets out, too."

Donna put her hands on her hips. "And who made you lord and master?"

"It's a dirty job," said Walt, "but somebody has to do it."

He watched her bend down under the sink to toss some sloppy plates into a bus bin and had an idea.

It was a town hall wedding with just Bonnie and Troy and two regulars she grabbed from the restaurant to act as witnesses. Standing in the sterile hallway in her princess gown and the velvet bodice with the too-large bust, Bonnie felt like a child playing dress-up. She was blushing with shame by the time the justice of the peace conducted the ceremony, then handed her a photocopied booklet entitled "Recipe for a Good Marriage" with pictures of happy-faced measuring cups drawn in the margins, which Bonnie crumpled into a ball and tossed into the ladies' room garbage on her way out.

Down at the Cataraqui the Maple Leaf girls set up a trestle table draped in crepe paper and two intertwined garlands of the Hawaiian flowers. A couple of the other girls, Candice and Amber, had pinned pink and orange garlands and paper bells on the ceiling and walls. As a final touch Amber pinned a pink bell on the muskie's tail.

"I wonder how long it'll last," said Candice, staring up at the muskie's fluorescent grimace.

Shelley reached up on her tiptoes and tore the bell off. "It's disrespectful," she said.

"To what?" said Amber. "The marriage or the muskie?"

The room filled up quickly with Troy's hulking brothers and the other Maple Leaf girls in tropical-themed dresses, their hair twisted into mountains of stiff curls that didn't move even when they were spinning on the dance floor under the DJ's rental strobe lights.

"Oh look," said Candice. "It's the homecoming king and queen."

Bonnie peered across the darkened room to see Walt arm-in-arm with Donna, who was already drunk enough to be unsteady in her heels. Walt looked over at Bonnie and waved. She bunched her hand into a fist and bashed the pink bell nearest to her, felt its thin accordion tissue paper collapsing before the wall bruised her knuckles. She found Troy in the far corner by the battered dartboard.

"I don't want them here," she said.

"He's my boss. He's your ex-stepfather."

"Whose wedding is this?" said Bonnie, her eyes filling with tears.

"Hush," he said, encircling her in his arms and squeezing so hard she gasped. She closed her eyes and saw her own self ten years back, standing in Walt's junk-strewn lawn, waiting for him to answer the door she'd been knocking and knocking.

She'd gone and kept going. Kept going back after he told her to quit bugging. She had begged and wheedled in his dirty kitchen, wanting him to hold her. And then when he held her, she wanted him to kiss her the same way she saw him kissing her mother when they thought she was upstairs in bed.

One day he took her hard on the rough carpet on the living room floor, so hard that she screamed each time she felt him bashing inside of her.

"Is this what you want?" he'd asked. "Is it? Is it?"

In spite of the pain she'd only started to cry when he reached out and absent-mindedly smoothed her hair. Not even the bleeding that followed and the thought of the dirty carpet stopped her going back the next week and the week after. Bugging, was what Walt called it. No matter how rough it got there was always that moment of tenderness like a candle snuffed out in a dark room when he reached out to touch her cheek or smooth her sweat-plastered hair.

The little bitch wouldn't leave me alone, was what he'd said to Bonnie's mother when she caught them behind an upturned car seat on his back porch.

I'm only human, was what he'd said to Bonnie's mother when she threatened to go to the police.

I don't want you here again, was what he'd said when Bonnie escaped from her locked bedroom to tell him she was in love with him. She was halfway down the drive when he called down to her from the porch, the sadness half breaking his voice. "Didn't anybody ever teach you what we did together was wrong?"

That was ten years and a ton and a half of scrap snowmobiles and car parts ago. Walt's house was a fortress, barely visible now from the road that Bonnie still caught herself walking down, and she had never once, since moving back, caught a whiff of tenderness in that saw-toothed rasp of his. She saw Walt's face when she conjured spells and when she pulled the devil card out of her Tarot pack. Ten years later and her mother still hadn't forgiven her, or Walt either. Hadn't budged enough to even come to the wedding.

She'd said, "I know you didn't come back here to marry that meathead so I don't see why I should celebrate."

Bonnie wriggled out of Troy's embrace and saw Walt hand

Donna another drink and whisper for a good while in her ear. Donna tilted her head back and laughed like the half-crazed woman she was.

Donna was still laughing when Walt took her out onto the floor, had her shimmying *Saturday Night Fever* style before spinning her loose into the centre for a solo dance. Her snake-skin belt was the first thing to come off, then the shoes. She had her blouse up over her head by the time Troy got her in one of his bear hugs and led her off the dance floor, but not before everyone had a good long look at the battleground of scar tissue, red as raw hamburger in places and cut so deep that the thought of it made Bonnie wince hours after the party was over and she and Troy were back in her apartment with all the beads and the incense.

"I'm not taking it off," she said, folding her arms over the velvet bodice of her dress. Troy shrugged and pushed her down onto the bed, pulled the tulle skirt up with one hand while he unzipped his fly with the other. After they were done, she pulled the tulle back down from her midriff and drew the blankets up to her chin. She would make the other girls believe in her powers and join her coven. She would find a way to turn Troy and all the others against Walt. She would go and see Walt at his house one day and give him a taste of what was coming. But for now she nestled against Troy and listened to the drum of his heart deep in his barrel chest. She thought to herself that every woman, at least once, should marry a man of few words.

The Prince of Chang

How am I fallen from myself, for a long time now
I have not seen the Prince of Chang in my dreams.
—Khoung-fou-tseu

A cartoon voice penetrates the waves of nausea for a moment before receding. It gets louder and is accompanied by reinforcements. I open my eyes. A blonde shaped like a Mayan fertility idol stares down at me. Behind her stand two line-order cooks swathed in bloodied aprons. Maybe they will perform a dance routine like backup singers. Maybe they'll draw and quarter me. She flings her head back and trebles her chin. This is a family eatery, she says. She'll call the police, she says. I have gone too far. I heave myself onto my elbows and squint through the pine railings to my left. Two children sit in the restaurant section with their hefty mother, smearing ketchup onto a tablecloth. One of them gives me the finger.

I'm in Honkers, the family-style roadhouse next to the Conestoga Mall with its famous glowing wagon wheel and western-themed food court. I have gone too far. I've been fondling the fibreglass effigy of a rock star. Honkers has several of these. Some are placed in alcoves above the bar like saints in a cathedral.

I grab the blonde by the ankle and hold on.

The cooks accompany me to the parking lot. A boy in a Burger King uniform waves me a casual hello. The mall people are getting to know me. Someday I will take my place among the regulars by the phony Roman fountains and engage in mock fist fights that sometimes turn real.

I cross the parking lot and the highway, then walk up the street lined with six-foot saplings that I sometimes also mistake for people.

My neighbourhood has a temporary feel, like a film set or a camp thrown together for disaster victims. The houses look as though they've been assembled out of ill-fitting plywood pieces with bricks and doors painted on them. If I went up close and stared through the chinks I might see the real interior, with half-starved inhabitants crouching on dirt floors, gnawing on bones or bright red strips of meat.

My own house feels so insubstantial that each time I open the front door I'm surprised to find a three-dimensional space with walls and ceilings. One day I will step into a whiteness.

I can't mention this to my wife because our house was more or less a wedding gift from her father, who built the subdivision. He lives in a kingly ten-thousand-square-foot semi-castle with Disney turrets and a cinema room, built out of the same salmon-pink bricks and beige vinyl siding that he uses in all his projects.

As I approach my house I see that a section of our guttering has broken off and is lying like a toppled column on the front lawn. I bring it inside with me and lay it on the kitchen table. There are voices in the other room. My wife and her friends, the horse-faced one and the dog-headed one, getting ready for their night out. I fold into a chair, lay my head next to the guttering, and doze off.

I open my eyes and my golden-haired wife is standing before me in a green sparkling minidress with her arms outstretched. She asks me to guess what she has in each clenched fist. Poisonous spiders. Cyanide capsules. No. The fists unfurl. In each palm lies a miniature silver temple with tiny minarets and rows of carved windows. Each temple has a doorway that by some clever design seems actually to lead somewhere. Her hands become fists again and the temples vanish.

They are earrings, she announces. She is planning to import them. This will be her new thing now since the pottery thing didn't work out. She is wearing a pair. They sparkle and spin on the ends of frail hooks as she moves through the kitchen collecting vodka and ice cubes. There are wooden boxes on the floor stamped in foreign markings, smelling of camphor. A car horn sounds. The women gather in the hallway. The screen door bangs against the vinyl siding, and they race out to the taxi, their voices dispersing like a flock of crows in a high wind.

"Is it like the white light?"

After my wife and her friends leave, I walk over to my friend Leland's house. We sit in his basement room and I try to explain the experience I had standing in line at the bank earlier on that made me clutch at the velvet rope. It happens quite a lot. The sensation starts in my stomach and makes me feel like I'm not part of my own body. I see things in a different way, as if I had been spun around in circles, a blindfold ripped from my eyes. The people at the mall are no longer just people shopping but sides of beef swaying up and down corridors filled with bright, unfamiliar objects. I can smell the meat and the fat underneath their clothes, clinging to slowly moving bones. It's pretty much what drives me into Honkers to drink.

Leland lives in his mother's basement in a house identical to mine in size and shape. It was the first house I noticed when I moved here because it has a chipped blue upturned half hull of a rowboat with a statue of the Virgin Mary in the front yard. Leland's mother is a religious freak. Figurines line the window ledges and she has a big manger scene in the backyard, garlanded with plastic Hawaiian flowers. The sight of these things in the sea of beige saps me. It's like coming across children's toys at the scene of a catastrophe.

While his mother sits upstairs with posters of Jesus, chunky Leland has dedicated his basement life to unlocking the mysteries of the occult. The walls of his room are lined with paperbacks announcing newly discovered Gnostic writings and revelations of ancient secrets born in the fires of Egypt and passed down through the writings of Hermes Trismegistus to Madame Blavatsky and the Hermetic Order of the Golden Dawn. There are books about how the secrets were lost, covered up in a conspiracy funded by the Vatican or a gang of nefarious billionaires. I know all this because at one point or another I've borrowed them off Leland. It's amazing, the stuff you get into when you have a lot of free time on your hands.

There are times when Leland doesn't read at all but sits empty-handed with the lips in his bloated cherub's face downturned. I don't need to remind him then that there are no white-robed priestesses singing in nearby groves or half gods brandishing tridents around the corner. He knows as well as I do that there are only the disintegrating houses and the grey, unending hiss of the highway.

I can hear his mother overhead, drifting through the unlit upstairs of the house like a jellyfish in her semi-transparent nightgown.

"If you mean the white light where you are dying and going down the tunnel, then no," I reply.

Leland frowns and strokes an imaginary beard. Because he lives in a dream world, he is always reaching for a metaphysical explanation.

"The thing that worries me the most," I say, leaning forward for extra emphasis, "is that I may possess some extraordinary, or even supernatural, power that I'm not fully harnessing."

Leland stares at me with his cherub's mouth open. Even he hasn't thought of this.

I used to know a man named Beauregard. He had a long, thin face and black hair cut to chin length. Women stared when he walked into a room. He didn't care for the attention. Instead, he'd find the sorriest customer in the bar and buy them drinks all night, listening to them rave about how terrifying the world was. That was how I met him. I didn't even know his name until he left hours later and I was groping in my pockets to pay my tab at the Magic Lantern. "Beauregard took care of it," the bartender told me.

I looked for him after that night. He was never far from my mind. At first I thought it was so I could repay him for his kindness. But after a while I realized that I just wanted to see him again. He had a gift for listening, with his head slightly bowed, soaking up each word. When I asked about Beauregard a week later, the bartender told me he often dropped out of sight for a while and then reappeared. Who was he? The bartender shrugged. Nobody knew. There were rumours that he was rich, a Westmount rajah with a trust fund who slummed it between trips to the Orient or Biarritz. But these were only rumours, the bartender told me.

I saw him again one night at two in the morning in the window of an all-night restaurant, sitting with an acne-scarred prostitute who slid out of the booth and swaggered towards the exit in a pair of high black boots. He stayed on, contemplating the empty bowl in front of him. He seemed pleased to see me when I tapped on the glass. I went in and sat down.

He was a night person, he told me. An insomniac. Whenever he did fall asleep he was harassed by nightmares so intense they drove him out of the small house he lived in with his elderly father. He told me how he liked to walk through the city and unearth strange places, a hidden bar at the end of an alley, a sagging dance hall frequented by elderly alcoholics. He pushed his empty dish away and offered to show me around.

He loved the outsized props and theatre of the nightclub scene. I remember him rapping the hollow Corinthian fibreglass pillars in a nightclub foyer with a wide, childish smile on his face. He had a theory that the fakeness was more representative of human endeavour than the trappings and contrivances of high culture they were meant to mimic. A complete shambles, he called it, waving his arms in delight at the undulating crowds of dancers.

We became friendly. Whenever I arranged to meet him somewhere he'd turn up with, for example, a Johnny Cash lookalike, a toothless bum with a yellow beard, an angry Pakistani man who spoke little English, a pair of elderly, doll-sized Inuit women. The only thing his friends had in common was that none of us liked each other. We all wanted Beauregard to ourselves.

It was a gift he had. People felt ennobled while he listened to them, as if their private suffering was part of a vast repository of human grief. He sat in silence, his back hunched, his black curtain of hair hanging over his face. No detail was lost on him. He only ever interrupted to clarify a time frame or to murmur consolingly.

Of course, the money poured out of him too. For a while he was everywhere, surrounded by an ever-changing gang of street people and down-on-their-lucks. Then things fell slowly and horribly apart. The hollows under his eyes deepened. He started to carry around little baggies filled with different-coloured pills, tucking stashes into the crevices behind fire escapes, jamming them in between seats at peep shows, wedging them between an alley wall and an electric meter. He would stagger out of the bar with his ragged followers and start a scavenger hunt for the baggies, flying into an agonized tantrum when he couldn't find them.

Bars started to refuse him tabs. Men in black leather

blazers came looking for him. The bartender at the Magic Lantern shrugged and told me that Beauregard had gone through all of this before. It was a cycle. He appeared out of nowhere and then he disappeared. But each time, the bartender told me, was a little more intense than the last.

There were rumours that he'd stopped eating. I saw him sitting alone in the apex of the brown, triangular city park across from the metro. The corners of his lips had begun to crack. The serene mask was slipping, and in its place an anguished human face appeared. I wonder if he was solely listening to people out of a sense of compassion. Maybe he was collecting evidence to support a conclusion he had already arrived at.

I watch my wife dress in front of the full-length mirror. It's like watching a pair of ritual dancers approaching and retreating, twirling at the same impeccably timed moment. She has erased the outward traces of her hangover with a flesh-coloured wand. Now she paints her lips and makes a movie-star pout. She glances at me and her face bunches into its habitual fist. We are not speaking. She arranges her lace blouse and leaves me with my own murky-green reflection in the TV screen opposite the bed. The front door slams.

We had a fight after she came in from the bar. I was sitting in the kitchen when she staggered through the door, the sparkly dress covered in twigs and tiny leaves, as if she'd become ensnared in a shrub on the way home. After I walked back from Leland's, an unknown force had compelled me to draw Magic Marker eyes and nose-holes on the fluted piece of guttering. She picked it up and threatened me with it.

"You don't take anything seriously," she said. "Not the house. Not me. Not us."

Then she cast the guttering to the floor. Whatever else caught her eye then followed. The Japanese display plates, her hutch full of squat mugs with ear-shaped handles. Then she sank onto her haunches and screamed until the vowels gurgled in her throat. Hard to take someone seriously when they're gurgling next to a piece of drainpipe with Magic Marker eyes.

I haul myself downstairs after I hear her car pull out of the driveway. I'm in the kitchen picking up the pieces of broken pottery when the doorbell rings. It's the dog-headed friend, no doubt on a mission to punish me for last night's fracas. She pushes past me into the living room and drapes her raincoat over a chair. She has maroon streaks in her hair and is wearing a necklace with yellow beads shaped like teeth.

"That's a nice necklace," I tell her.

She folds her arms across her chest and advises me that it is probably too late to save my marriage. She asks me how I would feel if there was someone else. A rival. Would I be shocked? Her lipstick has bled into the taut lines around her mouth.

My wife is a barbarian princess riding across a beige-vinyl and salmon-brick wasteland. She is a tribeswoman of the first order, smashing icons, arching the small of her back when a virile male walks into the room. The world was made for her to drag home, only to exile it to a distant landfill after crooking her neck disapprovingly: every reproduction candelabra, every Chinese vase full of sharp sticks. And all the while with those demagogue eyes staring out of her face, calculating and monitoring, measuring her strength against the weakness or goodwill of others. She has her father's eyes.

"No," I answer. "I wouldn't be surprised at all."

"I'm not saying that anything is actually going on," says the dog-headed friend, slipping back into her raincoat. "But you need to be aware of the infinite possibilities."

I am summoned to the semi-castle a few days later. My father-in-law opens the front door and steps aside with a flourish. He has a thin, tapered white moustache and yellow eyes. He closes the door behind me and punches me in the stomach. It's a hard, dry little punch. He wrestles me halfway into the hall closet where he pins me down with a quivering forearm. My head nestles quite comfortably against one of my mother-in-law's many fur coats.

"My daughter isn't happy," he says, and gives me a final shove. The fur coats dance and empty hangers rattle. He stands and picks an imaginary speck from his sweater before walking down the corridor. I hoist myself to my feet and follow him.

My wife and mother-in-law are both sitting in wingback chairs on either side of an electric fireplace. The fake flames realistically flicker. My pink-faced father-in-law pours himself a snifter of brandy and leans against the mantel, swirling his glass. It is a moment worthy of the mall's sole artist, who switched to portraits after his autumnal landscapes failed to shift. My wife sits with her eyes downcast, ankles demurely crossed. I am so absorbed in admiring her artifice that it takes me a moment to realize my mother-in-law is speaking to me in the tones of a concerned benefactress. We understand that life is difficult, she says. She tells me that she too has struggled. Has had moments of darkness. People have seen me at the mall, she adds in a quiet, menacing voice that is several tones lower than her usual benefactress register. People they know. My father-in-law interrupts her to ask me what the fuck I do with myself all day while everyone else is out at work.

Their words whistle through me. The veils lift. There is no velvet rope to cling to. Each object in my line of vision becomes sharply defined: my father-in-law's mottled cheeks above the snifter that he lifts to his lips like a chalice. The hardened webs of spittle at the corners of his mouth. The room is flooded with a wavering authenticity, as if a magic wand has been brandished and waved. The history of civilization has culminated in this moment—our faces hang in the air like masks in an ancient drama, suspended among the gunshot noises and screams drifting in from a barely audible TV in another room.

The moment loses its lustre. Once again we are in a pink-brick cartoon house with chubby turrets. The driveway is a long, pebbled tongue leading down to a pair of idiotic plaster lions. We are in a mock English lord's mock library exchanging suspicious glances from primitive eyes that pivot from side to side like the cut-out portraits in a haunted house. I take my leave, accidentally setting off the musical doorbell as I close the front door, head past the lions towards the nearest bar.

A few years ago I went back to see if I could find out what happened to Beauregard. I got off a bus on a highway and walked under the crumbling underpasses from the station to my old neighbourhood. I went to the one remaining restaurant that seemed familiar and sat between a pile of plates coated in cold gravy and a row of scarecrows plunging spoons into goblets of Jell-O. I took a stroll. All the old haunts had been turned into dollar stores and Vietnamese groceries.

Only Honkers is real, with its fibreglass rock stars and its family-value meal deals on Tuesday and Thursday evenings. Real and scarily permanent, like a pair of polyester golf slacks.

Beauregard would have loved Honkers. He would have loved the subdivision. He would have gotten down on his knees and kissed my father-in-law's clenched buttocks for creating such a magnificent work of art, one that so amply evoked the human condition in all its tawdry desolation. He would have praised the glowing wagon wheel in the sky. He would have hung out by the phony Roman fountains in the mall. He would have found someone to save.

I searched for his house when I heard he had died. His old father answered the door. He took me to Beauregard's room. There was a single bed with a pair of twisted sheets and a ragged wool blanket, a few milk crates full of wrinkled clothes that were starting to smell musty. He told me to take something as a memento. His shoulders started to heave a little, and he told me about the funeral home where his son's body had lain and how the funeral home had cheated him. He had paid too much, he said, for that wreath and the ugly casket. And hardly anybody came. We went up to his living room, which was cluttered with yellowy papers and smelled like a birdcage. He had nobody now, he told me. Beauregard had bought the groceries. Beauregard had done the chores. Someone from social services would come to help him, I said. I promised to visit again, but never went back.

KERRY LEE POWELL

I'm sitting with Murray by a stranger's pool. Like me, he's a regular at Honkers. He has long black hair and is wearing a T-shirt that says something in Gothic lettering. He used to be in a band. We are accompanied by two girls we met at the bar, who may or may not be underage. He has brought us all to a house he is looking after while the owners are in Athens. They are Greeks who run a restaurant called the Minotaur in another strip mall nearby. The house is a street or two away from my father-in-law's place, and composed of the same pink and beige building materials. The pool area takes up nearly all of the enclosed backyard. Plaster-cast statues dot the remaining strip of lawn. There's a grotto made of what looks like the remnants of actual monumental stones set in cement. There's a heap of fluorescent toys and inflatable dinosaurs beside the pool shed. Murray struts into the grotto and puts his arm around one of the statues.

"This is Venus," he says. "And the guy over there is what's-his-name."

"Aquaman," says one of the girls. They both start to giggle. They regain their composure, light coloured cocktail cigarettes, and cross their legs, leaning back in the white patio chairs. One of them arches her eyebrow and the other blows a smoke ring.

Murray steps through the sliding doors into the house to hunt for more booze. Bored with looking bored, the girls frolic in the grotto, squealing and posing like starlets beside one of the statues. I close my eyes and hear a loud shriek accompanied by a splash. One has fallen or jumped into the pool. Her face is streaked with mascara, and a string of snot dangles from her nose. The other girl helps to fish her out. They disappear into the house, laughing and leaning into each other. A few moments later Murray returns with a bottle. The girls are in the master bedroom, going through the jewellery, trying on the Greek lady's evening clothes.

I went one night to the place where Beauregard died, in the stairwell of a high-rise insurance building downtown. I never knew which floor he died on exactly, but in my mind he was laid out like an Egyptian prince in the centre. I got past security and climbed the fire escape up to the roof. When I looked down it was as though the rest of the city was a necropolis that had built itself around him, the lit staircases of the fire escapes zigging and zagging up to the sky, the polished stone facades of the skyscrapers mirroring the moon and clouds, and all of it sprawling out into suburbs and ragged clumps of darkness. It's been so long since Beauregard died now that I can only make out a blurred shape slipping past in my mind, a shadowy figure clinking glasses with other imaginary figures in a badly lit bar.

The sun sinks behind the grotto. An automatic lamp switches on. The girls will descend from the master bedroom in gold lamé and rhinestones. They will come out bundled like child brides in embroidered headdresses. Like Ishtar returning to the underworld. A choice will be made. One will be taken inside by Murray and unwrapped with trembling, predatory fingers. The other will remain outside in the chilly twilight, staring into the empty pool. Until then, Murray and I are statues in white patio chairs, waiting for the flash in the pan, the dance of the seven veils. For the whole shambling, glittering machine to heave itself into motion again.

SOCIAL STUDIES

She was still new enough to the city to gawk at the skyscrapers like a tourist when she came out of the subway. Today a window cleaner leaned over a scaffold to meet her upward gaze, and the shock of his raw, crab-red face against the clouds sent Ada reeling off the pavement into the curb. She brushed the grit off her hands and walked on, glancing at her reflection in the shop windows every few moments, as if to make sure it hadn't abandoned her. She slowed up after she passed an X-rated video store and a beat-up strip club with posters of dancers weathered to a blur of beige, then paused beneath a rusting neon giantess whose legs straddled the sidewalk to dig around at the bottom of her purse. The address she retrieved, scribbled on a scrap of disintegrating paper and further bleared with a coffee stain, was illegible, and it was only by luck she found the place she was looking for a few blocks up.

There was no sign other than the word "Macy's" painted on the streaky plate glass, and it was hard to tell, peering in with her hands wrapped around her eye sockets like binoculars, if it was open, or still in business, or even what kind of business was conducted there. The door had a set of jester bells attached that jangled harshly as she walked in. The gloom swallowed her up and temporarily blinded her. After a few moments, a wooden bar began to emerge out of the cavernous dark, and she made out her own reflection distorted into a kind of elongated mask in a dusty mirror behind a row of bottles. Farther down, a thicket of tables and chairs faced a low stage at the back.

She had been intrigued by the newspaper ad's brevity and dizzying potential: GIRL WANTED TO SERVE, MUST BE PEOPLE-ORIENTED. She had imagined a dozen scenarios, some of them really off-colour, none of which had prevented her coming for the interview. She wanted a foray into a riskier world. But this wasn't a sex club, she decided, or some set-up where they groomed white slaves. This was the kind of place her uncle used to go before he died of some kind of organ failure. She was almost, but not quite, disappointed by the bar's down-trodden ordinariness. She made a face in the mirror, baring her teeth and flaring her nostrils. Then, hearing footsteps and the sound of voices approaching, she resumed her usual vacant expression.

A small, partially concealed door behind the bar opened and two men stepped out. The taller of the two, a man with an intensely sombre face, frowned at her and started wiping down the bar top with a filthy rag. The much stumpier man led her to a table at the back. He had the largest head Ada had ever seen on a human being and seemed oddly distracted. She assumed he was the owner, Macy, whom she'd spoken to on the telephone earlier. She gave him her most professional smile.

"Tell me about yourself," he said. Instead of returning her smile, he stared over her shoulder at the door.

KERRY LEE POWELL

"I'm a people person," she said, but the words sounded alien as they left her mouth, the way people might refer to a species of insect.

"I'll be damned," said Macy. "Another people person! Did you hear that, Theo? The city's practically infested with them."

Theo rolled his eyes and looked even more sombre in response.

"Like I already mentioned on the phone," she said, "I worked at Paradiso and at Labyrinth."

In truth, she had only worked two shifts in Labyrinth and she had never set foot in Paradiso.

Macy narrowed his eyes. "So what's happening over at Labyrinth these days? Give me the dirt."

She gave him another, hopefully even more professional, smile while she thought of a reply.

"They redecorated the interior," she said.

"So no more Egyptian pillars?"

"They spray-painted them silver. To match the new ceiling."

"And the grottoes?"

"Still there. They had to resurface some of the rocks."

Macy frowned and drummed the tabletop again. He was jealous of Labyrinth, she realized.

"They made us smile all the time," she said. "We were punished if we didn't. It was really only wonderful on the outside."

This was true. She had been taken to one side and told to smile by the front house manager at Labyrinth on both occasions before being told to not bother coming back. Despite being fired, she had loved weaving through the semi-darkness between the pillars and laser lights and the slick dancers in her skimpy uniform, and staring at the fish-mouths of customers trying to make themselves heard over the blare. Sometimes she had pretended she was a slave girl in ancient times, someone whose life had already been lived and who therefore technically no longer mattered.

"Well, that's tragic," said Macy. "Did you hear that, Theo? It was only wonderful on the outside."

Macy's eyes were like yellow marbles unearthed from a dry summer yard. She felt like reaching over and plucking them out of his face. He looked a thousand years old, with his Easter Island head attached to that hairy little denim-clad body. He tilted it towards her.

"Look," he said. "We have our share of phonies and pimps and weirdos in tight pants, but we're also a home to folks who need a little human warmth."

"Human warmth," she said, suddenly wanting a glass of ice water. She matched his frown with a look of concern.

"We're not going to have you walking over hot coals or whatever they do at Labyrinth to initiate the new staff. But I'm warning you, today is going to be a really crazy day."

He stared past her again and she turned to see that a few silhouettes had already gathered at the bar.

"You want me to start now?"

"On a trial basis," he said, glancing at his watch.

Ada barely had a chance to answer before he was up and scurrying towards the door in his white sneakers, like the rabbit in *Alice in Wonderland*, which he now reminded her of.

She would have agreed under almost any terms. Apart from the two twenties folded in her back pocket, she was broke. She had moved to the city to go to college but had flunked her exams and spent the better part of the year in her foul shoebox of a dorm room, staring at the oily pigeons on the opposite window ledge. She could hear her room-mates fleeing from the common areas on the rare occasions she sought their company. Now she owed so much back rent on the bachelor apartment she'd moved into after dropping out that her landlord had started unlocking her front door without knocking, and looking mock-surprised that she still existed. She walked up to the bar where Theo stood like a sentry with his arms crossed.

"Let's pretend, among other things, that you really are who you claim to be," said Theo. "Pour me a beer and charge me for it."

He spoke with the trace of an accent Ada couldn't identify, but didn't dare ask him about it. She found a glass, turned to the pumps, and poured him a foamy beer, then went to the cash register and pecked at the grimy buttons until the drawer sprang open.

"Congratulations," said Theo, "you're a bartender. You get an imaginary gold star. If anything terrifying happens, stamp on the floor. Or scream if you prefer."

He unlatched the door to the basement and disappeared down the stairs with his beer. She turned then, reluctantly, towards the shapes gathered on the other side of the counter. Their faces had a mushroom tint in the murky light and a few, judging by their glazed eyes, were already drunk or otherwise medicated. She had decided, while pouring Theo's beer, to use on them the stern voice her mother used with beggars and lunatics and Jehovah's Witnesses. She was clearing her throat to introduce herself when a man the size of a twelve-year-old boy, with oily hair and a varnished black handlebar moustache, held out a monkey-sized hand for her to shake.

"Sonny," he said, jabbing at his chest with his thumb. "Don't mind Theo. He's Transylvanian. You know what they say about Transylvanians. All blood and guts. No sense of humour."

"Nonsense. He's nowhere near a Transylvanian," said a sour-faced man at the end of the bar. "You'll frighten her off with your guff."

"People go down to his basement lair and they never come back up," said Sonny, winking at her.

"If they don't come back it's because they can't stand the thought of contemplating your ugly mug," said the sour-faced man. He turned to Ada. "You should know that Theo is a man of considerable refinement."

"Sure," said Sonny. "Vampires always are."

Their surreal banter made her feel lightheaded. In contrast to the dutifully smiling wait staff, the patrons of Labyrinth had pursued and conquered each other with reptilian seriousness. Ada was unsure how to respond, but she couldn't imagine using her mother's voice on Sonny or the sour-faced man, and so she dabbed at the bar top unconvincingly with a rag, then rummaged in the fridge where she found a few withered lemons and a crusted-over jar of maraschino cherries. She began to assemble garnishes with a dull knife, tucking a cherry into a lemon slice and spearing them together with toothpicks. She had seen bartenders prepare garnishes this way at Labyrinth and was happy to do something that at least seemed practical.

The jester bells jangled. An ivory-bearded man appeared in the doorway. He was a tramp or a lunatic like the others, she thought, with his frayed raincoat and his long, greasy scarf. He tottered up to the bar, squinting at her pile of festive lemons and cherries.

"What, is it your birthday or something?" he said. "I personally have my birthday parties at McDonald's."

The thought of him hunched with his nicotine-stained beard in a pointy party hat made her laugh out loud.

He grinned at her. "It's grand," he said. "They give you presents. Puppets. The plastic kind that slide over your hand. Ronald and that big purple thing. What's that thing's name?"

"Grimace," said the sour-faced man.

"That's the one. Grimace. Why would anybody create such a horrible, unformed thing? It doesn't make sense."

"It makes sense if you think about it allegorically. Ronald is Jesus," said the sour-faced man. "Hamburglar is the thief on the cross. Grimace is the Holy Ghost. Amorphous and inscrutable."

"Grimace is my favourite," said Ada, although she'd never given the matter any consideration before.

"Hamburglar's my man," said Sonny. "He gets the job done."

"I didn't get you a birthday present," said the bearded man in a forlorn tone, tracing a mock tear with his nicotine-stained finger.

"That's fine," she said. "It's not really my birthday."

His jaw dropped, and she caught a sickening glimpse of his tongue.

"That's a nasty trick, fooling us into thinking it's your birthday." He gestured at her angrily, unleashing a multitude of unpleasant odours from the depths of his coat, then stumbled towards the stage at the back of the bar.

"You've hurt his feelings," said the sour-faced man. "Is this what you want to do with your life, make old men howl?"

"Of course not," she said. "I'm in college, majoring in social studies. And criminology."

Ada *had* taken social studies during her first term, but hadn't attended class after the first week of pie charts and incomprehensible diagrams and fellow students sweeping past her on the steps of the stone-fronted buildings. She had not taken any criminology classes, but she *had* stolen from her roommates. Small things mostly, but so regularly and often that it was a shock when they confronted her one evening. She had looked up at the ring of flustered, pretty faces and not known how to answer. She had learned so much about each of them by going through their drawers and closets and peering into their diaries while they were out. How could she explain that stealing their things was the closest she'd ever felt to anybody at all? She smiled at the sour-faced man.

"What I hate about college is how there's always some awful explanation for everything," she said.

"You are sure to find all sort of things for which there is no possible explanation if you stick around here," said the sour-faced man.

The jester bells now began to jangle at regular intervals, and the murky space beyond the bar filled with voices and shapes backslapping and high-fiving each other, re-enacting dust-ups they'd either been in or watched on TV. The old man with the ivory-coloured beard stood on the low stage with a vacant expression that transformed into a glower each time she scurried past him on her way to and from the bar, where, for the next ten minutes or so, she clumsily poured drinks, reached among the unfamiliar shelves for glasses, and slid around on the beer-slicked floor. Once the rush subsided she turned back to the sour-faced man to pick up where they'd left off.

"It's the statistics that bother me," she said. "Even though I know they make half of them up."

"I imagine they're terrible," said the sour-faced man.

"I want to learn," she said. "I'm just not great with numbers."

"How are you with figments?" he asked.

A man with glowing white dentures and wavy blond hair had appeared at her elbow. His suit had a silvery sheen and he reminded her of a game show host or crooner.

"Leslie Howard," he said, holding out his hand.

"I'm bad with names too," she said.

"If you can't think of me as an individual then think of me as a phenomenon," said Leslie Howard.

He had the same mellifluous voice as her high school drama teacher, a man she'd never trusted. Something else nagged at her.

"Isn't Leslie Howard the name of a movie star?"

Sonny said, "He was the guy who didn't make it under Scarlett's hoop in *Gone with the Wind*."

"Have you noticed," said the sour-faced man, "how all the best stories have young ladies as heroines? So enslaved by circumstance and yet full of hope and fruitless rebellion. So representative of the human condition."

"That's just what I hate," said Ada. "How everyone expects you to be a certain kind of girl."

"And yet here you are, the heroine of your own story."

"The movie did make me a hit with the ladies," said Leslie Howard. "But I prefer to think it was the qualities that I represented rather than my good looks. A kind of long-vanished gallantry."

"Leslie Howard died in a plane crash," said the sour-faced man.

"Someone of my calibre never dies," said Leslie Howard. "You could be in a terrible plane crash and still, you live. A couple of scratches. A few flickers and glitches. The show must go on!" He winked and gave Ada a movie-star smile. "You have to admit I have a kind of timeless quality," he said.

The sour-faced man drained his glass and leaned towards her, cupping his hand against her ear. "Every month the man who calls himself Leslie Howard gets his welfare cheque, goes to the barber, and has a shave and a fresh wave. He checks into the Ambassador. They treat him like royalty, give him room service each morning and change his sheets every other day. He has a suitcase he leaves in their lost and found when he checks out. Then it's back to the bus stations and the park benches, and wherever else he happens to drift in and out of consciousness."

"That's amazing," she said.

Her mind raced ahead into the future. If Macy's didn't work out, she could become a part-time person like Leslie Howard. There would be no need to be a busy young lady rushing out to museums or appointments, always looking nervously for her own reflection in the plate glass or the convex mirrors at the convenience stores or on the smeared bulbous surface of the chrome-plated kettle in her apartment. There would be no need to make monumental life decisions, decipher scrawled comments in her diary, or call telephone numbers on the scraps of paper she occasionally woke up with. No need to be a fully fleshed somebody at all.

"Who cares," she said, "if you drool into your sleeve for half the month when you can spend the other half at a hotel pretending to be a completely different person?"

"Maybe you haven't fully considered the reality of the situation," said the sour-faced man.

"That's the whole point," she said.

She was so taken up by the idea of Leslie Howard and how it might apply to her own problems that she had failed to notice the jangling bells. A throng of new customers was now elbowing and waving and thumping at the far end of the bar. The next few minutes passed in a blur as she whirled from shape to shape, doling out foamy glasses of beer.

"Maybe you don't like people," said the sour-faced man. "Maybe that's why you can't remember their names."

Ada wiped the sweat from her face with a bar towel that stank like the inside of an old sneaker. She considered pounding her foot on the floor to raise Theo from his lair and then decided, as a matter of pride, that she wouldn't. She had a grasp of the situation.

"Do you like the neighbourhood?" asked the sour-faced man.

She thought of the rusting giantess and the weathered photographs of the dancers she'd walked past. "It's none of my business how people choose to live their lives."

"Of course it isn't," said the sour-faced man. "You don't even want to acquaint yourself with their statistics. But you ought to know that every regular in here has been thrown out of at least one of those strip clubs. For groping and being unruly. Even Mr. Gone with the Wind and his sun-kissed hair."

"Speak for yourself," said Sonny. "I was snatching the bills out of their G-strings."

She turned back to the forgotten garnishes. In the hour or so since she'd made them they'd become limp and slimy. They reminded her of when she was a kid and had made a crown out of flowers, weeds most likely, from an empty lot near their house. She had worn the crown all afternoon, parading up and down the street like a princess, but had yanked it from her head in shame and disgust when she got home and saw in the bathroom mirror the shrivelled ring of flowers.

The sour-faced man left his stool for the men's room.

"Don't let him get to you," Sonny said. "He's mean because he killed somebody and now he's living a life of torment and regret."

"Who did he kill?"

"I don't know. But if there's a type I know how to identify, it's a killer."

"Maybe it was his wife," said Leslie Howard.

"Yeah," said Sonny. "That makes sense. He killed his wife because she tried to poison him. I mean, who wouldn't try to poison him?"

"I can see her now," said Leslie Howard. "Creeping down the staircase in her dowdy dressing gown in the middle of the night to crush pills in the pantry."

Sonny beckoned her towards him and she forced another smile. The thought had just occurred to her that Theo might not arise from his basement lair.

"Have you ever done time?"

"Of course not."

"I just thought you might have for criminology purposes," said Sonny. He stuck his tongue out and waggled his eyebrows. "I read a lot of detective stuff when I was inside. Wild West books too." He pulled a pair of imaginary six-shooters out of his side pockets and pointed them in the air.

"There he goes," said Leslie Howard.

She watched Sonny play pantomime cowboys and Indians, making bang-bang noises with his wet lips, and thought about her mother's hands and the things they had done. Snapping loose threads, clapping slices of Wonder Bread and Cheez Whiz together when Ada kept bawling for food. Reaching down to smack Ada so hard that her head spun, for reasons that were never clear.

By the time she'd snapped out of her reverie, the sour-faced man was back at his bar stool and staring intently at her again.

"You do realize it's welfare day," he said.

"Busiest day of the month," said Sonny, smacking his lips. "Macy jumps ship every time. He can't stand to see us in our finery." He stood upright on his stool and tweaked an imaginary bow tie with his tiny hands. "But don't worry. When the going gets tough, I'll show you the ropes." He held an imaginary noose above his head, made a choking noise, crooked his neck and stuck out his tongue.

"That's why Macy hired you," said the sour-faced man. "Neither he nor Theo can stand the guilt of robbing us of so many future cans of soup, so they hire a sacrificial lamb. The lamb, which is you, usually puts in a shift before running out onto the streets to bleat for her sanity. Then they hire a new one the next month. There's never a shortage.

"It's a lamb-eat-lamb world," said Sonny. "But don't worry, Theo comes up to do the night shift. That's where the real money is."

She had so far only thought of the customers with a sense of panic as they pushed through the jangling door and into her consciousness. Now the room seemed awash in sad profundity, like a European movie. Instead of an assortment of creeps and lowlifes with bad breath, here was raw humanity, defiantly festive in the face of poverty and despair.

Moreover, much that had been mysterious appeared to now be resolved: Macy's White Rabbit retreat, Theo's abandonment, the fact that she was scrambling alone on a weekday afternoon to serve watered-down beer to what felt like the population of a small village. But just as the pieces of the puzzle began to fall into place, her sense of clarity began to waver. Leslie Howard was a human pipe dream. Sonny was clearly some kind of low-level trickster, and the sour-faced man, at first so inquisitive and friendly-seeming, was starting to seem more and more like the sour old bastard he looked a lot like.

What were the odds this wasn't a practical joke, a delusion within a larger delusion the three of them had sniggered over while she was playing with her silly garnishes? Maybe Macy was just a busy guy. Maybe Theo was going through a bad patch or a divorce. And apart from the obvious tramps and disturbed street people who appeared to form the bulk of Macy's regulars, it was hard to tell in the badly lit bar who might be poverty-stricken and who might just be casually dressed. Who could say if the straggly men almost coming to blows in the corner had chosen the loud T-shirts with the Make Love Not War logos or if they had been foisted upon them by a charity worker with a sick sense of humour.

The jester bells jangled again and more customers piled in, including a group of heavy-set women who seated themselves at a table near the battered stage. The largest among them wore a leopard-print sweater in need of a wash, and reminded Ada of an ogress in a fairy-tale book she'd had nightmares about as a child. The woman hoisted her belly up over her thighs as she sat down and began to bellow at the ivory-bearded man, who crouched down on the stage with his hands over his ears. Ada couldn't quite make out what the woman was saying above the general clamour. She turned to Sonny, who was throwing mini punches in the air beside her.

"Is that his wife?"

"Just bad blood," said Sonny. "They go way, way back. To the Dark Ages."

"Before the Ark," said Leslie Howard.

"They're both cuckoo," said Sonny. "It's always the same argument. She says he took something of hers. She thinks everybody took something of hers."

"Maybe they did," said the sour-faced man.

Whatever the root cause, the argument caused a ripple of animosity to spread through the bar. Ada stamped her foot on the floor. The only violence she'd witnessed in Labyrinth was between two drunk men in one of the back grottoes. Both had been ejected from the club's torch-lit portico by the sleek bouncers before coming to blows. The event had been seamless, as though choreographed to the trance-like music and the endlessly flowing lava projected on the dance floor walls. But Macy's felt as though it was on the brink of outright chaos. Even the laughter she could still hear from various pockets of the bar sounded less like drunken merriment and more like the angry laughter of baboons she'd seen on nature documentaries, just before they launched into a frenzied attack. One of the fake brawls in the corner turned into a shoving match.

Ada approached the table of heavy-set women with her cocktail tray pressed to her chest like a shield. The women were too engrossed in their own quarrels to do more than snarl at her. She scribbled orders for several complicated cocktails, then watched the ink bloom into illegible blue squiggles as the paper on her pad soaked up the slops on her tray. The pages of the drinks manual behind the bar were gummed together and so grimy she could barely make out the ingredients.

She looked to see how the leopard-print woman and the old tramp's argument was progressing but saw that the stage was empty. She caught a glimpse of the muttering old man as he pushed his way to the door. The leopard-print woman was wiping a gob of something off the front of her sweater, her chin tripled as she peered down. Leslie Howard had been replaced by a bulbous-nosed drunk who stirred the brimming puddle on the bar top in front of him with a half-shredded straw. The sour-faced man had also vanished, and along with him, the feeling that she was half-immersed in someone else's dream.

She overfilled the blender and the froth spewed across the room, flecks of it landing like green snow on the heads of nearby customers while Sonny expertly weaved through the crowd, draining the dregs from stray glasses.

She glugged vodka into the blender without measuring, then crouched behind the bar and took a long guzzle herself, assembled the drinks with the browning, withered garnishes, and placed them on the tray that brimmed once again with slops. Sonny came behind the bar and flipped the stereo on, filling the air with thudding drums. Her forehead began to throb, as though someone on the inside was pounding on it like a door. She stamped her foot and banged. She poured. She tossed the blurred instruction manual into the clogged sink and waded back out among the customers, many of whom had now laced their arms together at the shoulder and burst into off-key song.

After serving the women, she tripped over one of their immense handbags and plunged forward, her fall broken by someone's paunch. She lay motionless, the blood pounding in her head, the din muffled by an underworld of low-hanging buttocks and bedraggled outerwear. Her tip jar slid off the tray and loose change spewed into a puddle of spilled beer and rolled between customers' feet. She contemplated simply lying there. She was quite comfortable despite the fact that the muggy air stank of urine and vomit and that someone had just kicked her in the kidney.

"I ordered a grasshopper. There's no way this is a grasshopper!" A woman loomed over her with a half-drunk green cocktail in her hand.

Ada hoisted herself onto her knees with the help of a random pant leg and began to sift through the sludge, scooping coins back into the cracked tip jar. Then she spotted the tooth.

It was a chunky molar with what looked like a raw, glistening root still attached and a glob of half-clotted blood on one of the root tips. Had any of the phantom brawls and scuffles been real? Surely she would have noticed, would have heard screams. Might even have run over to help or call for an ambulance. Could anybody have a tooth knocked out without screaming? Maybe the brutal act had occurred while the blender was on. She wondered if she should ask around, or put a sign up at the bar, or if a tooth knocked out at the root could even be reattached. She was about to pick it up and see if anybody was crying or holding their hands to their mouths when an undersized hand reached down and plucked it off the floor. Sonny winked at her and slipped it into the front pocket of his western shirt.

A hundred faces distorted in the mirror, laughed and cried, their mouths ringed with foam.

Sonny had promised to show her the ropes and now he was, ducking and diving, draining the dregs of abandoned drinks before collecting them up in a tower that swerved and swayed above his head like a glass snake, forming a brief conga line, dancing back towards the bar on the pointy black cowboy boots that reminded her now of hooves. He was in his element, an enormous smile beneath the handlebar moustache that Ada now believed was fake. She was sure too that he was pocketing her tips while her back was turned. Each time she spun around to catch him in the act he was hovering close to the glass jar on her tray, his lips puckered in the ghost of a whistle.

He flipped the volume on the stereo higher and then higher again, snaked out again into the lurching crowd and the thudding rhythm. A moment later she watched transfixed while, with the delicacy of a jeweller, he placed the tooth on the bar top. The customer nearest the tooth stared down at it in mesmerized horror while Sonny reached into his pocket and helped himself to his wallet, and Ada felt around in her back pocket for the two twenties that she already knew weren't there.

When he came behind the bar again to deposit another tower of empty glasses, she slammed him into the sharp sink corner. His face behind the glasses and handlebar moustache was smooth and unlined. He was like a kid in some shyster Halloween costume. That didn't stop her from wanting to open the partially concealed door and kick him down the basement steps.

She felt as though she had finally worn through whatever polite veneer civilization demanded of her. A more brutal self would emerge, the way it happened to people marooned in the wilderness after a plane crash. The new her would make jabbering noises as it rushed around the room bashing heads with the duct-taped baseball bat she had spied at the side of the cash register.

"Hey," he said, rubbing his hip. "What's the big idea?"

A moment later she spotted him heading out the fire exit with the grasshopper woman and what looked like a purloined bottle of crème de menthe tucked under his arm. She looked over at the duct-taped bat, tempted to test out her newfound brutishness. But the crowd, she noticed, was magically dispersing. Stragglers lolled open-mouthed at the bar, and a few more were huddled in a circle at the back, as though gathered around a campfire.

A stack of glasses toppled near the clogged sink and she caught sight of a gleam of white in the murk. The tooth lay partially submerged in the sink's muck, like a pirate's skull and crossbones in an aquarium. Sonny must have been too distracted by the bruise on his hip to notice that the shove had dislodged it from his pocket.

She plucked it out of the sink just as Theo opened the small door to the basement. His eyes travelled from the pools of beer and green foam on the bar top to the crumpled napkins and overflowing ashtrays and pieces of glass still littered among the coins she hadn't yet scooped up from the sludge. She followed his gaze to a small clock above the cash register that she hadn't noticed before.

It seemed impossible that only three hours had passed. The clock leered at her like a comedian's face after a cheap joke.

She thought of Macy's white shoes and his Easter Island head. Leslie Howard and his fluorescent smile. The three-chinned leopard-print woman. The sloped-headed customers bursting into raucous song, the drums throbbing in a primitive accompaniment. Sonny's dancing hooves as he criss-crossed the floor. The mouths ringed in foam. The coins on the black floor like a night sky in reverse, and the bar door opening and opening, filling the space with shapes who drifted in and out of consciousness, hers and their own.

What had passed seemed, on reflection, less a measure of time than an immensity, an expanse where images and fragments of lives, snatches of conversation circulated like deep ocean fish. She could survive in this flux while a new Ada, more impersonal and more plausible, bulged at the seams of her meagre old self like a flexed muscle. She was not required to smile. She could slip beneath the crowd into a netherworld of barn-like warmth and odours. And she had the tooth tucked deep in her apron, like a witch doctor's amulet.

"I'm free to come back anytime," she said.

Talking of Michelangelo

I took my kung fu instructor off speed-dial today. I was leaning on him too much for advice. Calling him up to ask if it was okay to buy goods made in China. Calling him at midnight to see if he was as lonely as I was. Which he was. He always was.

When I moved here I was too broke to live near the college so I rented half a duplex in a neighbourhood full of barking dogs and visits from the police. I knew it was a mistake as soon as I closed the front door and heard the voice of my next-door neighbour explaining through the wall, maybe to a room full of nodding thugs, maybe to nobody at all, the many ways in which he was going to take a guy called Angelo to pieces. By the time he'd reached number ten, I'd unpacked my suitcase, blown up my air mattress, and run out of cigarettes.

I left to look for a store and walked along the duplex-lined streets until I saw the 7-Eleven sign up ahead. I bought a pack and lit up, then strolled down the adjoining strip mall, which contained a particularly shabby Salvation Army, a boarded-up law practice, a knitting supplies store, and the Double Dragon Kung Fu Academy.

For a place that called itself an academy it was nothing special: there was a peeling double dragon decal on the door, frayed black mats, and four walls lined with dusty, bubbled mirrors. There was a small class going on. I've never been a martial arts kind of girl, but the arcing, whirling bodies caught my eye and soon I was mesmerized by the flock of graceful pant legs flaring out, each foot looking like it yearned to fly off at the ankle and up into the sky.

The instructor was a small brown-skinned man dressed in baggy black. I found out later he'd been a world-class welterweight boxer but you wouldn't know to look. Some accident of fate had spared his nose and face, which conformed as closely to a Grecian ideal as any man's I've ever seen. He wore a black prayer cap embroidered with tiny mirrors and silver thread.

I got so flustered when he paused mid-kick to wink at me that I dropped my cigarette. Being broke, I debated on whether or not to pick it up, then decided to leave it smoking on the sewer grate. I'd reached the Salvation Army when I heard a voice behind me.

"What are you afraid of?"

He was leaning out the door with half a smile, the other half hidden by peeling coils of double dragon tail. You could have knocked me down with a feather when he picked up the still-burning cigarette and took a deep haul before flicking it back into the gutter.

"Everything," I said.

I always end up back in these chilly eastern college towns where the wind sweeps down from the Arctic in November and freezes everything to an opaque blank. There's always a row or two of sagging clapboard mansions and a department store having a bankruptcy sale and a manicured expanse between the campus and the local millwork's rusting minarets. It didn't take me long the next day to find the Humanities building and my cubicle beside an obese Chaucer adjunct who spent the hour I sat beside him filling a jumbo notepad page with raunchy doodles. At three o'clock I found the door to my professor's office at the end of a long corridor. There was no answer when I knocked. I'd just turned to go when a high, querulous voice told me to enter and I stepped into another world. A Victorian world.

Only the overhead strip of fluorescent lighting gave the game away. The book-lined walls were deep olive offset by turquoise curtains drawn to hide the dreary courtyard. The professor's beard was streaked with silver. He was seated at a walnut desk piled with papers and a green glass lamp. After a few moments he motioned for me to sit down. By the time he made eye contact with me I was almost prepared for the concentrated sourness of his face.

He took his glasses off and polished them with a silk handkerchief.

"Your job is to mark the Shakespeare papers," he said. "Mark them hard, but not so hard we get the parents in for a pitched battle. They will fight to the death for an A minus."

He handed me the syllabus without looking up. I was beginning to understand why my predecessor had quit midterm. A thin smile hovered on his lips.

"We're reading *Romeo and Juliet*," he said. "So the trick for you will be to make sure they write about the actual play and not the movie starring what's-his-face."

I almost didn't recognize the kung fu instructor when I passed him on the street a few days later. There had been a cold snap and he wore a hoodie and a black tuque encrusted with frozen droplets pulled down low over his face.

"You look tired," I said. What I meant was puffy. Like he'd been crying. He spat onto the pavement in reply. We walked along together until he stopped beside a tall apartment building that overlooked the highway. His name was Sal. He was a newcomer to the town as well, having moved here a couple of years ago.

"This is where I live," he said, pointing upward. The flaking iron balconies climbed up into the clouds and disappeared.

"You can't," I said.

"Why not?"

"It's so grim and anonymous."

"That's probably why I feel so at home," he said.

Looking back, I wonder what kind of place I *had* imagined for him. Somewhere with mosaics and inlaid marquetry?

"Come on up," he said. "I'll show you my weapons."

When I was a kid my father covered the windows in opaque plastic during winter to keep out the cold. It was no good. The drafts seeped in through the floorboards, blasted through the roof shingles and the walls, had us shivering each night when we knelt by our beds to pray. But it made the rest of the world disappear. From November to May there was no sagging chain-link fence, no ugly neighbour with the junked lawn and the dog with the bald patch chained to a gnawed stump. Only the landlord's balloon face once a month collecting rent and a blur of oak shifting restlessly in the wind.

Sal's apartment was on the top floor and his window was a perfect blank of sky. Only if you went directly to the window ledge and peered down could you make out a curve of lake, a stripe of highway, the town's sprawling westerly mess of Quonset huts and rail yards and postwar bungalows. His walls were bare apart from a red pennant with Chinese characters. There was a polished wooden cabinet in the corner.

"You don't have visitors very often," I said.

"How did you guess?"

"Because most people don't keep porno magazines on their coffee tables."

He grinned, swept the magazines up in his arms, and thrust them into the drawer beneath his stereo. Then he walked over to the wooden cabinet and flung open the doors. It was lined in red velvet and contained a few carved, curving weapons and polished wands. He unsheathed a bronze-handled sword and balanced it in the palm of his hand.

"Shaolin," he said. He held the sword up to his nose and stared down the length of it, then looked up at me. "So," he said. "What do you do for kicks?"

I told him I was, or had just become, an assistant to a professor at the college. "Or maybe I'm just about to become a posthumous assistant to the professor," I said, staring at his sword.

"How'd you score a gig like that?" He swung the sword to the left and then to the right. The tip nearly grazed the walls on either side of him, and I wondered if he'd chosen the weapons, or the apartment, or both, in respect to their relative spans.

"I faked my way in."

"Well la-di-da," he said. But by the tone of his voice I could tell he meant la-di-fucking-da.

I hadn't lied on my résumé, just exaggerated a little. I went to grad school, but the truth is that I'm an academic the same way Charles Manson is a guitarist. By that I mean, I liked researching representations of the body in Middle English poetry well enough, but my own body couldn't run fast enough away from the library at the end of the afternoon to get on with its unfathomable business. The truth is that my last boyfriend broke my nose and then we both broke all the living room windows including every pane in the French doors. And even though it took me a month to pick all the glass out of my feet it was all I could do to not throw on a robe and run out to him when I heard his car creeping around and around my block on summer nights. Which is why I started applying for jobs. Any job, anywhere that took me far enough away to make the bus ride back to him a pain in the ass.

I took a long look at Sal and his ceremonial sword and decided not to fill him in on the details. He sheathed the sword and put it back in the cabinet, then walked over to the window.

"My family," he said, "is descended from a Persian dynasty of tribal chiefs who warred in Kurdistan and served the shah Nasser al-Din. For his bravery one of my ancestors was awarded part of the imperial hunting grounds in Tehran. Our family name comes from a warrior whose horse had golden shoes." He gestured out the window towards a squall of grey-white snow that had swept down out of the sky. "Here, people just call me a Paki."

He walked back to the cabinet and scowled at the array of weapons inside, as though whatever he was looking for had been mislaid. Then he turned to me.

"Look," he said. "It's awkward. I don't know why you think I brought you here but I'm not really up for a date. Or a relationship. Or anything like that."

"Fine with me," I said. "I'm just here to unlock the ancient secrets of the masters."

"The secret is that there is no secret," he said. "You wake up. You put your pants on before your shoes."

"Hold on a sec," I said. "I want to jot this down."

In bed that night, through the windows and the walls, I listened to the wind and to my neighbour issue vague threats to Angelo or anyone, until sleep swept me away in a thundering cloud of dark, edged at the bottom with a thousand gold hooves.

The squalls blasted through the night, and I waded to the campus for my first lecture through whirling flakes and knee-high drifts, the amber lights of a snowplow blinking on a far-off hill. I've always loved those forays into oblivion before the world digs out from underneath its mock burial mound.

The auditorium was empty when I arrived and I watched the rosy-faced students file in and shake crusts of snow from their coats and hats. My professor was late and even more contemptuous-seeming than he had been in his office. He looked directly at nobody, reading as if by rote from his sheaves about Shakespeare and his folios, about antecedents to *Romeo and Juliet* in European history.

He came magically back to life whenever he quoted from

the play, caressing each word in mid-air as it left his mouth. A yearning Romeo, a quavering Juliet, you could almost see the proscenium arch flowering above his head, the blackboard dissolving behind him into velvet swags. He enacted the balcony scene in a breathless swoon, his body rocking gently back and forth, his face so nakedly vulnerable that I had to look away. Later on by the cafeteria I saw two students mimicking his tremulous Romeo, their chests expanding outward until they collapsed laughing in the snow.

"Picture a monastery high on the top of a lonely mountain, carved over the centuries out of stone by a million monks. Feel the weight of your feet rooted to the earth," he said. But none of us can take our eyes off his bare chest, the way his hands or feet wing past, stopping a few millimetres short of the mirrored wall, someone else's neck, my solar plexus.

It's not even Sal who's got me signed up at the Double Dragon Kung Fu Academy so much as the idea of Sal. And it isn't even so much the idea of Sal as the idea of who he isn't. I've burned every photograph, banished myself from within a hundred-mile radius of him, but my ex keeps creeping deeper and deeper into my thoughts. Whenever I close my eyes at night, his green eyes open in my mind. In the morning I'm like a kid on an Easter egg hunt, looking under the bushes by my balcony and in the backyard for evidence that he's been stalking me. There's a bus schedule in the kitchen drawer I don't need to look at because I already have it memorized.

We move through the stances, our legs spread wide and low, our fingers curled into loose fists, trying to replicate Sal's grace and sinuousness. Tiger and crane, snake and dragon. Each stance, he tells us, is a letter in an alphabet. Strung together they form words, lines, whole poems of violence. I stumble onto the black mats and the girl beside me holds out her hand to help me up.

She filled me in on everybody's stories while we moved through another sequence. Dara had watched from behind a bush while her family was beaten and then loaded onto a truck by soldiers. Graham was mugged at knifepoint. Rita behind him had seen one too many fatalities as a paramedic. Douglas was the classic skinny kid who'd been bullied. Sherry was assaulted at a party, while the girl behind her with the furious look and the whip-fast strike had been raped by a complete stranger. Wanda worked as a teller and signed up after her bank was robbed for the second time. The robbers wore pantyhose masks, and she still had nightmares about the faces distorted underneath. I see them here too, she said, lunging at the empty space in front of her.

I lingered by the doorway after the rest of the class had gone and asked Sal about the country he'd originally come from. The truth is that I would have said anything to keep us standing there alone, our reflections multiplied to infinity in the dusty wall mirrors.

"We left when I was too young to remember what it was like," he said. "And now it doesn't even officially exist."

"Nobody comes from anywhere these days," I said. "We're all in the same boat."

That was true in my family's case. We've never known if we were Irish Travellers or Scottish beggars or descended from Huguenots escaping persecution in France. My father used to say we were descended from pilgrims, but that was just after he'd done his correspondence course to become an ordained minister and would have said anything to convince himself that God had forgiven him.

"My family hangs on to their old way of life," said Sal. "They won't let go."

I asked him why he gave up boxing.

"I'll give this up too one day," he said.

"What will you do instead?"

"I don't know. Sit cross-legged in my apartment for a few years. Stare at the empty walls."

The snow laid siege to the town for a week, burying the streets and the campus and all the public buildings beneath domes of sparkling white. On Wednesday kids were out making snow angels. On Friday they were charging up ten-foot snowbanks like knights in a fairy tale. By Sunday morning they'd built a walk-in castle with a moat. Classes, kung fu and otherwise, were cancelled and I stayed home rereading *Romeo and Juliet* while listening to my neighbour's threats escalate through the walls. When I couldn't concentrate enough to read anymore, I hurled my book repeatedly at whatever spot I imagined my neighbour was. I performed every stance in the alphabet I could remember, my fingers and toes stopping just short of the white plaster dividing us. I paced up and down. I picked up the phone and called my kung fu instructor.

"This neighbour of yours, how do you know he isn't a voice in your head?"

"How do I know you're not?"

"Okay, so maybe Angelo is a figment of your neighbour's imagination. Maybe," he said, "I'm Angelo."

"Let me check my notes," I said. "I'll let you know when I find out."

The truth is that I just wanted to hear him listening to my voice in the dark. When I got up later to marvel at the suddenly clear sky, I saw tiny mirrors on a prayer cap instead of stars.

My professor wrote out the essay question on the blackboard and turned to the class with a smile thin as a knife's edge. Discuss the significance of Romeo's love for Rosaline.

"I don't want quotes from fancy academics and French philosophers," he said. "I want to know how you feel. In your own words. Pour your hearts out."

The auditorium went quiet. Then the whispers began, with students leaning towards each other to shrug or express their disbelief. A gang of them surrounded me after class.

"Who the fuck is Rosaline?" they asked.

The professor had warned me in advance, telling me he often threw that essay question to shake them, in his words, out of their slumber. I turned to the beginning of the play.

"Act 1, scene 1. Tybalt swings his sword into a wind that hisses back at him in scorn and Romeo is so in love with Rosaline that he wanders through the orchards sighing until dawn."

A girl in floral tights said, "He wants us to write a whole essay about someone who isn't even in the play?"

Sal's family chose him a bride just after his eighteenth birthday. He told me about it while I leaned against his window and watched the men drag their ice huts out onto the frozen lake. Clustered in the whiteness, they looked like something out of a Siberian fairy tale, a hamlet suspended above the deep on two feet of solid glass.

"You've got to understand," he said. "There's a whole other side to these customs. It's not as barbaric as it seems."

I thought about the glass splinters in my feet still working their way to the surface of my skin six months after my breakup.

His mother had shown him a photo of a girl with hair to her waist and a wry smile, as if she was mocking the portrait photographer and the white arch of artificial roses she was posing under. They had taken into consideration his aloofness and his wit. They were matched because they shared auspicious stars and because both families enjoyed a similar social status. And because they were both zany, his mother had said in her thick accent. The fact that she had bothered to learn this odd little Western word and consider how it might apply to him melted the last icicle in his heart. He started to meditate upon what it was to be a man.

"I was wild before that," he said. "Ran with a bad crowd and hated everything my parents stood for. Did stuff I regret."

"What kind of stuff?"

"The usual kind of stuff."

He thought about duty and sacrifice and honour. About earning the respect of his community and becoming an elder himself one day, handing down his own hard-won wisdom to others. To his children. After a week of deliberating he agreed to marry her.

His parents paid for the entire extended family to be flown in for the wedding feast. A hall was booked and flowers and trays full of almond-scented sweets were ordered. But the bride ran away, vanished a few nights before the wedding. To where, nobody knew. Off the face of the earth, perhaps, if her father ever found her.

She left him a note, said it had nothing to do with him. She wanted to find herself first before giving herself away in marriage. He took the news hard, moved away from the place where his family had branched and blossomed, filling their calendars with ceremonies and picnic gatherings where children tumbled in the grass and women in gold-threaded robes handed out plates heaped with food. At first nobody knew where he was. He had a year, two years of solitude. Then they started to show up, in the foyer of his building or at his door if they got through the security system. A brother. An uncle. They told him to come home, that all would be forgiven. Then the younger cousins started to come.

"Asking, is it better on the outside? Is it more fun? I sent them home. But there's no going back for me."

"Why not?"

"I fell between worlds," he said. "I don't belong anywhere."

It had been a while now since anyone had come.

"What if she came back?" I asked. "Would you marry her now?"

"Now? I couldn't pick her out of a police lineup."

Over the next few days the students came to see me in my cubicle, singly and in small, perplexed groups. Did the professor want us to talk about actual love? Was Romeo for real? Would a play called *Romeo and Rosaline* have been a boisterous comedy, or would the fates have ensured their tragic demise as well? Was it all a cosmic joke? The questions led to other questions, which drove me to the telephone, where I always held my breath until he answered. And he did. He always did.

"The truth is that there is no truth," he said.

"You already told me that," I said.

"How's this? There's a fine line between transcendence and self-annihilation."

"Let me know when you find where the line is," I said, "and I'll cross it out for you with my red pen."

I met my ex at a patio bar. He was sitting by a row of potted palms, his leg jogging out of time to the Latin music everyone else was dancing around to, as they spilled off the patio onto the night lawns with their drinks. He screamed in my ear to tell me how he never picked up women in bars. But when he saw me in the crowd it was like he'd known me already for a thousand years.

The next day my doorbell rang and his green eyes stared at me over a bouquet of spiky lilies. Then the phone calls started coming, a few at first and then a flurry. I want to make sure, he'd say, that you are where you say you're going to be. I'd see his car flit past my window at night and wonder if I'd imagined it. I can't help myself, he said. My lizard brain takes control of me and all of a sudden I'm driving past your front door.

After our first fight he turned away from me with an astonished look, his hands outstretched like a defence lawyer appealing to an invisible jury. A religious kook's daughter, he'd say, and look how she behaves. He got me in a chokehold and said he'd seen me with other men. He said that underneath my lies, I was a monster like all the rest.

The longer we were together, the less we got to know each other. Hello, he'd say, waving his hands in front of my face. Is anybody home? Every time he hit me I flew all the way back to my childhood bedroom with its opaque windows, the plastic sheaths rippling like ship's sails in the wind while my father prowled downstairs. I could have called the police, but something inside me must have wanted his car nosing around the block, the hum of its engine through the slit of my barely opened window.

When we made up he folded my hands inside his to make a double prayer before we kissed. This was what his father had always done to ask forgiveness, he told me. That's how love is handed down through generations, in gestures, empty or otherwise, like a family sword or an old candlestick.

Once you've been knocked out by a man like that you slip into a pit that you only ever half drag yourself out of. Underneath my lies, I'm a monster like all the rest.

A clear Perspex panel separated my desk from the four-storey drop into the library's central foyer. I carved the whole stack up with my red pen, each essay as full of folly and outrage as any letter from a star-crossed lover. I contemplated taking them to the panel and letting them waft, like the lazy snowflakes beyond the library's amber-lit window, and amass in loose drifts on the marble floor below.

Instead, I took them to my professor's office and opened the door without knocking. He'd drawn the curtain back and was looking out at the opposing courtyard wall, its dull grey brick flecked with frost. He let the curtain drop. The face he turned to greet me with was as expressionless as a funeral mask. I placed the stack beside his green lamp along with my resignation letter.

"Congratulations," I said. "You just broke everybody's heart."

It was packed to capacity at the Double Dragon. Dara put paid to the Khmer Rouge while Graham and Douglas gave their old tormentors some grief. Wanda and Sherry made short work of the pantyhose gang and the frat crowd. And I kicked the shit out of every last Montague and Capulet, knocked the Prince of Cats out cold before he could plunge the tip of his rapier deep into the heart of everything and give it a little twist.

After the last car pulled out of the parking lot, Sal told me about the day he almost packed his bags and went back to the city where his parents lived.

"You don't know what it's like to be a brown face in a sea of white, in a college town where the rednecks throw beer cans at you from their pickup trucks."

He rolled his weapons into a cloth and put the cabinet up for sale and gave notice to the owner of the strip mall. He wrote a letter to his mother. He was on his way to the mailbox when he walked past an electronics store, glanced at a stack of two dozen televisions in the window, and saw the planes flying into the twin towers of the World Trade Center. And then over and over again for the foreseeable future, the same skies filling with fire and shattered glass. On every TV, in the imagined eyes of all the people who cancelled his classes, on the faces of the people who muttered under their breath at him when he walked past.

"The same clip," he said. "Of the same couple holding hands, their clothes flapping in the wind as they fell."

He unrolled his weapons and tore up his notices. Moving back was out of the question. Everyone would assume he'd come home because he was a coward. And after he contemplated the matter a little more, he knew it wasn't even just a matter of pride.

"Feel the weight of your feet," he said, "rooted to the earth."

He looked so alone that I couldn't stop myself from putting my arms around him, although the truth is that I was always looking for the right moment to make a move. I knew part of him wanted me, even when he peeled my arm off his shoulder and gave me the gentlest of shoves.

"You've got me confused with someone else," he said.

I didn't feel a thing, the thin material of my kung fu robe rippling over my skin as I slipped and slid all the way from the strip mall out onto the lake. The stars had come out and the ice huts were abandoned by the time I got there, and it was only when I saw how far away the town looked that I started to feel the cold.

He helped me up from the asphalt to make sure I hadn't broken anything after I fell. He offered to walk me home or anywhere. I know he's alone like me, lying high up in the dark in his bedroom in the sky.

But I'm not going to call. I'm not going to call.

THE SPIRIT OF THINGS

Christoff stood in the alleyway behind the European Fine Meats and Delicatessen. He had worked here since he was a child, wrapping meat in wads of pink paper and helping his parents with their English-speaking customers. Now that he was sixteen and had left school he presided over the electric cutting machine, transfiguring stumps of cured sausage and ham into slivers transparent as stained glass. The vibrations from the machine numbed his arms and upper body, so he slipped out into the stillness of the alleyway as often as he could to shake loose and breathe deeply. It had snowed earlier in the afternoon and all the crates and trash cans were cloaked in sparkling white.

He was about to go back in when he saw a young man in an army surplus coat with a sleek black guitar case approaching. Christoff almost exclaimed out loud as he walked by because, apart from his long dark hair, the young man appeared to be his exact double. Christoff had heard of doppelgängers and evil twins in books and movies. He was aware that these stories didn't always end well for either party.

He could also hear his father crashing and banging in the storeroom, a sure sign that he was about to call out for him. Nonetheless, he followed the receding figure. He had lived in the town his whole life and had played in the alleyways behind the mock-Victorian shopfronts as a child. This evening the snow-covered alleys began to seem unfamiliar, like a maze that had been arranged overnight to trick him. He was almost ready to give up when he turned a corner and caught sight of the young man, who had just opened a large steel door.

The alleyway was flooded with discordant music. Christoff broke into a run, arriving just as the door, which was made of painted steel and heavily engraved with graffiti and strange symbols, clanged shut. He could still hear the music, hive-like, when he pressed his ear to the cold door.

He retraced his own snowy footsteps back to the European Fine Meats just as his father stepped out of the back storeroom to call for him. Hunched once again over his cutting machine, Christoff promised himself he would return to the strange door and find out more about the young man who looked so much like himself.

After dinner, Christoff's father liked going down to the basement where he kept flagons of homemade plum brandy. He would drink his fill and start to bellow, his angry voice echoing off the concrete walls, travelling up the heating ducts and throughout the house. When Christoff read the story about the Minotaur in school he had thought to himself: that's my father. As a child he had crept down once to see who or what his father was screaming at, and caught him with his face a few inches from his own bleared reflection in the oil furnace. Sometimes Christoff stuffed cotton wool in his ears to shut him out, but his father's voice was nearly always ringing in his head, long before the real shouting started, and long after it stopped.

Because his father had been so furious to find him missing from the store that evening, Christoff kept to his bedroom until he heard the slow thud of his father's footsteps down the basement stairs, then tiptoed down into the kitchen in his sock feet to make himself a sandwich. He had just taken a loaf from the basket when his father barrelled back up the stairs to threaten Christoff again with the thrashing he'd promised him earlier.

Christoff darted past him into the front parlour where his mother kept all her treasures: a gilt painted claw-foot table and brocaded drapes, a thick velvet sofa with embroidered gold cushions, and a set of crystal glassware displayed in a carved cabinet. When he was small he used to hide at the back of his bedroom closet to escape his father's raw hands. He had recently discovered that his father seemed reluctant to beat him in the parlour. At first Christoff thought the objects themselves exerted a magical influence. Now he realized that his father was afraid of breaking something valuable.

But not even the parlour afforded him sanctuary that night. His father, a heavy-set man with sad jowls, pummelled him rhythmically with glazed eyes while Christoff's mother wrung her hands in the doorway, wincing when blood from her son's nose sprayed onto the figured rug. She hadn't learned to read or write, but she had nonetheless picked up various household tips and tricks over the years. How to cover a bruised eye with rice powder and a pancake stick of Maybelline. How to rinse blood out of fabrics with ice water. After her husband disappeared back down to the basement she dabbed at Christoff's lip with a rag.

"You shouldn't make him angry," she said.

"He's always angry," said Christoff.

"You know how he suffered in the war."

"Why won't you tell me what happened to him? He's not even beating *me* when he beats me. I wouldn't mind so much if he was."

"It should be enough for you to know that he suffered," said his mother. "One day you'll own the shop, and then you'll be thankful to your father."

"I wouldn't care if it vanished off the face of the earth," said Christoff.

His mother shook her head and crouched down to blot the rug. The European Fine Meats and Delicatessen had made them quite well off, but hiring household help went against her nature. When she wasn't working in the shop she skivvied around the house in a patched dressing gown. She almost never sat in her parlour, but preferred to gaze at its splendour from the doorway, rapt as a farm girl at every ornate curlicue.

Christoff looked down at her bent head and felt a surge of tenderness and sorrow. Despite his father's brutality both his parents had a child-like innocence, needed his help to fill out even the simplest of forms, were as suspicious as medieval peasants about all manner of things in their adoptive country. Nonetheless, he often dreamed about running far away, of simply disappearing into the mists. That night, however, his thoughts returned to the young man who was, or so it seemed, his army surplus–coated double.

The next day at school he told his girlfriend, Hanna, about the strange encounter. She was a small girl with tawny hair that fell to her waist. She spent a great deal of time filling notebooks with flowers and fantastical creatures surrounded by twisting vines. Their families had both emigrated from the same Silesian village and belonged to the same dimly lit church on the outskirts of town.

She didn't seem at all surprised. "I knew something strange would happen because I dreamed about you last night," she said. "You were running in the woods behind the school."

Hanna took her dreams seriously, and wrote them all down in a white leatherette diary with a little gold lock that she kept on her night table. She had books on dream interpretation and spent hours flipping through them to decipher her own and Christoff's dreams and nightmares. He had always thought to himself that it was all superstitious nonsense, but after his experience in the alley he was no longer sure.

"Was I running towards something," he asked her, "or was I running away from something?"

"Both," she said, looking vague for a moment. "It was definitely both."

"A monster?"

"I don't know. Maybe it was your own self," she said, reaching out to touch his hurt lip.

The next day Christoff cut slice after slice of cured meat, wrapped thick wedges of hock in paper, helped his father prepare heaps of blood sausage in the back room. He scooped quivering mounds of liver into the display case tray and lined pigs' hooves into neat rows against strips of artificial grass. When he had finished his chores and his father was preoccupied with a delivery, he slipped out back to retrace his steps through the snowy maze. He found his way to the steel door in no time at all, pressed his ear against the metal, and heard the hive-like din once again, then felt a hand on his shoulder and spun around.

It was the young man in the army surplus coat. His features, Christoff was disappointed to note, while similar to his own, were not by any stretch identical. It must have been a trick of the light, he decided, or a product of his own wishful imagination.

The young man who was not quite his double held out his hand. "Luka," he said.

"Christoff."

Luka heaved open the door, and a gust of chaotic music blasted, each note seeming to whirl in the air like metallic snowflakes in a miniature storm. A staircase twisted down into darkness.

"Welcome to the maelstrom," he said.

The stairs led to a dimly lit hall with several closed metal doors, where the clamour was so loud it pulsed in the pit of Christoff's stomach and made his hair stand on end. He followed Luka to the farthest doorway into a windowless space that contained several rolls of mildewed carpet. Here, Luka was able to shout above the music and explain to Christoff that the owner of the antique shop upstairs rented his basement out as a music practice hall.

"Now he complains that all his china and his knick-knacks are leaping off the shelves to their deaths because of the noise."

Christoff wasn't surprised. Even in the dank inner room in which they stood, his body felt as though it might fly into pieces at any moment.

"What kind of music do the bands play?" he asked.

"All the same," said Luka. "Loud."

Luka led him to a lit space with a large black banner on the wall with a graveyard embroidered on it. Beneath the banner was a drum kit that looked, to Christoff, like a small city made of silver under siege by a giant.

An angry giant, judging by the drummer's face. He was bare-chested beneath his army surplus coat and had a mane of tangled dark hair. The bass drum began to thud and suddenly the drummer's beefy hands and large, powerful arms were everywhere, smashing the cymbals and the hi-hats, swiping at the tom-toms and snares with a pair of scarred drumsticks. A thin blond-haired man, also wearing an army surplus coat, aimed his bass guitar at Luka and Christoff like it was a machine gun.

"Sit and listen," said Luka. "But say nothing or they'll kick you out. Or worse."

Christoff squatted on an old carpet roll while Luka opened his case and slung a red guitar around his neck, then plugged it into a black amplifier. The three bandmates then began to argue. The drummer, whose name was Drago, kept his hi-hats hissing while he shouted and rattled on his snare for emphasis. The bass player, whose name was Kugel, flicked the back of Luka's head a couple of times with his fingers. Finally, the drummer signalled for the band to start, and Christoff was struck by a fusillade of noise that nearly knocked him off his roll of carpet.

He had heard heavy metal music before, but never at a volume that assaulted his entire body. This was music he could relate to. He had also never seen a band where the lead singer was a drummer. If you could call it singing. Drago sounded like a man being tortured, at other times like a drill sergeant barking orders. It was Luka, however, who commanded Christoff's attention. He writhed and wrestled with his guitar like it was an animal, flung his head back like a man possessed while his fingers needled the strings. At times, though, it sounded as though Luka's guitar was trying to climb up out of the blistering chaos into a solo. It sounded, Christoff thought, like a soul.

He gave himself over to the noise for a while and then remembered the European Fine Meats and Delicatessen and his father. Even though he knew he'd be punished for his absence, the music surged through him as he ran back through the snow-covered alley. He felt certain that fate had led him to follow Luka down into the practice hall.

Over the next while Christoff found that he shared more than just a slight resemblance to Luka, who lived on the other side of the same sprawling suburb, in a house almost identical to Christoff's. His parents were also from Eastern Europe and spoke little English. When Christoff visited his new friend's house for the first time he gasped, for their parlour was a mirror image of his mother's, with gilt furniture and a marble coffee table, and the same crystal glassware in an ornate cabinet.

"Except my father drinks rakia," said Luka. "Not Silesian plum brandy."

Christoff asked Luka if his grim-looking father had also suffered a terrible experience during the war.

"Yes, but he won't talk about it," said Luka.

"My father is the same," said Christoff.

"So we'll never know if they're fucked up because of something terrible they did to some bastard, or if it's because something terrible was done to them."

KERRY LEE POWELL

"Either way," said Christoff, "the end result is the same."

"Yes," said Luka. "And the town is full of bastards just like them."

"I come from a long line of bastards," said Christoff.

"Me too," said Luka.

They stared thoughtfully at each other.

"I want to play the guitar like you," said Christoff.

Upstairs in his bedroom Luka taught Christoff a few scales and told him how he had joined the band recently after answering an ad in the classifieds. They were supposed to be practising for a battle of the bands competition. That, Kugel told him, was simply their first step towards world domination. They would soon be playing to stadiums full of chanting, swaying fans. But every time Luka asked Drago when the battle was supposed to take place, he became enraged, then accused Luka of holding them back.

Luka had too many ideas. He wanted to experiment and create his own guitar solos.

"Drago wants me to play each note exactly the same as the last guitarist did," said Luka. "Which is the same way as the guitarist before him."

"What happened to them?"

"I don't know." Luka grinned. "Maybe one day we'll find out."

At the end of the month, Christoff took his savings out of the bank and, without telling his parents, bought a pearl-white Flying V guitar with gilt hardware.

"Be careful where that thing takes you," said the music shop owner.

"As long as it takes me far away from here," said Christoff.

He practised scales unamplified, under his quilt at night; pictured himself climbing up and up an intricate mountain stairway, higher and higher until there was nothing but notes hanging like ice crystals in the cold, pure air. He played until his fingers bled. When he'd mastered some scales and chords he pieced together whole songs, copying Luka's agonized contortions in front of his mirror. He summoned up the courage to play in front of Hanna in her family's kitchen, singing in a shaky off-key voice.

"You have to imagine the songs being screamed," he said.

Hanna frowned. "It sounds like they're from the old myths about the world being destroyed in a war with the gods," she said. She liked gentle music that harkened back to olden times, played with lutes and harps.

"I wouldn't care if the world *was* destroyed," said Christoff. He caressed the deep bruises on his rib cage from his father's most recent outburst.

"Be careful what you wish for," said Hanna.

She brought some books about legends and myths down from her bedroom and she read to him about seven-headed serpents and men with black worms inside them whose tails were big enough to curl around the world. Stories that reminded Christoff a great deal of Drago. And Drago's songs.

"He's stolen all the lyrics straight from here."

"You can't steal from myths," she said. "They belong to everyone." She reached out and stroked the hem of Christoff's army surplus coat. "This band, are they some kind of neo-Nazis?"

"I don't think so. They just sing about death and destruction in general. Or Drago does. The others do whatever he screams at them to do."

KERRY LEE POWELL

"It's funny," she said. "You try to escape from under your father's thumb and you end up with some other angry bastard screaming at you."

"This is different," said Christoff. "It's art."

He took the books home and pored over them, hid them under the bed with his guitar. For the first time in his life he no longer heard his father's angry voice twining up through the heating ducts into his ears at night. When he closed his eyes he saw wolves running through snowy woods, eagles wheeling in night skies. He dreamed about distant battles fought between monsters and knights with shining swords. He told Luka how sometimes the monsters had Drago's face.

"Everybody has nightmares about Drago," said Luka.

Drago had grown up poor on a farm and his parents had worked him hard. Too hard, some people said.

"That's why his hands are so strong," said Luka. "He wasn't just slicing little bits of sausage like you. He was killing whole cows, hacking the heads off pigs and filling old bathtubs with their guts. He'll tell you all about his lovely childhood memories if you ask him."

"Aren't you afraid he might hurt you?"

"He already has," said Luka.

Drago had pinned him to the floor, sat on his chest, and eaten an entire pizza. He had battered Luka's forehead with his drumsticks. He and Kugel had rolled Luka up in a musty carpet and threatened to leave him overnight. When Christoff asked him why he put up with it, Luka shrugged and said that at first he'd thought it was all part of being in a band or that if only he got better at playing, Drago would leave him alone.

"Now I think Drago is just another crazy bastard," said Luka. "And maybe I'm a crazy bastard too."

It was true that Luka was looking paler and more hollow-eyed, and that he was often too lost in thought to answer Christoff's many questions. More and more often, Drago interrupted the music with an enormous crash of cymbals, flinging his drumsticks at the back of Luka's head, startling Christoff out of the exact point in his reverie where he imagined himself on his own mountain peak with his white guitar. One evening Luka stopped playing completely, unslung his guitar, and threw it to the floor. The distortions resounded like thunderbolts.

"You're speeding up the rhythm and then slowing it down to throw me off," he said. "It's because of your endless bullying we never play outside of this hole."

"You guitarists think you're above everything," said Drago. "But you're no better than any one of us down here in the real world."

"I would rather play alone in a cave for a thousand years than another minute with you," said Luka, packing his guitar into its case. He stormed past Christoff.

"Anyone could play better than that bastard. Even you," said Kugel, looking over at Christoff. "Yes," said Drago, peering at him over his drum kit. "Why not you?"

Christoff hesitated. A part of him felt that he should also storm out of the hall and join his friend. Another part of him thought of his own agonized contortions in front of the mirror, and the scales he'd practised until his fingers bled. He thought about the feeling he'd had, since stepping through the embellished steel door, of being destined for something higher than the European Fine Meats and Delicatessen. Perhaps, in the grand scheme of things, he had been meant to take Luka's place. He unsheathed his guitar from its case and plugged it into the abandoned amplifier. He was shocked at how easily his fingers flew up and down the neck. But then, he had learned the songs and followed Luka's movements so slavishly that it seemed just— but only just—within the realm of possibility.

"You can play with us for now," said Drago.

"But only until we find someone else," said Kugel, again aiming his bass guitar at Christoff like it was a gun.

Now, instead of at Luka, Drago's hi-hats clapped together behind Christoff like the beak of a prehistoric bird, slackened off mid-song so that Christoff stumbled over his own fingers. Whenever Christoff heard his own heart thudding in his chest, he saw Drago's foot on the bass drum. At night practising scales on his white guitar, he heard Drago clubbing harder and harder, until it felt as though he was being hunted down by a whole tribe of drummers.

He was so exhausted that he started wrapping the wrong meats for customers, falling asleep in the back storeroom only to be shaken awake by his furious father. He slit his finger on the cutting machine and swore to his mother, as she wrapped the finger and wiped the blood from the steel blade, that he wouldn't work at the European Fine Meats and Delicatessen anymore. When she pleaded with him, he threw his apron on the floor.

He went home and reached under the bed for his guitar, climbed up and up through the scales despite the throbbing in his cut finger. He had hidden the guitar and spirited it in and out of the house so often without either of his parents catching sight of the thing that it was a shock to open his eyes and see both of them standing open-mouthed in his bedroom doorway. He leapt to his feet when his father staggered into the room with his fists clenched, then swung his guitar over his head like it was an axe. The two men stood transfixed.

"I'll smash your bastard head," said Christoff.

Slowly, miraculously, his father backed out of the room. Christoff filled a bag with clothes while his mother begged him not to leave. He looked pityingly at the embroidered kerchief she always wore around the house.

"I'll find somewhere for us," he said. "I'll send for you."

As he walked down the street he imagined filling a house with the golden furniture she loved. They would live happily ever after while his father raged and sputtered elsewhere. In the meantime, Christoff rented a room with a rickety bed and table in a rundown house with blocked drains and a host of other inhabitants he heard pausing in the corridor outside but who seemed to vanish down the hallway every time he cracked open the flimsy door.

"They're like ghosts," he told Hanna. "I never see their faces."

He was beginning to feel like a ghost himself, turning up at practices that Drago had arranged only to find the space empty and dark. He had haunted the alleyway behind the European Fine Meats and Delicatessen, hoping that his mother might slip him a few slivers of sausage. He had called at Hanna's only to be turned away at the door by her parents, who had heard at church about his running away from home. Christoff had finally managed to get through to her on the phone, and she had promised to bring him some money and something to eat.

But Hanna had come empty-handed, twisting her tawny hair nervously with her fingers. Her parents had caught her filling a basket from the refrigerator.

"It's not just the basket," she said in a low voice, avoiding his gaze. "I dreamt last night that we didn't love each other anymore."

"You can't just believe in stupid dreams," said Christoff.

"You're the one who wanted the world to end," she said.

Christoff contemplated his guitar after Hanna left. He'd hoped it might be magical for a while. Now he wondered if it might not be cursed. There was no practice arranged for that day, but Christoff went down to the hall, heard Drago's bass drum thudding like a heartbeat, and knew before he reached the doorway what he would see in the brightly lit space. Kugel with his sneer. Bare-chested Drago with his mane of snarled hair, his drum kit spread beneath his muscled torso. And Christoff's replacement, bent over a black guitar, his face obscured by the hood of an army surplus jacket.

He wondered what his life would have been like if he'd walked through any of the other steel doors in the practice hall, or if each one contained its own Drago. It occurred to Christoff that Drago could no more stop bullying than the seven-headed serpent he reminded Christoff of could stop wanting to wrap its tail around the world. The anger blasting from his father's mouth didn't belong to him any more than the music that Christoff had slaved over belonged to his white guitar. When his father died the rage would blare from someone else's mouth, and its fists would find another face, just as someone other than Christoff was now setting the ham hocks and pigs' feet in neat rows beneath the glass countertops at the European Fine Meats and Delicatessen.

He was lightheaded and not at all hungry on his way back through the snow-covered alley to his rooming house. When he saw that the padlock on his door had been broken, he knew before looking under his bed that the guitar had been stolen. He stood in the centre of the room with his head bowed, and his fingers needled the air. He writhed like a knight with a mythical beast. He staggered like a man in a death scene. He didn't need Drago's drums, or slivers of meat fine as stained glass. He had the notes in his head climbing higher than ever, and they were more real than anything.

In the Company of Others

A dozen of us were dressed up as low-budget ghosts outside Earl's Court tube station. We'd gathered there for a night shoot, and my instructions from the director were to stand stock-still staring up at the sky. The evening was chilly, and while my fellow ghosts flitted and capered among the tube-goers, I entered the initial stages of rigor mortis. I went AWOL when my teeth started chattering uncontrollably, and ducked into a nearby tea room. What good is a chattering ghost? I sat down opposite a large woman who had the expression of a person who had been both lured in and contented by the pink frosted angel cake positioned on a revolving cake stand in the window. Apart from a few crumbs and a smear of icing, the plate in front of her was empty. When some of my fellow ghosts drifted past the window clutching fuzzy microphones, she asked me what the hell we were doing. I held my jaw steady to stop the chattering.

"We're interviewing people to find out what they most want to do before they die."

She looked at my white-sheeted body and stared at my hood with its cut-out eye sockets. It occurred to me that we might look like something altogether more sinister than dress-up ghosts.

"We're ghosts," I explained. "We're a performance group making a movie."

"Oh," she said, in a tone that made it clear she not only didn't understand me but also thought I was crazy. She eyed me suspiciously again. "What's it about?"

The overarching idea, I explained, was to splice the interviews together into a collage: a shimmering spool of collective dreams interspersed with ghostly antics. It was a film, I said, about the dream that is life. At least, that was the spiel that Warren, our director, told us to tell. Who knows what alchemical processes the footage would undergo back at the studio, and what Warren would make of their earnestness or desperation.

"That sounds nice," she said. Her expression softened and her voice mellowed. "I'd like to see it sometime."

I actually voted against having Warren as director, and I hated the new name he'd persuaded everyone to vote on: *The Company of Others*. Sure, he has a lot of administrative experience. Sure, he knows how to write a good proposal. But his creative work has always struck me as a little superficial. I tore a corner off my paper napkin and offered to send her an invitation to our first screening.

"If we ever have a screening."

"I'm sure you will," she said. "After going to so much trouble and making such, ahem, authentic-looking costumes."

Neither of us had a pen, and so we both stared up instead at a fancy brass hook that had been screwed high into the tea room wall for no apparent reason. My hands, in the meantime, were still shaking enough that when I took a sip of the tea my waitress brought me it leapt from its cup and splashed onto the table.

The woman slung me her overcoat—a pearl-coloured affair lined in sateen. It slithered across the table at me.

"That ought to bring you back to the land of the living," she said, chuckling to herself.

I draped it over my shoulders and the shuddering eased. I leaned back and thanked her for the loan.

"It's nothing," she said. "Just an old thing from a few seasons ago."

She was quite elegantly dressed, I noticed, in the way that women with good taste and not a lot of money often are: the composition was artful but the materials let her down. The skirt and matching jacket were cut from pale green polyester. She wore a fake cameo brooch and matching ring set, the ivory plastic mounted onto a backdrop of washed coral.

When I started art school they encouraged us to make sculptures and installations out of anything we found in the street: TV parts, milk crates. The message was that with a little innovation, a concept, a little inspiration, anything could be art. Of course, nobody, especially the department, could supply us with the materials we needed otherwise. Our garbage picking was a necessity, but we were crazy for it. We were looting abandoned buildings, stripping copper wire, getting mildly electrocuted, gashing ourselves in junkyards and needing tetanus shots. We were filming ourselves in stolen cars, making sculptures out of household refuse and movies about our favourite brand of hot sauce. Most of us were reasonably well-off kids roughing it for the first time, and the students who'd grown up tough and poor became like minor cult figures because they could navigate their way around the slums we all roomed in and knew a thing or two about living on almost nothing.

By the time my final year rolled around the department got a fancy donor and decided to hold their first international festival around our final-year show. The plan was to add some serious glitz, make it a big hit on the art circuit. The festival director invited some expensive acts. A full brass orchestra playing dance music. A man dressed in a steel angel suit with a twenty-foot wingspan who planned to suspend himself in the main hall. There were some questionable live animal shows off campus, one involving a herd of pantomime horses. For the final act, the director hired two performance artists who billed themselves as the Naked Siberian Poets and did some kind of shamanistic sideshow with drums she thought would be perfect to wrap up the evening.

Nobody in the company knows this, but I joined the army straight after I graduated from secondary school. I did it to impress my father. He served in the war and always made a big deal out of military stuff, said the discipline was what made him a man. I knew even before basic training was finished what a colossal mistake I'd made and quit as soon as I could. Then I spent a year living in Marseille trying to figure out what to do with the rest of my life. There was a beach I liked to go to in the early evening where the sun set just right. It was right next to a rehabilitation facility for men who'd served in the French Foreign Legion. The stuff they got up to in the facility's yard rivalled anything I've ever witnessed in terms of radiant, crazy weirdness. There were guys screaming, performing Olympics-worthy gymnastics and bizarre feats of strength, guys with post-traumatic stress disorder rocking back and forth with towels over their heads, guys re-enacting scenes of torture, guys on too much medication taking those giant tiptoe steps you mostly associate with pale inner-city ex-psychiatric patients. But these guys were buff and bronzed as Greek gods, standing on a clifftop looking out over the Mediterranean. They were like centaurs or some kind of mythical creature that might suddenly appear in your humdrum life, and they exerted a near-magical hold over anyone who laid eyes on them. Most of the facility was fenced off, but there were a few metres that adjoined the public beach leading down to the sea. Some of the most beautiful girls I've ever seen in my life flocked to those adjoining sections to lay themselves out like human sacrifices on beach towels and score a date.

Those legionnaires were the first thing that came to my mind when I saw the Naked Siberians. It was hard to tell where their dense body hair ended and the mangy bits of fur that made up their costumes began. But beneath the layer of fur their bodies were chiselled. They were at least half a head taller than anyone else in the room, and looked even more imposing with the tawny, gnarled antlers they had strapped, somehow seamlessly, to their hair-matted heads. They had a rank, feral smell and their eyes burned with the intensity of biblical prophets.

They were not, by any stretch, the arty male strippers the festival director had imagined she was hiring. Moreover, they were furious about headlining for a depraved Eurotrash audience in a tricked-out golden cafeteria. Rumours about their previous feats flew across campus. The word was, for example, that they had once roller-skied from Finland to St. Petersburg attired solely in fur loincloths and antlers so they could sabotage a performance piece they disapproved of. Sometimes they simply menaced, their antlered shapes appearing like ill omens in background photos and video documentation. Often, though, they sabotaged with holy fervour, purging anything they considered pretentious and finding ways to humiliate its maker. For months after a visitation, every artist in a community they'd made an appearance in would glance nervously out into the audience to see if two pairs of antlers were there.

Their vengeance, in our case, was swift and brutal. Onstage, they howled their earth-shattering Siberian shaman songs to a spellbound audience and banged on goatskin drums with what looked like two sets of mastodon bones. Only at the end of the performance did they approach two microphones and call the festival director a bourgeois cunt. Then they dared the flabby oil men sponsoring the festival to remove their sinister overcoats and join them naked onstage.

The next day, they set about sabotaging the whole of our final-year show, dismantling our star pupil's wall of cracked TV screens playing slo-mo footage from a horror movie, smashing key pieces from installations into smithereens, unbolting the angel suit and leaving it in a pile of little steel jigsaw pieces on the floor. But the crucial thing was that they weren't without mercy. They cloaked a crude robot in some of their rank fur and placed it on a tump of grass, transforming an otherwise blah piece into something extraordinary. They set fire to a spooky dollhouse and filmed the burning on video, and the ruined house, with the accompanying video, got picked up by the best gallery in the country the following year. By the time the festival director called the police these guys were fucking heroes, living gods we searched for at afterparties just to catch a glimpse of those antlers, those eyes, and, at least in my case, hope that a little of their fire might rub off. But they left as quickly as they'd appeared, and as far as I know, nobody from my graduating year ever saw them in real life again.

Ghosts flew past the tea room window. My large companion laughed and we craned our necks and watched as a pair tumbled between two parked cars.

"You know," she said, "I ought to go out and tell them about Vienna. This is going to sound crazy to you." She paused for a moment, and then feigned a comical look at the ghost costume. "Or maybe not."

It started after she read a book where the characters moved to Vienna for a while. Something about the way the author described the city took root and opened up inside her like the petals of a hothouse flower.

"I couldn't even point out Austria on a map before then," she said.

She told me how she started going to the library during her lunch hours and reading up on Viennese culture. The more she read, the more she fell in love with the idea of going there. She fantasized about scenarios with archdukes encountered on museum staircases or in the cloisters of medieval abbeys. But in the end, all she really wanted was to just wander around soaking up the atmosphere.

"I wanted to *live* there," she said. "Not visit. If you know what I mean."

She wanted to lose herself completely, shed her old life and explore the boulevards and the avenues, sit on a bench in a gated park and eat chestnuts. She wanted to frequent the famous Viennese coffee houses and eat pastries as elaborate as Venetian facades served by flaxen-haired maidens in frilled caps. She wanted to open her balcony doors and breathe cool air blown in from a snow-tipped Alp.

"I opened a savings account," she told me. "And I started to put by for moving day."

She kept the account hidden from her no-good husband and her troublesome son, stuffing ten dollars here and there into an envelope, tucking loose change into a stocking in her underwear drawer. She kept reading and learning about the city and the ways of its people. She knew her stuff too—the names of all the imperial palaces and the principal buildings on the Hofburg boulevard. She acquainted herself with the various empires and occupations.

"I knew it was crazy," she said. "It was a fever. Like falling in love. It was glorious."

Sometimes she relented and decided to take the boy along with her. He was young enough to become fluent in German, she thought. And sometimes she also allowed the husband to join them in her daydreams. It would do him good to be out of his element. She could picture him—a surly, badly dressed man strolling down the avenues among the elegant Viennese.

He would be slowly transformed and arrive at some important realizations, like a character in a novel.

And of course the idea of all those Viennese balls dazzled her. From dusk to dawn, all those gloved hands meeting above a sea of rustling silks. The way she described it all, I felt I was right there with her in the ballroom, spinning under a gold-leaf chandelier. She said she'd met a girl of Austrian descent at the library who flew back to attend as many as she had time and money for. There were over two hundred balls a year, she told me.

The statistic brought me back to the real world—or at least to the tea room with its yellowing posters of Corfu. She noted the way my eyes dropped and then looked quickly away from her enormous bust. Lolling on folds of thick, green-suited flesh, each one of her breasts was easily the size of my head. Her eyes narrowed.

"I know what you're thinking. But that Austrian girl wasn't your average Cinderella either. In fact, she had to sew an elasticized panel in her gown after her baby was born. Trust me, she was big-boned to begin with."

And anyway, she continued, just knowing that the balls were happening all around her was the important thing. The idea of her surrounded by all that swirling lace and silk had me picturing her as a kind of kitsch plus-sized Venus rising from the foam. I looked around to see if any of my fellow ghosts were near the restaurant. Someone, I thought, should make a note of all this.

She smiled and blushed and shook her head, mashing a few crumbs on her plate with her thumb. She never went, of course. Things got in the way. There were bills and setbacks, illnesses and surgeries. And it was no good just going for a vacation with what little savings were left, she explained. She had invested too much time and energy to turn around and come back again. She sighed, and the waitress, noting her air of dissatisfaction, refilled our cups with tea.

I knew the book she was talking about. It was on the best-seller list for years and was then made into a movie. I was warm by now and getting a little restless. What was I supposed to say to this woman who'd just told me her story and who sat across from me now smoothing the folds of her cheap skirt, humming tunelessly?

The cameraman appeared in the window, his shoulder sagging with the weight of his ancient camera as he panned the street for ghosts or potential interviewees. Instead of motioning to him, I leaned back in my chair. Fuck Warren, I thought. Ghosts, okay. But hopes and dreams? I stretched my legs out carefully so as not to disturb the coat draped over my shoulders. Then I told her about a similar experience I'd had myself.

A few of us formed the company after art school, lived out in a big barn owned by Warren's parents for a while to develop our mission. We went back and forth between absurdism and minimalism, staged a few performances, and were perennially strapped for cash. Then Warren got us a small starter grant to stage a deconstructed version of *A Doll's House* using elements of kabuki theatre. The kabuki was my idea. Not everybody knows this, but kabuki was originally performed from morning until sunset in the dry riverbeds of medieval Kyoto.

I researched all the revolving stages and trap doors used to realize kabuki themes of revelation and transformation, and the way the actors layered their costumes and whipped them off in order to reveal their character's nature. The way we put it in the grant proposal was that we wanted to find a way to use those devices to expose our own imaginings of ourselves, to undo the premises of realism by emphasizing the strings attached.

The woman was still listening politely at this point, but I noticed how her eyes lingered more and more often on the poster of Corfu closest to our table.

"In the meantime," I said, "the members of our troupe fell victim to a series of personal disasters."

She looked at me with renewed interest. I wasn't lying. Gary, one of the founders, developed a case of shingles so severe he was blinded in one eye. Then Katia went into rehab and the Ibsen-kabuki grant application was turned down. When one of our stagehands suggested that maybe the universe was trying to tell us something, we agreed to disband temporarily.

But I couldn't let it go. Every day I went to the public library and leafed through books about Japan. I read guidebooks and histories and squinted at sepia photographs of rigid, tiny royal figures. I daydreamed about moving to one of the mountainous lesser islands in the north, where the waters of the ceremonial basins froze overnight, and I could live cheaply with a tatami mat and a simple futon that I rolled up in the morning and tied with a rope.

"Oh yes," said the woman. "I had my dream worked out right down to the last detail of my apartment building's foyer."

The more I immersed myself in Japan, the more the real world became an unchanging place to which I returned like a hotel room between forays to the library.

"I've never been a spiritual person," I told her. "I didn't want to go to Japan to meditate or study Zen Buddhism or pray at Shinto temples or worship the flowering cherry."

What I wanted was to stroll around with my hands empty, the same way this nice lady wanted to sit on a bench in a gated Viennese park. I wanted to take in the air. I wanted to be done once and for all with that division between art and life.

"For a few days," I told her, "everything was distilled and perfect in a way I've never known before or since."

She brushed a stray crumb from her blouse. The epiphany came during an Elvis Presley competition at a cheap bar near our studio. The walls were painted black and it was a very cave-like space. Elvis after Elvis went on, each one replicating the familiar Elvis movements like florid priests performing a series of rites. You could almost imagine the crowd lighting incense sticks and making sacrificial offerings.

Time, I thought, will hollow out the specificities of these gestures the way the sea empties and polishes a shell. The gyrations we were watching would lose their particular Elvis attributes, become formalized into the glyph-like movements performed by dancers of the future, the way primitive drawings became the letters of an alphabet. From that moment on, I've been a little obsessed. I once arranged and rearranged the same table and four chairs for eleven hours onstage at a festival.

"It's funny," I said to her. "It was such a defining moment, and yet I forgot all about it until just now."

But it wasn't *the* defining moment. The defining moment, if there ever is one, happened on the day those Naked Siberians blazed a trail in and out of my life. I looked for them, I

KERRY LEE POWELL

asked after them everywhere I went. There were sightings of antlers at festivals and performances, probably fakes. There was some dumb gossip among the more salacious that the oil guys had had them hunted down and offed for trying to humiliate them. I heard from a friend that one of the Siberians had made his living all along as a fencing master, and that the other was a practising psychoanalyst, that the whole shaman thing was just a radical gimmick. I didn't buy it then and I don't buy it now. Their eyes still burn a hole right through me, as if they had a direct line back to a more primitive, mysterious world.

Every piece, every show I ever did after that, I was looking for those antlers in the crowd, waiting for those sometimes kind or sometimes wrathful hands to descend. The longer they don't appear, the starker and flatter my world becomes. All my work, even that big Japanese diversion, has been addressed to their absence.

My companion shifted in her seat and motioned towards the window. "I think your friends are looking for you," she said.

I turned to see two ghosts with their hoods removed: Warren with the neck of his dirty sweater showing and Rufus with his straggly goatee trembling in the tea room's reflected light.

"You know, I realized a while ago that I was never going to make it to Vienna," said the woman. "But I still throw five dollars or so into my drawer every now and again just to keep the dream alive. It's too good to let it go completely."

The cameraman joined the two ghosts and looked at me inquiringly. I probably should have told Warren the woman's story. But it felt good to keep another secret and let her dream go unmolested. The thing about Warren is that he's always trying to make things so human. Whereas me, I'm all about the empty gesture. I shrugged the coat off my shoulders and handed it back to her. We both became awkward, like people stuck in an elevator who trade their deepest hopes and fears only to walk away strangers after the doors have been prised apart. I felt my face stiffen into a mask of good manners. I might have even bowed to her slightly before pulling the hood over my head. Warm now and feeling more than a little foolish, I joined my fellow ghosts outside.

VULNERABLE ADULTS

When the pamphlet came through the slot they were in the middle of a small fight. A small fight being when they teased each other but with higher than normal voices and more rigid than usual faces. It could have turned into a big fight: things were getting higher and stiffer by the minute, but the pamphlet stopped all that.

WANTED: GOOD HOMES FOR VULNERABLE ADULTS

"Give me that," said Lauren. The pamphlet said that the social services were desperate to find good homes where vulnerable adults could reintegrate themselves into the community.

"Pretty good money," said Jacko, leaning over Lauren's shoulder.

She frowned. "This is crazy. Anybody could get hold of this and mistreat them."

"Who cares," said Jacko. "They're retards."

"Who are?"

"Vulnerable adults." He smiled. "I'm just fooling with you," he said.

"Oh," said Lauren. She had moved to London a few years previously from Illinois and sometimes had trouble knowing if British people were being crass or ironic. Perhaps, also, the word "retard" was acceptable here.

"Let's get some! We could train them to clean," said Jacko. "We could get them to build a shed out back. They could live in it and do our bidding. Bring us tea and make our beds."

"I could train one to be my personal maid," said Lauren, joining in on the joke.

"She could iron your shoulder pads," said Jacko.

"I can't believe we just said that," said Lauren.

He put the pamphlet in his miscellaneous folder.

Jacko was an artist. A real artist, Lauren liked to say, especially to members of her family who questioned her decision-making skills.

"More wacko than Jacko," was how her Illinois aunt had put it after a week-long visit that went askew.

He'd had a brush with fame with some pen-and-ink sketches of stills from eighties porno movies that he'd had made into toile wallpaper. The toile had appeared in a few art magazines and got him represented by a high-end gallery. But Jacko hadn't liked the attention, insisted the whole toile thing was a prank. Then a celebrity had bought the piece from Jacko's gallery and had his dressing room papered with it. The bathroom got into all the main rags and Jacko had gone berserk, assaulting an arts beat reporter and threatening to strap a bomb under a tabloid journalist's car.

That was three years ago. Since then, he'd drunk a lot of tea and watched a lot of daytime TV. Lauren respected the reasons behind Jacko's withdrawal from the art scene. He wasn't in it for fame or money. He wanted to make work that disrupted comfortable or shallow-minded notions about reality. He wanted to go deep, delve into nether regions where even other artists feared to go. He needed to come up with something that undid the damage that the porno toile had done to his reputation. So that people wouldn't think he was, in his words, a fucking decorator. To this end he kept a miscellaneous folder of potential ideas. So far, nothing had seriously spoken to him.

Lauren was not an artist. She was an art lover in the most primitive sense, drawn to certain shapes and colours, scenes that reminded her of something else. In the beginning she had seen her relationship with Jacko as a kind of anthropological journey that might lead her into a more profound understanding of herself and the world. After a few months of having Jacko poke holes in her comments and sneer at her vacuous questions, art had become a sensitive topic in the house. Even now she felt jumpy, slicing vegetables with a diagonal slant and arranging them on the cutting board in a pretty pattern while the radio played soothing music. She quickly disarranged them when she heard Jacko come in from the living room.

"I can't believe she's gone and shagged the next-door neighbour," he said, grabbing her by the shoulders from behind. "The silly tart."

"Who?" she asked. He kept a running commentary of soap operas he watched, weaving their narratives with events from their actual lives so that she was never sure if what he was saying was real or not. "As if our own lives aren't ridiculous enough," she said. But Jacko had already gone back into the living room.

She heated the wok until it smoked, then tossed the pretty vegetables in. The soothing music was gone, replaced with some opera that was heavy on the cymbals. She switched the radio off and listened instead to the boom of the TV through the wall.

Later on when she couldn't sleep, she switched the bedside light back on and tried to distract herself by reading an article about feng shui and how to keep evil spirits at bay through the careful arrangement of household items. It was difficult to understand the diagrams and instructions. She threw the magazine down and turned off the light and thought of all the spirits that might, according to the article, be whirling around overhead.

When she came home from work a few days later, Jacko had made two more of his puppets. This was the single artistic endeavour he'd embarked upon since the toile debacle. They were featureless, crudely hand-stitched from a bolt of yellowing flannelette he'd found at a car boot sale. He had never taken them out of the house and she often found them in odd places, falling out of the kitchen cupboard, or half-buried in the laundry hamper. They looked to Lauren like the ghosts of Victorian orphans, and it startled her to come upon their blank faces, although he had explained to her he'd left them blank intentionally because he felt it was up to him to make them seem happy or sad with the movements of his hands.

On her way upstairs to the bedroom she glanced out the landing window into the back garden of her neighbour's terraced house. There was a small, stumpy girl sitting on an ornamental bench between two gaudy gnomes and a small blue plastic pond. Her hands were folded together and the corners of her mouth were turned down. She was wearing a red corduroy dress and a red jacket. Beneath the jacket's hood, two slightly slanted eyes stared up at her.

"The neighbours have got a vulnerable adult," she said.

He came upstairs to look, wiping the glue from his hands. They both stared at the girl, who had turned her face away from them and now appeared to be staring into the empty plastic pond.

"That was fast," said Jacko.

"She looks unhappy," said Lauren.

Lauren and her friend were sitting in the kitchen drinking ginger tea and eating sun-dried bananas.

"I'm a sucker for details," said Lauren's friend. "Sometimes I watch movies just for the scenery and to see what outfits the actresses are wearing."

Lauren poured more tea.

"Even if it's a really stupid movie."

"I wish I was a character in a movie," said Lauren. "A different movie."

"I always pretend I'm a character in a book or movie," said Lauren's friend. "It's what makes life worth living."

They laughed again and ate more bananas.

Jacko came into the kitchen. He held his arms up high in the air so that the two puppets appeared to stare down at them.

"I'd like to interrupt this program with another message from the department of social services."

"Now is not the time," said Lauren. She put her hands over her eyes.

Jacko lowered one puppet and curled his hand inward to

make the puppet look sad. "Mommy bit me," he said in a high tremolo, his lips only barely moving.

They all stared at the puppets and then at each other.

"Oh my God," Lauren's friend said. "That is so funny, Jacko. You're a scream!" She got up and snatched the puppet off his hand and examined it. "Look at the stitching," she said. "Did you make this yourself?"

He smiled weakly at her and took the puppet back, then went back into the living room.

Lauren looked at her friend and felt as though there was very little left to chat about. It was getting dark so quickly now that fall was here. They both sat for a moment in silence.

"Oh, I get it," said Lauren's friend, sitting upright. "It's like those dolls they use to get children to talk in the police stations."

After Lauren's friend left Jacko came back into the kitchen with his hands curled into fists, the puppets like floppy boxing gloves over top of them.

"You were trying to *belittle* me in front of your friend," he said.

"You were being a creep."

"Your friend didn't think so," said Jacko.

"How do you know? She could have just been humouring you."

"I saw the way she was looking at me."

"This isn't one of your soap operas," said Lauren.

"It is if I say so," said Jacko.

Later, in bed, she thought about what else the visiting aunt from Illinois had said about Jacko after the first evening she'd spent in his company.

"I get that he's a real artist. But maybe he's *more* than just a real artist. Maybe he's also a real crazy guy."

Lauren had sulked and said something trite about how all artists were blessed with a touch of madness, and the aunt had snorted.

"Honey, who wants to shack up with van Gogh?"

The girl was so often there, wedged between the two gaudy gnomes, staring ahead into the plastic pond that had been drained for winter and was now covered with a ragged piece of black tarpaulin. Lauren found herself looking down every time she went upstairs, contemplating what the girl might be thinking or experiencing as she sat so quietly, with her hands laced in her lap. When Lauren switched the hall landing light on she saw tea rings on the window ledge, and realized Jacko was also looking down on her. He came up the stairs behind Lauren and put his arms around her shoulders.

"She seems quiet and peaceful," said Lauren. "I don't understand how she doesn't get cold sitting out there."

"I hear it's a big problem in the group homes," said Jacko. "Keeping them from fucking each other all the time. They don't acquire all the niceties and mores that go along with conventional courtship. I bet she's missing the freewheeling orgiastic days squirming around on the floor with all her buddies."

"That's not a nice thing to say," said Lauren.

"I only say what everyone else is thinking," said Jacko.

This was one of his favourite pronouncements, as though everyone's darkest thoughts were connected in a series of underground caverns.

"They bring them out here and let them get all lonely," said Lauren.

"It's called reintegrating them into the community," said Jacko.

Lauren came in, dropped her grocery bags on the floor in front of the couch, and sat down. Jacko was watching TV with the sound turned down. He sometimes liked to scrutinize the facial expressions of the actors without knowing what they were saying.

"I think I'm losing my mind," she said. "I'm looking at everyone now and wondering if they're vulnerable adults too."

"Me too," said Jacko. "I mean, I'm wondering if everybody is a vulnerable adult too."

"I bought one of those aromatherapy steamers for the house," she said, kicking the bag in front of her. "To make it smell nicer. Have you noticed how stale and damp the house is smelling lately?"

Jacko turned the sound back up while Lauren went into the kitchen and tried to assemble the new steamer. The instructions were difficult to follow and no matter how hard she tried, she couldn't find a place for all the pieces. She pushed the steamer off the table and watched the pieces scatter across the floor.

"Feeling vulnerable?" said Jacko. She threw the empty box at him.

"Why don't I take care of dinner," he said. "I'll bake a hamster. I'll build a shed and fill it with vulnerable adults to do our bidding and make us feel powerful and all-knowing."

She went upstairs to collect her thoughts, but instead of going to their bedroom she went to the guest room and lay down on the single bed. It was the chilliest room in the house and she lay motionless for a while, getting colder and colder. She could hear the sound of pots and pans and cutlery, and what sounded like the pieces of the new steamer being swept up in the kitchen. She was almost too cold to get up and wrap herself in the blanket she knew was draped across the rocking chair in the corner. It was a mystery to her how she, a grown woman with a sensible job, could allow herself to feel so helpless. The mysteriousness of her own actions made her nervous. What else was going on beneath the surface of her daily life? She forced herself up finally, and walked stiffly over to the blanket, knowing that if she looked out the window she would have a direct view into the neighbouring garden. Lauren had a sudden horror of seeing the squat little girl there in the dusk.

"I'm not going to look," she said to herself, but she glimpsed the red jacket out of the corner of her eye, deepened to maroon in the darkened garden. Lauren went back to the bed and curled up into a fetal position under the wool until Jacko came up the stairs.

"Your morsels are served," he said.

She was crying by then, but she brushed the tears away, smiling gratefully at Jacko's silhouette in the hallway. She was hungry, and the morsels, whatever they were, smelled good.

She had actually, literally, gone beneath the surface once, with a boyfriend from college who belonged to a speleological club.

"It's like a palace beneath the earth," he'd said, inviting her to accompany them on their day trip.

She had agreed despite having a mild case of claustrophobia, thinking of the rainbow-lit caves on tourist pamphlets she'd seen on trips as a child. She only really started to panic when the speleological club's van deposited them at a hole in the ground no bigger than a manhole, with a single iron rail and ladder leading down. There wasn't a kiosk in sight, nor any of the well-meaning guides with soft drawls she'd become accustomed to on her own adventures into the wilds. They had closed the caves to the general public years ago, the driver of the van told her, without explaining why.

The group, ten in all, got out, put on hardhats, and armed themselves with flashlights.

"Everyone is required to carry three sources of light in case there's a problem," said the boyfriend, whose name she had long ago banished from her memory. She still remembered, though, the sound of each rung on the ladder as they descended, and the way his words echoed in her mind. Three sources of light for three problems, like a gift from a fairy-tale witch. Each light extinguishing itself after the battery wore out.

"What kind of problems?"

He was too far down by then to hear her. The person below her on the ladder called up.

"Some of the caves are man-made from dynamiting they did for minerals a hundred years ago."

She was halfway down the ladder, looking up at the clouds above the tiny opening.

"That doesn't make me feel any better," she'd said.

She was the odd one out, the only non-science major. They

had laughed at, instead of with, her. She had an urge to skitter back up, but the thought of the club members waiting at the bottom, possibly staring in disdain at her rump and rather chunky legs, made her quickly descend despite the clammy feeling in the pit of her stomach.

There were no rainbow lights. The pencil beams from the flashlights and the larger beams from their hats lit up the draped crags slick with damp and the tunnels veering off like tentacles in all directions. Several of them were barricaded with chain links and wooden boards branded with the words "Access Forbidden."

"I'm surprised we're not seeing any bats," said the only other girl among them, a blonde who looked like the Norwegian troll dolls that Lauren had played with as a child. When they headed, single file, towards one of the lesser tunnels, Lauren had lingered behind them and then tripped. She turned back towards the ladder, intending to go back up to the surface for a Band-Aid.

"Don't worry about me," she called out while her boyfriend lifted the chain link so that the other members could enter more easily into the forbidden area. "I'll wait in the van."

In fact she stayed down in the cavern for another twenty minutes, too paralyzed with fear to take a step in case the earth's crust might crumble overhead and bury her alive. It was only when she heard movements, possibly echoes from the vanished group as they explored whatever deeper caverns they'd been intent on reaching, or possibly something much more sinister, that she'd scrambled back up the iron rungs and hoisted herself through the hole.

The van was locked, the keys tucked in the driver's pocket, and it was far colder on the surface than she'd expected, the sun obscured by heavy clouds. For the first hour she'd circled around the vehicle, hugging her arms for warmth and squatting when she felt tired. She did jumping jacks to warm up after she started shivering uncontrollably. Then the panic started to overwhelm her again. She was alone in a barren waste, prey to any ranging beast that might spot her from a distance. She remembered reading in the newspaper about a girl who had been torn to pieces by coyotes that surrounded her while she hiked with a pair of headphones on. It had sounded like something from an old ballad, she'd thought. Well, except for the headphones. Now it sounded like a harbinger of her own demise.

After four hours she was numb enough from the wind and terrified enough of the animals she imagined were surrounding her in invisible droves to wedge herself underneath the van.

Who was dumber in the end, her or the club members down below with their foolish grins as they ducked under the chain link into the forbidden caves? They had all resurfaced singing the "Heigh-Ho" song from *Snow White*, giddy with in-jokes from their underworld journey. They had seen walls whorled with semi-precious stones and a winding river full of albino cave fish. She had managed, at least, to scramble up from beneath the van before they caught her under there. Because it was dusk they couldn't make out the grease stains or her face, with its look of terror mingled with abandonment.

The boyfriend she'd dumped after the rumbling van ride home. A month later she'd applied for a grant to come to

England, had clung to the genteel landscapes and revelled in the enclosures and little pockets of ancient forest where there always seemed to be a yellow field shining through the gaps in the trees. The panic had come back once or twice in the labyrinthine basements of big museums, but on the whole she'd felt safe flitting between lecture halls and libraries, bashfully unfurling a Klimt print in her bedsit after swooning at an exhibit of his swaddled women.

When she met Jacko at an opening, she had been half-giddy and half-frightened by his pitiless, freewheeling commentary on the artworks hanging in the gallery. He had depth and daring. After a few dates she thought that he might not just be the "the one," but that he might also help her make sense of her own puzzling interior.

After a couple of years of watching him slip from living room to kitchen with his cups of tea and his endless gloss on soap operas and minor household events, she'd come to realize he was wedged, like her, under the speleological club's van, scared of descending into the underworld, but just as terrified of whatever might be wandering vicious and free on the surface.

Lately, though, with his frantic pacings up and down, and the tea rings on the landing window, she wasn't sure if Jacko was still under the van with her. She often woke up in the middle of the night and felt the cold space where his body ought to have been. And then she invariably remembered her aunt's nasal voice and the way her eyes bulged for emphasis as she spun her finger slowly in the air around her ear. Wacko Jacko. Loco in the Coco.

"I'd like us to enrol," she said. "It would be good for our bodies and our minds. Very cleansing."

"Ethnically?"

"Very funny," said Lauren. "I'm serious. They say if you practise a lot it actually changes the way you see the world. The way you experience reality."

"We could get a black belt in meditation," said Jacko, striking a karate-chop pose.

She threw the folder down on the coffee table. "It's better than playing with puppets all day and watching TV. I want us to do something together. To grow as a couple."

Jacko narrowed his eyes. "Have you been playing with my puppets?"

"Look," she said again. "We've got to find our way out from under all this. I want both of us to be happy. Fulfilled. And other things like that."

Jacko crossed his arms and pressed them against his chest. "I'm not going to a local community centre to sit around with a bunch of cretins and hairdressers searching for inner harmony."

Lauren felt tacky and grubby all of a sudden, like one of those spritely do-gooders that nobody talked to if they could help it. She chewed her lip and decided not to tell him how she'd spent the afternoon quelling a panic attack by leafing through *The Children's Book of Illustrated Bible Stories* in a second-hand bookstore. She remembered all the stories from when she was a little girl, with their primitive blue, pink, and yellow pictures.

It was useless, she knew, to ask him to do anything he hadn't dreamed up himself. When she left the living room to go for a walk, she saw him slide the tai chi pamphlet into his miscellaneous folder.

She turned to him later that night after she slipped under the duvet, jogging his shoulder until he grunted softly.

He'd said, "We'll both be a lot happier if you keep quiet and things stay nice and simple."

It was the kind of thing a kidnapper might say to a hostage as he led her into some frightful hiding place.

"Have you ever believed in God?" she asked. "Or were you born like this?"

She spent the whole of the next day out, roaming from store to store, stopping in the park to stare at the ornamental trees wrapped in burlap now for the winter. When she returned, the house felt colder and damper than the afternoon air outside. Where was Jacko, who was always home? She went into the living room but it was empty, without so much as a faceless puppet in sight. She ran upstairs and looked in their bedroom and then in the guest bedroom, where the blankets were still mussed from the evening she'd spent lying curled up. She moved towards the window to look down into the neighbouring garden and then stopped herself from opening the curtain, grabbing her own wrist as though it was a stranger's.

"I'm not going to look," she said.

There Are Two Pools You May Drink From

My childhood friends have all disappeared. People die or get
unlisted numbers. Some people don't want to be found. I have
moved from place to place all my life, and the only time I ever
looked back was to make sure nobody was following. Lately,
though, even moving hasn't done the trick, and I've given up
on the idea that there's a mythical place where I'll find ever-
lasting happiness. A hell of a conversation with a fellow suf-
ferer on my lunch break got me thinking that the only way
to truly make peace with my former self was to face the people I'd spent so long trying to forget. And so one by one I've
started hunting down those hazy figures from my past, the
children hiding in the bodies of adults, tucked away in pockets
of the countryside like witnesses in a protection program.

The ones who bothered to answer my letters or phone calls
hadn't made much of their lives. They were scattered across
the country, but they all seemed to live in the same town,
encircled by the same fast-food chains and the same gleaming
megachurch, and the same crumbling elementary school with
a roof that leaked the way our old school roof leaked twenty

years ago. Maybe they'd gravitated to places that reminded them of back home. Maybe we were all under some kind of spell, the kind that dooms you to repeat your mistakes. A few were unemployed due to personal problems or what one of them called "the way things are heading in the world." More than a few had oxycodone issues and couldn't remember last week let alone what happened back in the mists. Eventually I found Sherry, my second-grade desk partner, living out of her trailer in a Walmart parking lot. She remembered everything, I could see by the look in her eyes while she handed me a cup of instant coffee, but she didn't want to talk. She especially didn't want to talk about Tully Blanchard.

"I put all that way behind me," she said. "And you should too."

"I did," I said. "But now it's so far behind me it's come up around the other end to smack me in the face."

She chuckled when I told her how Mickey Dodge and Lewis Calhoun—two of the worst bullies—had both built shelters they were filling up with canned food and ammunition for the coming apocalypse.

"They're practically frothing at the mouth about it," I said.

"That's poetic justice."

"Especially if the apocalypse *does* come. For them."

"It should," she said.

She took a flask out of her windbreaker and livened up our coffees. The one thing I managed to squeeze out of her was that the person I wanted to find the most lived less than fifty miles from my current address.

Lindy had married and changed her name from Moon to

Weeks. Her number was right there in my telephone book, and she answered before the first ring ended, as if she'd been waiting for my call.

She was an administrative assistant at one of those blank, mirrored buildings along the side of the highway. She lived in a bungalow. She told me these things in a flat, matter-of-fact voice. There was a long pause before she agreed to see me. It wasn't until I was halfway down the leaky tunnel headed out of town that I started to have doubts about seeing her. I decided not to tell her that I'd been looking for her for a long time.

I had met Lindy on the first day of school. I was new in town and trying to find the bus stop when I spotted her skipping ahead of me in a diamond-patterned dress with a ribbon that splayed out from her backside like a pair of red polyester wings. She heard my footsteps behind her and turned around to look. Her hair was curled into two ram's horns on either side of her forehead. The face was not quite a child's face. The eyes were set close. The nose was long and foxy. She turned her back on me and went ahead. I followed her down the hill.

The bus stop was by the marina. Broken hulls and pieces of rusting machinery were strewn around the boatyard and along the weedy riverfront. A set of crumbling green steps led down into the water. A group of boys writhed in a far corner, and the air was filled with high-pitched cries and gurgling noises. Lindy Moon paid no attention to any of this but stood in front of the marina's office window and stared at her reflection in the dusty glass, occasionally lifting up the corners of her stiff dress as if she was about to curtsy.

Over time I learned that the cries and gurgles belonged to Tully Blanchard, a small boy with the features that I associate now with fetal alcohol syndrome. He lived in an apartment across from the marina with his mother, who liked to sit on her balcony on hot days in a beige girdle and red-framed eyeglasses. When she was drunk she peered over the railings to slur at the people passing beneath her. More often she sat empress-like on her folding chair while her son was given Indian burns or dunked into the water. Her face was too far away for me to see whether she approved of the goings-on.

When the water froze they made him go out onto the ice. They bullied until he walked into the blasting wind, his hair blown up off his face like the cartoon survivor of an explosion. Bent-backed like an old pilgrim he crept towards the gash of open water while the ice cracked and shifted under his feet. He walked out so far I was sure he didn't mean to come back. Then the same hard, high voices were calling out to him from the shore to turn around.

But on that first day I crouched on the pavement and waited. I sat next to Lindy on the bus and admired the way her dress fanned out around her as we wound our way to a part of town where the river widened into a lake. We passed a yacht club and a large blue sign with WHITE LAKE ESTATES written on it in white sail cord. Rich kids poured onto the bus at each stop, filling the air with talk of music lessons and summer camps. Mothers and nannies waved from flower beds and circular driveways, from the doorways of houses with porticoes and Ionian columns.

Lindy lived across the street from me in a row house backing onto the town's water tower, a crumbling minaret surrounded by rusted chain-link fence. Drunks slept in the tall, parched grasses of the water tower yard on summer nights.

She was the youngest in a family of five boys. Each morning her mother dressed her up in doll-like outfits she bought at Woolworth's and Zellers. In spite of the fact that the Moons were as poor as, if not poorer than, anyone else in our neighbourhood, Lindy was an object of worship in her house and received one of every new kind of candy and flashy plastic toy that ever appeared in TV commercials. I have an image of her at Christmas, standing like a tiny priestess with a sea of sparkling presents at her feet.

I loved visiting the Moon kitchen, a grease-laden cave that stank of meat. The table had a plastic covering patterned with wagon wheels and rustic scenes. The Moons cooked foods I'd never seen before, in vats studded with dumplings. At dinner the Moon men mopped up their stews with slices of white bread and guzzled cartons of milk. They had a big cat-killing dog that they had trained to sit upright on a chair at the table, and they took turns feeding it buttered toast smeared with jam. After dinner, Mr. Moon sat in the kitchen if he wasn't at the tavern, drinking beer and bluing the air with swear words and tobacco smoke.

I used to stand next to the brown bear-shaped jar full of store-bought cookies and frosted industrial cakes. I was a hungry child. All the Moons teased me cruelly, describing the things they'd eaten before I came, or would eat soon after I left. Mrs. Moon called out to me from the living room whenever she thought she heard me sneaking into the jar. I remember one evening when a raw-boned Moon brother tossed cookie after cookie in an arcing rainbow to the dog, which caught each one in a delicate motion between its teeth before looking at me, flipping it back up into the air, and then swallowing it whole.

They say that kind of hunger never really leaves. It's all I can do to not pull up at every corner store I see and wolf down candy until I'm sick. The floor of my car is littered with empty wrappers: they rustle like autumn leaves when I open the door or roll down the window to ask for directions.

When we were kids, my brother used to say we'd be better off running away and learning how to live in the wilds. He had a Boy Scout handbook he'd picked up at a garage sale and was always flipping through it, learning about which berries weren't poisonous. But I don't blame my mother. She wasn't much more than a kid herself, alone and going through hell. If she could've snapped her fingers and had a chicken dinner appear at the table every night I'm sure she would have.

I thought about these things as I pulled up to the bungalow's long driveway. It was set so far back that it looked like a doll's house with taupe shutters and beige-coloured bricks. Beside it was a sagging white gazebo, the kind you buy at a hardware store and assemble at home. The gazebo's flapping curtains reminded me of a nomad's tent.

She unlocked the front door without looking at me and let me in. She wore a stone-grey skirt and blazer and was heavy limbed like her mother. The foxy nose and close-set eyes were encased in a marbling of fat. Her pink scalp showed through her cropped bronzy hair. Her face was taut and shiny, and I saw that it was also finely and elaborately scabbed. Her eczema had flared up, and moving her face too much cracked the skin and made the sores open again. She told me these things in the same privileged tone that always impressed me as a child, as if these were the glamorous markings of a tribe I would never belong to.

For almost as long as I've been alive, I've wanted to be someone else. Not a rock star or a millionaire but almost any stranger disappearing down the street or glanced at through a window on a darkened lawn. At one point during our friendship, I tried to curl my hair into Lindy's ram horns and branded the side of my neck with the curling iron. Even now with her eczema I felt my old jealousy stir.

I followed her into the kitchen and she made tea. Despite being so near, she had never visited the city where I lived. I described the lights and the cathedral, the fields and stunted pine forests that I had driven through on my way out.

"It couldn't be more different than the place we grew up," I said, as a way to introduce the subject.

We moved into her beige living room, balancing our overfull teacups. The walls were bare apart from a luminous rectangular clock that hung above her electric fireplace. She had lived there for ten years. She wrinkled her large, slightly pitted nose when I mentioned the gazebo. It was a disaster, she said. She couldn't bear to hear it flapping. It was coming down in the spring. She would pull it down with her own two hands. She frowned and stared at her lap.

We sat for a moment, not speaking, and I realized that what I thought was Turkish zither music being played in another room was the twang of her electric brazier's heating element.

She explained to me how she had moved to the bungalow after her father was diagnosed with Alzheimer's. They had put him in a home down the road, but sometimes he got out and wandered through the fields like an escaped convict in his striped pyjamas.

Mr. Moon had danced in the kitchen with his dog on hind legs. He had swaggered and brawled and been tossed out of taverns. He had gone on midnight raids and stolen sacks full of apples from a nearby orchard. He'd beaten his raw-knuckled sons when he thought they had shamed the Moon name and laughed when they told him about their pranks and adventures, some serious enough to involve visits from the police and the high school principal. Nobody realized how far gone he was until Mrs. Moon died. Now he remembered nothing, raging and sputtering at trees and telephone poles and birds passing overhead.

The Moons couldn't afford a babysitter, so we used to drive out with Mrs. Moon in her blue Nova to the White Lakes Estates where she dusted and scrubbed for the big houses. I loved going from house to house, out into the snow and the chilly lake wind and then back again into the long rooms full of African statues and Oriental vases.

Some of the White Lakes ladies took a shine to Mrs. Moon and followed her around in their silk hostess robes so they could talk about soap operas and Mrs. Moon's other customers. Mrs. Wallis gave her old clothes. Mrs. Lilic used to pour Mrs. Moon a thick, sweet liqueur and invite her to put her feet up in the parlour. She and her husband had escaped from an evil regime and come here as refugees. Look at us now, she would say to Mrs. Moon in her sticky accent. You never know what's going to happen. Lady Luck may lean down from the clouds and hand you a bouquet full of blank cheques. Mrs. Lilic was never satisfied, cruising the department stores and raiding the antique places. Mrs. Moon's living room was full of her cast-offs.

When the Lilics went on vacation to Florida, they gave Mrs. Moon a house key and asked her to keep an eye on things. After work Mr. and Mrs. Moon, the Moon boys, and Lindy piled into the blue Nova and sneaked over to the Lilic house, crammed themselves into a small den off the kitchen to watch TV and drink Coke out of Mrs. Lilic's crystal glassware while Lindy and I wandered through the house touching all the vases and the figurines.

In the master bedroom we climbed onto the four-poster Gothic-style bed and lay down on the satin spread. Maybe it was the solemnness of the room, the high spires of dark twisting wood that made it look like it belonged more in a cathedral than a bedroom, that made Lindy lift up her dress and confess to me what somebody did to her with their hands and then with their thing, and what always happened afterwards, and how the stuff that came out always wet the sheets or spoiled her nightie. I can still hear her voice whispering those things in my mind, and see the outline of her expressionless face against the carved headboard.

Now she sat across from me in her bland living room, fussing with the bow of her high-necked blouse. I have come all this way, I wanted to say, and across all these years for you to tell me whose face it was that loomed over yours while you cried or pretended to sleep. I wanted her to tell me so that I could then tell her about some of the things that had happened to me. I thought that we might then embrace each other, or weep like women at a funeral.

The light outside her window changed, and the brown field turned to ochre. She lifted up her head and looked out. It was hard to tell if she looked sadder now, or if it was just a trick of the light. She told me how the Lilics lost their money and their house. Mrs. Lilic's hair had fallen out with the shock. She wore a wig and lived in a stuffy apartment crammed with the things that she'd saved from the auction house. Mr. Lilic drove a taxi. Sometimes at night he pulled up outside the darkened old house and wept for the rooms he could no longer walk through. He confessed these things to Lindy at Mrs. Moon's funeral.

Mrs. Moon with her swollen ankles, lugging her bags of groceries from the car. Tossing buttered toast to the dog. Making the Moon beds each morning. Stripping the sheets. Turning a blind eye to the soiled things she must have seen. Driving away in her old blue Nova and then back again.

She never met the owners of the house she died in. It was her first day on a new contract with a big cleaning company. The woman who found her body saw it from the foyer and hadn't known what it was at first. She told Lindy how Mrs. Moon, swathed in a grey pinafore and drenched in the coffee that had spilled from the pot as she fell, looked like a creature washed up from the lake.

After the funeral the Moon household broke up. The Moon boys married and got jobs and multiplied. Lindy looked after Mr. Moon until it became impossible. She wouldn't move again, she said. She liked it where she was.

I always end up wringing my hands and pacing when I stay in the same place for too long. Then I'm in my car driving around with the loose wrappers rustling like leaves. But looking at Lindy I see for a moment, as if through a chink in a stone wall, how it is possible to keep steady while the hands travel across the clock's face, how the smallest variations in the yard might give comfort as the years pass, why children beg to be told the same story again and again.

The sky clouded over once more, and the lines in her face deepened. She bowed her head. No. She didn't remember the crumbling green steps leading down into the water. She didn't remember the winter boats shrouded in the tattered, flapping plastic. She didn't remember how they made Tully Blanchard walk out on the ice, and how he never made it back to the shore. She smoothed her skirt over her knees and stared straight through me. What kind of people would do such a terrible thing?

RIGHT OR WRONG

Driving across Lawrence County was like heading back into prehistory. With their ragged clefts of burst rock, the hills seemed freshly buckled. Even the locals had a primeval look, rough-hewn and heavy-set, cruising around in muddy pickups or low-slung reptilian sedans. Blasting through to make this stretch of highway ten years back, the road crews unearthed a trove of fossils. Three-hundred-million-year-old shark-tooth, millipede, and scorpion fossils were etched into the outcrops that loomed like cathedrals as Maitland sped beneath them, a pop star caterwauling on his car radio.

He squinted, recalled the singer gyrating in a skin-tight dress on a music video, and then fiddled with the dial to find the weather report. He didn't like too much sun: the glare skewed his aim. He took his exit off the highway, waved at the pump attendant as he drove past McCalley's gas bar and motel, then turned onto the red dirt road that swept down to where the land broke into jigsaw puzzle pieces in the lake.

A few moments later his SUV was creeping underneath a canopy of low-hanging trees towards the weather-beaten group of outbuildings where his mother had lived with her second husband until her death three years previously. Selma and Barry had been among the first to build hunting camps out here on the cusp of what some now called wetlands but older folks called swamp. Their acres were buggy and humid, full of rotten boughs colonized by yellow ear-shaped fungi, ankle-snapping ditches and gulches that widened into emerald ponds during the wetter months.

Barry had been in the family for over forty years but even so, nobody knew too much about him. They knew he was Irish, crooned off-key folk songs that made Maitland's stomach sink to his shoes. They knew something had happened between the day Barry was born and the day he stepped into Selma's living room, smothered in Brylcreem and Old Spice, to see them all piled like a raccoon family onto the caved-in sofa. Something that made him prowl up and down on the kitchen linoleum, groan in his sleep, slump on the porch with his head in his heads.

Whatever he was, wherever he'd been, Barry was big on justice with a small *j*. Red-faced and flying off the handle, he was always getting fired from this or that factory job, coming home with stories in which he was the underdog or unsung hero. But he'd stuck by them all these years, piously shaking his head whenever their real father, who had walked out on them without a goodbye or explanation, was mentioned. He'd put food on the table and had taken care, in his rough way, of Selma when she had her stroke and went into her long fade.

Maitland pulled up next to a freshly delivered mound of the gravel that was forever being raked around by locals to stave off the encroaching marsh. As the years passed, Barry had added more and more rooms to the camping shack, until people joked that it looked like a fugitive's long-term hideout, the kind of lair a drug lord would lie low in. Selma had decorated the hell out of it in her final years. There was a wide-screen TV and a microwave and a million frilly pillows that Barry threw around the living room when he was mad.

Maitland stepped onto the porch just as his brother William, having heard his car on the gravel drive, emerged from the hammock he was partially cocooned in. The two brothers stared at each other. Then William, standing at his full height, looked away through the trees to the lake's edge, alive now with the sound of splashing. Through the leaves Maitland caught a glimpse of William's blond children and golden retrievers, the vivid pinks and greens of his younger wife's dress. He turned back to face William again.

"Where is he?"

William nodded towards the screen door. Maitland peered into the shadows, made out the brass spokes of the sunburst clock mounted on the wood-panelled living room wall, heard the muted sound of a television or radio in a distant room.

"They called. Won't know any more until later this week," said William.

"That doesn't change anything."

"No."

Not wanting to waken Barry, the two brothers stepped down from the porch and onto the gravel drive. They were fit, long-legged, middle-aged men, often mistaken by strangers for twins although Maitland was five years older. William was still golden-haired. Maitland was ashy, had always been darker. In their youth they had both been champion runners, and still ran now although they'd worn away so much cartilage in their knees that they hobbled out of bed each morning. William was faster, came a few seconds shy of making the Olympics while his college rival had raced on a shorter track in the States and qualified, a story the family retold in the hushed tones of a Greek tragedy.

But what they did on a racetrack with a stopwatch in the broad light of day was nothing compared to what they'd done out here in the woods. It made Maitland catch his breath just thinking about them racing on cloudless nights, so fast they felt weightless, two disembodied spirits flying over the raised logs that Barry set up as a makeshift obstacle course, the ruins of which still rotted in the undergrowth beside the driveway.

"There will be hell to pay when he finds out," said Maitland.

"It's not up to him anymore," said William. "There are other people now. People who might get hurt."

He gestured towards the small beach that Barry had carved out when the grandchildren started to arrive, heaping bulrushes onto his boat, slashing the high weeds on the shoreline. Maitland followed his gaze, glanced at the bright colours flitting in the sunlight, made out a child's bonnet and snatches of picnic things. It was an Indian summer, July in September. If he wasn't too cranky or exhausted, Barry might tell stories to the wide-eyed children by the flushed light of the woodstove tonight, his voice pitched to a disturbing sotto voce.

He was always the life and soul of any party. When Maitland and William were small, their faces, terrified or elated, followed him from their nest of comic books and afghans as he whirled their mother around the kitchen or staggered back and forth with a quart of whiskey. Even after he joined AA there was never really anyone else in the room when Barry was around. He didn't get old the way other people did. He just got Barry-er, his body wizened to beef jerky, emerging, whenever their cars pulled into the driveway, from the wall of green undergrowth like some creature out of a legend.

His hold over them was still powerful enough that they had dropped their weekend plans when he summoned them here, ostensibly for an off-season duck hunt. The summons wasn't unusual; he had a long and flagrant history of flouting local enforcers. What was unusual was his tone of voice on the phone: harsh and hollow, as though calling out from a great distance. It made Maitland wonder if Barry was hitting the bottle again.

William was too young to remember, but in the beginning Maitland had been the retriever, wading up to his waist in the marsh to clasp the ducks by their limp necks. He stacked them on land with their beaks facing the same direction, marvelling at the ovoid skulls, peacock sheen, and sculpted nostrils, the occult mystery of their lifeless eyes, staring out into blackness.

Lying in bed at night in town, he could still hear the rhythmic plash of the oars dipping into silty water as he drifted off to sleep. His keenest memories were of gliding beyond the craggy inlets past chamber after chamber of walled rushes, a vast, rustling palace in the pre-dawn night. The darkness felt so endless and absolute he was surprised each time the inks faded into the chilly steels and blues of early morning, his body stiff from crouching beneath the camouflage nets that Barry draped over the boat as a blind. Maitland was nine when he shot his first duck, could still remember the surge of startled panic, the hollow sound of the flapping wings, the hull tilting beneath him as he fired and watched the bird softly crash through the rushes.

Barry taught him that if you couldn't make a clean kill it was better to not shoot or at least miss altogether. A wounded duck will flee and warn the others. Word spreads from flock to flock, passes down through generations. But if there's a legend of dead spots the ducks avoid or fly over high out of range, Barry has the inverse map, knows the pools and coves where he can lure greenheads from the sky with a wooden reed until the air is alive with wings and the green fire of their feathers, pike twitching in the eelgrass below.

The three men had headed out into the indigo mist the previous morning, paddling past the rocky point where Barry's hunting dogs were buried beneath stone cairns hauled up from the shore. Dressed in camouflage, faces scribbled with greasy pastel, the men almost disappeared into the landscape as they rowed past the branches of a newly toppled tree. It was here that Barry broke down and told them what the doctor said. How the secret he'd been keeping had spread into his bones and other organs. He spent the trip back to the camp in silence, his head cradled in his splayed hands.

The brothers had stared at each other across the curve of Barry's spine with the same expressions they wore now, a day later, standing on the gravel-strewn driveway. The silence deepened between them, the shrieks and splashing of the children having paused at an earlier point. Through the trees Maitland caught another flash of pink, a child's blond head darting from view. They were all still there, lost in a quiet game or contemplating the delicate life forms that teemed in the shallows. There was a stirring from within the cottage and he glanced over William's shoulder into the shadows beyond the screen door. Wordless, they moved down the rough stone path and into the woods.

In the beginning there was a one-room shack with a splintered porch and a bug net more duct tape than mesh that Barry called his getaway. The two of them, Maitland and Barry, left town on a Friday evening after Barry's shift at the pulp factory, drove out into miles of forest interrupted only by the odd waterfall cascading from the rocks, ivory white in the gloom. Exhausted from a week of humping sacks of wood chips, Barry lit a fire in the pot-bellied stove while Maitland opened cans of Vienna sausages and potatoes they wolfed down lukewarm. If it was off-season Barry sat by the stove's roaring mouth and drank bourbon by the quart until he blacked out, the canvas chair tipping him onto the rough planks in the early hours of dawn.

For the rest of the weekend it was Maitland standing tip-toe on Barry's tackle box to make himself a sandwich on the splintered counter. Maitland lost in the woods for hours, rid-dled with blackfly, miraculously spotting the river of red road through the trees just as the sun dipped out of view. Sinking into the river on a homemade raft. Soaked to the skin in cold rain, shuddering between the burnt-out mouth of the wood-stove and Barry's prostrate body. Sneaking Barry's .22 out to shoot rabbits and squirrels, turning their slack bodies with the tip of his shoe to stare at their dead faces.

It wasn't like Barry didn't try. Sometimes at night he told Maitland stories, tales that dissolved into a mist of unremembering or the saw-toothed rasp of a snore. If Maitland prodded him awake and pleaded with him to finish, Barry scrutinized the woods from his sunken armchair on the porch as though an ending might emerge from the foliage at any moment.

Maitland had waited for his real father to come for so long, listening in rapture for his footsteps on the bungalow's front path. He would come and save them all, take them to the white mansion in the hills they were sure he lived in. But in the end there was only Barry in his grime-stiffened pants, pulling into the driveway after a double shift, his Ramcharger cankered with rust. No matter how often Maitland ate stale Cheerios from the box, no matter that the shack reeked of Barry's pissed pants, he never breathed a word about what happened on those weekends to his mother or anyone else. Because anything was better than waiting for a man whose face was no more than a blank white oval to never come home.

They made an effort to be more civilized when William started coming along. Maitland could recall the bursts of love and panic he'd felt in his chest watching William's golden head, as fragile as a Christmas ornament, leaning from the car window as he reached out to frisk the passing branches, hovering over the boat's stern to watch the fish flickering in the deeps. There were weeks, maybe a whole July, where Barry kept his cool, blew smoke rings with his feet dangling over the gunwales, and the three of them ate beans by the stove, dozed off in a mess of old sleeping bags under the stars. Maitland thought he could even remember singing, by the stove-light and on the winding drives home.

Then it was Barry muttering at his own reflection in the window on the porch. Pacing back and forth, shielding his agitated face with his forearm, as though an unseen man was jabbing him. It was Barry, sick of his own torments, piling the kids into the truck and heading out, rifle on his lap, bourbon wedged between his knees, each rambling drive more reckless than the last.

Sometimes he got Maitland to lean across his lap and steer the wheel while he drew a bead on whatever he saw alongside of the road, which was sometimes a living creature, sometimes just the wind stirring in the brush. And once, a police car's high beams on a hilltop, illuminating Barry's hunched silhouette and cocked rifle to a radiance. The chase went on forever, William and Maitland rolling loose in the back after Barry told them to hunker down. The excitement jolted Barry out of his funk, seemed to give him a heightened awareness. Drunk, he handled the Ramcharger like a racetrack driver, had the cunning to sling his rifle out the window on a curve so the police car headlights didn't catch sight of it flying into the woods.

They ended up lost, creeping along a logging road with the lights off, the truck sinking into ruts so deep the wheels sank into the mud and squealed. They arrived at an escarpment, a rash of stars overhead and the blood still buzzing in their ears. A maze of bulrushes lay beneath them, as intricate as a figured carpet and overhung with a haze of fog. Barry rolled down his window. The air was clogged with the smell of fungus and rotting leaves and the drone of insects and frogs.

"Listen," he said. "Both of you, because he needs to hear it too. Take those fancy places in town, all those towers and fountains and pretty wallpaper and lists of what to do. Your mother cleaning the house in case someone important happens to swing by and ring the doorbell. It's all just bullshit people make up to fool themselves. *This* is all there is. There isn't anything else. I want you to remember that. The rest is bullshit people make up just to get by."

The next morning Barry lay wide-eyed and motionless on his bunk, even after Maitland waved his hand over his face and offered him a bowl of cereal. Maitland and William rooted around in the bushes along the roadside until they spotted the rifle's muzzle in the crotch of a trembling ash.

Golden-haired and smooth-skinned at fifty, dragging his pretty wife and children everywhere he went like the good luck charms on a bracelet, William had been too young at the time to remember any of this. Meanwhile Maitland had two broken marriages behind him, had never settled down. Was always rushing straight into the heart of any crisis. The two brothers faced each other once again. They had become estranged over the years, had headed out in different directions but had nonetheless both ended up back in the gloomy nave carved out of the woods by Barry, equidistant from the cluster of buildings and the shore, surreally bright beyond the undergrowth.

During hunting season there were trips out into the bay and up the river's wide mouth to meet grizzled men at the bottom of fire roads and on the porches of half-toppled shacks. Stinking of beer and 3-IN-ONE gun oil, muttering about sports or war, rolling cigarettes from cut-price jumbo tins. They all shared a sour reverence for Barry. He had a knack for being in the right place at the right time. He was luck personified, a mascot whose roughhousing and hijinks were tolerated because you were sure to bag a kill if Barry came along. On one trip the men had a large gathering and a bonfire at a shack ten miles upriver from their swamp. Maitland and William both felt something akin to terror as they watched the men nearly coming to blows and breaking off into fits of convulsive laughter, their faces devil red from the flames.

The moon was nearly full and they rowed home that night on a ribbon of blue glass, the bonfire shrinking to the size of a struck match behind them. Wrapped up in an old rain poncho, William nodded in and out of sleep. Barry crouched in the stern taking swigs from his bottle. They had arrived at a strait with a swifter current when Maitland turned and saw the shape in the water ahead of them. He thought at first that it was a felled bough, or a mass of wood broken loose from a beaver dam and snagged on a rock. Then Barry, possessed once more with that uncanny awareness, rose to his feet and shone his flashlight on the largest stag Maitland had ever seen, a twelve-point giant heading upstream, its white chest like the prow of a small ship.

Out of its element, struggling against the current, the stag seemed to know what was going to happen even before Barry groped for his rifle and took aim. He waited for the boat to steady, squinted into the shadows at Maitland and William to make sure they were watching, and squeezed the trigger. He looped a rope around the stag's antler and tied it to a cleat, then climbed over the seat to the bow, took a long, deep drink from his bottle. "It's all such a goddam struggle," he said. He lay down in the hull next to dumbstruck William, with his face turned up at the stars. At first Maitland thought Barry was laughing but when he looked over at him he saw tears silvering his cheeks. The sobs grew louder and louder, swelled into an outpouring of grief that Maitland had never heard from anyone before or since, not even his wife after her miscarriage.

For forty years Maitland has dreamed about the stag trailing behind the boat beneath the water's surface while Barry's ragged sobs tore the air. In his dreams the antlers branch upward, furnish the river's narrow corridor with their primordial elegance.

After what felt like a cold eternity Barry's sobs began to diminish. When the only noise Maitland could hear was the sound of the oars dipping into the water, he glanced at Barry's tear-streaked face and wondered what his own life might have been if this man hadn't turned up on their doorstop with his recklessness and his Ramcharger. Then, when he was sure that Barry had dozed off, he rowed inland and grabbed the bough of an overhanging tree, undid the slipknot around the antler with his free hand, and watched the stag's silhouette flow back into the expanse of darkness, like the final piece in a puzzle.

The next day Barry drained his remaining liquor bottles into the sumac grove, tossed the empties into the lake where they bobbed in the rushes for years. Every now and again one of William's children would dig one up on the beach, the dirty glass streaked with green. After Barry joined AA the wild drives were replaced by pilgrimages to the nearest towns that hosted meetings in church cellars. The boys waited out by the truck for Barry to emerge, head down, hands shaking so hard he couldn't get the keys back into the ignition.

There were good years. When Barry found out they could run fast, he took them out into the woods and urged them to go faster and faster, until Maitland felt as though he was being hauled along by the power of Barry's voice alone, lashing at their backsides like a bullwhip. When they started to train seriously for races, he chased them uphill in his Charger with the brights on so they could see the road ahead at night. For a few years the two boys were like Barry's own creation, a single two-headed animal racing through the woods at breakneck speed. Then William started to pull ahead and leave Maitland retching and bent over at the waist behind him, the world a pounding, dizzy blur.

Maitland always had the sense that it was never enough, that while they were dropping their medals into the new, reformed Barry's lap for him to shine with an old pyjama-striped flannel, they were doing it all for the old Barry, who they hoped somehow to summon up like a genie from the place deep inside himself that he had retreated to.

He never shot at anything other than waterfowl after that night on the water. Right or wrong, Maitland had always yearned to have the old Barry back with his fiery grief and restless rages, his face twisting into grotesques that had him and William rolling on the floor in laughter, and at the same time quaking inwardly in fear.

But now the wild, hectic look was back in spades. The night before, William had taken Barry out by the waterfront on a pretext while Maitland went into his room, stuffed all of Barry's hunting rifles from the gun cabinet at the back of his closet and the .44 from his night table into a duffel bag that he shoved in his trunk. Not knowing what else to do, he had driven back to town and stuffed the bag under his bed. It was William's idea to take the guns away, and Maitland had agreed. But he spent a long night awake in his bed, conscious of their cold mass and weight in the darkness beneath him, their acrid oils perfuming the air. Stepping out onto his driveway in the morning to head back here, he had an urge, an impulse that he didn't trust, to run back into the house and grab the .44. Sneak the gun back into Barry's night table drawer. Let him make his own choices out there in the woods.

"They have pills," said William. "Things he can take to make it easier on him. They know what they're doing these days."

The stern, somewhat impatient expression on his face made Maitland wonder briefly if his brother remembered more about the past than he claimed to. There was, just then, another commotion by the lake and the air was filled with cries and glittering arcs of spray. William turned to step through the last of the foliage towards the shore. Maitland swivelled back to look once again at the low buildings where Barry lay, asleep or awake, or in a world somewhere between, deep in the cave of his bedroom.

"Just tell me we're doing the right thing," said Maitland. But William didn't answer, or was already too far ahead to have heard.

ACKNOWLEDGEMENTS

I am grateful to the Canada Council for the Arts and to the Arts Council of New Brunswick for the financial assistance that allowed me to write these stories.

"In a Kingdom Beneath the Sea" was previously published under a different title in the Fall 2013 issue of *The Malahat Review*. It won the 2013 Far Horizons Award, and it also received a Pushcart Prize Special Mention in *The Pushcart Prize XXXIX: Best of the Small Presses 2015*. It was subsequently republished in *15: Best Canadian Stories* (John Metcalf, ed., Oberon Press, 2016).

"The Prince of Chang" appeared in *The Malahat Review's* Essential East Coast Writing issue (Autumn 2012).

An earlier version of "Vulnerable Adults" was published in *Wild Cards: The Second Virago Anthology of Writing Women* (Andrea Badenoch, Maggie Hannan, Pippa Little, and Debbie Taylor, eds., Virago Press, 1999).

"There Are Two Pools You May Drink From" won the *Boston Review's* 2013 Aura Estrada Short Story Contest and appeared in the July/August 2013 print issue.

I first came across the Prince of Chang in the poem "Responsibilities" by W. B. Yeats. The title story was inspired in part by Willem de Kooning's *Woman* series. "Talking of Michelangelo" was borrowed from *The Love Song of J. Alfred Prufrock* by T. S. Eliot. Thanks also to Jim Currie and family for lending me a powerful memory.

Grateful thanks to my editor, Jennifer Lambert, for her patience and brilliance, and to Natalie Meditsky, Shaun Oakey, Miranda Snyder, and the rest of the HarperCollins team. Thanks also to my agents, Chris Bucci and Jennifer Hewson.

Thanks to Dr. Heather Tait, Dr. Maged Salem, and all the staff at the Moncton Hospital Oncology Clinic.

For their kindness, solidarity, and inspiration: Arthur Leonoff, Nathan Englander, Alissa York, Stevie Howell, Carrie Anne Snyder, Caroline Adderson, Steven Heighton, John Metcalf, Marilyn Biderman, Gail and Gary Buzzell, Kim Jernigan, Amanda Jernigan, Pamela Mulloy, Shaena Lambert, my brother, Gareth Powell, Junot Díaz, Simon Waxman, Deborah Chasman, Pamela Stewart, Anthony Howell, Robin Robertson, Kate Bingham, Glyn Maxwell, Alan Jenkins, Daniel Wells, Rachel Lebowitz, Zach Wells, Lee Thompson, Elizabeth Blanchard, Beth Janzen, Jeff Bursey, Danny Jacobs, Kimberly Gautreau, André Touchburn, Karen Baird, Carol Steel, Allan Cooper, my mother, Lana Coe, and Frank Briggs, Brad Shapansky and family, Monica Carter and Cherie Sturm, David and Marlene Powell, Gareth and Brenda Powell, Erin Frey, Larry Arbuthnot and Ann Crammond, Alexander MacLeod, Michael Christie, Christos Tsiolkas, and Eliza Robertson.